The Marvelous Story of
Claire d'Amour

BY THE SAME AUTHOR

The Marvelous Story of Claire d'Amour and Other Stories

by
Maurice Magre

Translated, annotated and introduced by
Brian Stableford

A Black Coat Press Book

ISBN 978-1-61227-652-6. First Printing. August 2017. Published by Black Coat Press, an imprint of Hollywood Comics.com, LLC, P.O. Box 17270, Encino, CA 91416.
Printed in the United States of America.

TABLE OF CONTENTS

Introduction

This is the first volume of a twelve-volume set of translations of Maurice Magre's prose fiction. It contains as many of his early short stories as are readily available at the time of writing, including the contents of the collection *Histoire merveilleuse de Claire d'Amour suivie d'autres contes merveilleux* (1903) and six other stories from various sources published between 1901 and 1913.

Volume Two, *The Call of the Beast and Other Stories*, contains translations of his first three works of prose fiction in volume form, *Les Colombes poignardées* (1917), as "Stabbed Doves," *La Tendre camarade* (1918), as "The Tender Comrade" and *L'Appel de la bête* (1920), as "The Call of the Beast."

Volume Three, *Priscilla of Alexandria and Other Stories*, contains translations of the original version of the story collection *Vies des courtisanes*, first published in *Oeuvres Libres* 23 (1923), as "Courtesans' Lives," plus the additional story substituted for "Priscilla d'Alexandrie" in the version of the collection published in volume form in 1925, and the novel *Priscilla d'Alexandrie* (1925), as "Priscilla of Alexandria."

Volume Four, *The Angel of Lust*, contains translations of the novella, *La Vie amoureuse de Messaline* (1925), as "The Love Life of Messalina," the novel published as *La Luxure de Grenade* (1926), as "The Angel of Lust," and the chapter from *Magiciens et illuminés* (1930) entitled "Christian Rosenkreutz et les Rose-croix," as "Christian Rosenkreutz and the Rosicrucians."

Volume Five, *The Mystery of the Tiger*, contains translations of the novella *Le Roman de Confucius* (1927), as "The Story of Confucius," and the novel *Le Mystère du tigre* (1927), as "The Mystery of the Tiger."

Volume Six, *The Poison of Goa*, contains translations of the novel *Le Poison de Goa* (1928), as "The Poison of Goa," and the prose poems contained in *Le Livre des lotus entr'ouverts* (1926), as "Lotus Blossoms."

Volume Seven, *Lucifer*, contains a translation of the novel originally published under the same title in 1929 and the novella *La Nuit de haschich et d'opium* (1929), as "The Night of Hashish and Opium."

Volume Eight, *The Blood of Toulouse*, contains translations of the novel *Le Sang de Toulouse* (1931), as "The Blood of Toulouse," and the chapter from *Magiciens et illuminés* entitled "Le Maître inconnu des Albigeois," as "The Secret Master of the Albigensians."

Volume Nine, *The Albigensian Treasure*, contains translations of the novel *Le Trésor des Albigeois* (1938), as "The Albigensian Treasure," and the collection of vignettes "Communication avec la nature" from *La Beauté invisible* (1937), as "Communication with Nature."

Volume Ten, *Jean de Fodoas*, contains translations of the novel *Jean de Fodoas: aventures d'un Français à la cour de l'empereur Akbar* (1939) as "Jean de Fodoas" and the chapter from *Magiciens et illuminés* entitled "Le Mystère des Templiers," as "The Mystery of the Templars."

Volume Eleven, *Melusine*, contains translations of the novel *Mélusine, ou le secret de solitude* (1941) and the collections of vignettes "Le Côté d'ombre des âmes" and "Révélation des mondes invisibles" from *La Beauté invisible*, as "The Dark Side of Souls" and "The Revelation of Invisible Worlds."

Volume Twelve, *The Brothers of the Virgin Gold*, contains a translation of the novel *Les Frères de l'or vierge*, first published posthumously in 1949.

Maurice Magre was one of the most far-ranging and extravagant writers of fantastic fiction active in France in the first half of the 20th century, and perhaps the finest of them. All writers of fantastic fiction are, of course, extraordinary by definition, but there are degrees in their extraordinariness; they differ in the range and extravagance of the fantastic component of their work and they also differ in the purpose for which they introduce heterocosmic elements into their narratives. Magre was extraordinary even among the most extraordinary

The fertility and versatility of Magre's imagination were not the only things that distinguished him; the most interesting and intriguing aspects of his work were the manner and purpose for which he deployed the fantastic elements of his work. All of his fiction—and, for that matter, all of his poetry, his dramatic works and his many other prose works—was produced in the context of an exploratory quest in which he sought come to terms with certain personal and philosophical fascinations that evidently haunted him throughout his life. The nature of that quest played a large part in determining the idiosyncratic fashion in which fantastic elements are featured in his work.

Prose fiction was one of the media in which Magre sought answers to the questions that those fascinations led him to ask; he used it, alongside his poetry and other prose, to explore a number of different hypotheses at various times and with various degrees of seriousness. They were often hypotheses that he had tried to apply in his real life, although the fiction was usually retrospective, re-evaluating ideas that he had either already abandoned or had transformed in the context of his quotidian life. As his attitude to the hypothetical solutions that he considered changed over time, however, so did the narrative methods and voices of his fiction, producing a remarkable variety in his work while always retaining the same central obsessions. Although his works are invariably engaging when seen in isolation, they gain considerably in interest when they can be viewed in the context of his work as a whole, as elements in an ongoing artistic and intellectual endeavor.

Although he was essentially an earnest fantasist, primarily interested in exploring ideas seriously, Magre nevertheless set out in all his works of fiction to be entertaining, deliberately adopting forms and methods from popular fiction. Several of his longer novels are action-adventure novels replete with heroic exploits, battles, sieges, pogroms, murders, kidnappings, mysteries and treasure hunts. Many of them also have a forceful and flamboyant erotic component—naturally, given that one of the key elements of his central obsession was the role played in human life by erotic desire. His use of all those elements, however, is relentlessly unorthodox; his plots never follow the standardized story-arcs associated with the relevant motifs in formularized popular fiction, and his work routinely delights in contradicting the expectations tacitly put in place by their use, giving it a striking unpredictability that is rewarding for readers fond of the unexpected, although it compromised his popularity somewhat by denying readers the ritual satisfaction built into conventional endings.

Because Magre's fiction addresses, albeit obliquely, questions that were of great personal importance to him, much of it seems to contain autobiographical echoes. Several of his contemporary novels are first-person narratives featuring unnamed protagonists who are writers, thus tacitly inviting the reader to assume that the author is speaking for himself and about himself, although the events that occur within the stories clearly do not correspond with events in the author's own life—not so much because they are fantastic, as Magre appears to have been completely convinced that there are supernatural intrusions in real life closely akin to those featured in his fiction, as because they blatantly contradict the very few facts that are reliably known about his life.

In fact, few details are known about Magre's life, in spite of the fact that he wrote several volumes of supposed non-fiction in which he really does, ostensibly, address the reader in his own voice. One of them is entitled *Confessions sur les femmes, l'opium, l'amour, l'idéal, etc...* [Confessions regarding Women, Opium, Amour and the Ideal, etc.] (1930), and contains a great deal of revelatory information, but it is remarkably lacking in hard data, especially with regard to its chronology. There is also a biography of the author by Jean-Jacques Bedu, *Maurice Magre: Le Lotus perdu* [Maurice Magre: The Lost Lotus] (1999) which might contain fewer items of detailed factual information than any other biography ever penned, although Bedu did manage to obtain several certain key items of information that would surely have taken center stage in a comprehensive book of *Confessions*, but about which Magre maintained a strict silence in all of his writings. Magre's three-part collection of vignettes *La Beauté invisible* [Invisible Beauty] (1937) contains a great many first-person anecdotes, but most are blatantly fictitious, and his evident comfort in presenting fictions as if they were factual anecdotes suggests that almost everything he said about himself might have to be taken with a pinch of salt.

In that context it is worth noting that several of Magre's works of contemporary fiction—the first of which, "La dernière sirène" is translated in the present volume as "The Last Siren"—feature "the poet Jean Noël," who seems to have elements of wry self-portraiture about him. The most intense of his contemporary novels, *Lucifer* (1929; tr. as *Lucifer*), ends with an epilogue in which another first-person narrator suddenly takes over text, and what has gone before is revealed as a story told to him by "J. N***"—presumably Jean Noël, although it is not obvious why the name is not given in full. That duplication clearly invites consideration as a kind of psychological sidestep, an attempt to find a more distanced hypothetical standpoint for self-assessment: an introspective variant of the doubling intrinsic to an author's attempt to create any character and assume his or her skin for narrative purposes. The characters in his numerous historical novels clearly cannot pretend to be the author in the same sense as unnamed first-person narrators in works of contemporary fiction, but it is notable that the most famous one, *Le Sang de Toulouse* (1931; tr. as *The Blood of Toulouse*), concludes with an epilogue that does explicitly identify the 13th century protagonist with the 20th century author in an ingenious fashion licensed by its fantastic hypotheses.

In this context, it is also notable that there is one story by Magre told in the third person that features a protagonist named Maurice (with no surname) and that the story in question, although it is one of his most extravagantly fantastic—and perhaps for that very reason—appears to demand interpretation as a transfiguration of the author's own feelings and concerns: "Histoire merveilleuse de Claire d'Amour," translated in the present volume as "The Marvelous Story of Claire d'Amour." In that story, and the cluster of *contes* that were associated with it in the collection *Histoire merveilleuse de Claire d'Amour suivie d'autres contes merveilleux*, the seeds can be seen of almost everything that followed in the remainder of the author's literary career—except for the solutions to his perceived predicament that he tried out in vain, and the one that he claimed, in the end, to have succeeded.

It is as well to put the marvelous story of Claire d'Amour and its associated tales in context, both within the frame of the author's early life and within their declared genre, that of the *contes merveilleux*, sometimes known, somewhat inaptly, as *contes de fées* (often translated, even more inaptly, as "fairy tales").

Maurice Magre was born in Toulouse on 2 March 1877, and he concluded his education at the University of Toulouse. Long before completing his studies, however, he had developed an intense interest in literature, particularly in the poetry of the Symbolist Movement, which was in its heyday in the early 1890s, and especially the fraction of it that attracted the alternative title of the Decadent Movement. He published some of his early poems in *Éveils* (1895), along with contributions by his elder brother André (1873-1949), who was also one of the co-founders, with other friends, of the short-lived literary periodical *L'Effort*.

André Magre published a further volume of poetry in 1899, not long after Maurice's first solo collection, *La Chanson des hommes* (1898), but André did not move to Paris and he went on to become a career civil servant. The two brothers seem to have become estranged eventually, as André's politics moved inexorably to the right and his religion remained dogmatically Catholic, while Maurice never entirely abandoned his early Anarchist sympathies and usually categorized himself as a Buddhist, but they remained close until the Great War, when Maurice often expressed anxieties about André's fate. André's subsequent career, however, was one of the things that Magre never mentioned in his autobiographical writings, and he is even effaced from many of his memoirs of childhood.

Their father, who was a municipal administrator, might well have preferred it if Maurice had followed in André's footsteps, but when Maurice decided instead that he was had to Paris in order to follow is destiny and become a poet, he agreed to give him a small monthly allowance—just enough to live on—which he continued to pay from 1897, when Maurice set forth, until shortly after the turn of the century. It is no coincidence that it was when that allowance stopped that Magre, who had previously only written poetry, and had won some critical acclaim therefrom, began to write prose in some quantity, albeit with limited success in the early days.

Magre was poor during his first few years in Paris, although, as he later observed in *Confessions*, he was surprised to find that there were a good many poets in Paris, including reputable ones, who were even poorer than he was, having no parental allowance to help them stave off starvation. He eventually published an embittered essay, *Conseils à un jeune homme pauvre qui vient faire de la littérature à Paris* [Advice to a Poor Young Man Coming to Paris in order to Practice Literature] (1908), in which he reflected on his early difficulties, while deliberately giving the impression that he had had a harder time than he actually had. To some extent, that was because he was reflecting on the experience of others less fortunate than himself, but it was also a component of a determined attempt to cultivate the image of a Decadent Bohemian that he thought appropriate to a poet.

The anecdotes in *Confessions* mention many of the literary acquaintances that Magre made in Paris, but are vague about his amities. He does not mention attendance any literary salons, and does not seem to have attended any on a regular basis, although he was certainly acquainted with several members of José-Maria Heredia's salon, including Jean de Tinan, and he later became friendly with Gabriel de Lautrec, who also hosted a weekly salon. The only circle with which Bedu found evidence of consistent association prior to the turn of the century was centered on the American exile Stuart Merrill, which frequented a café near the Panthéon, and it was in that milieu that he undertook his first tentative amorous adventures.

Those first adventures do not appear to have been very successful. In the preface to his elaborately sarcastic *La Conquête des femmes: conseils à un jeune homme* [The Conquest of Women: Advice to a Young Man] (1908), which might be slightly more trustworthy than the rest of the text, he says that it was during a summer vacation spent with his family in the Midi when he was twenty-six—i.e., in the summer of 1903—that he changed his philosophy with regard to women and decided that his objective ought to be to sleep with as many of them as possible rather than, as before, trying to find a single satisfactory and long-lasting relationship. According to *Confessions*, that calculated promiscuity quickly became an obsession. The 1908 essay was ostensibly an account of the experience gleaned in the previous five years, based as much on failed trials as successful ones. "Histoire merveilleuse de Claire d'Amour" must have been written shortly before that crucial summer of 1903, and as a self-analytical exercise it might well have contributed to his determined change of direction, deliberately calculated to avoid the fate to which the unfortunate Maurice, blinded by illusion, delivers himself in the story.

Between 1897 and 1902 Magre was living in the Latin Quarter, which, as well as pullulating with would-be poets, was replete with prostitutes and poor working women hovering on the brink of prostitution, and mostly doomed to fall into it. Magre's allowance, although it kept him from starvation, did not stretch to paying for sex, but it was a standard aspect of the mores of the time and milieu that prostitutes and kept women had, as well as paying clients, a "lover of the heart" with whom they slept for free. Such lovers had had a rich literary mythology attached to them since the pioneering endeavors of Honoré de Balzac, and their association with literary Bohemia had been solidly cemented by Henri Murger. The quest to be a "lover of the heart" in the *fin-de-siècle* Latin Quarter was one that seems routinely to have delivered rewards, and doubtless did for Magre as well as many others, but it was not the kind of romantic career that would suit a young man enthusiastic to find true love, or one vulnerable to fervent jealousy, like the narrator of the earliest story translated in the present volume, "Marcelle."

One of the anecdotes in *Confessions* relates how Magre broke up with the first woman with whom he became infatuated as soon as he discovered that she had slept with someone— someone he found particularly loathsome—and that motif recurs incessantly throughout his works. Although he certainly did not say so, it is possible that if Magre really did change his philosophy of amorous relationships abruptly in 1903, it was largely an attempt to conquer or set aside the deleterious effects of his irrepressible jealousy. At any rate, it is probably not a coincidence that Maurice, in "Histoire merveilleuse de Claire d'Amour," is blinded by illusion, and thus immunized against jealousy.

Such, so far as it can be determined, is the personal context of Magre's early fiction, insofar as it deals with *claire d'amour*—i.e., the bright light of amour—in the broad sense.

All the stories in *Histoire merveilleuse de Claire d'Amour suivie d'autres contes merveilleux*, and most of the other stories included in the present collection, belong to the genre identified in that title. When the genre in question had been invented in the literary salons associated with the court

15

of Louis XIV in the late 17th century, it had been called *contes de fées* by one of its leading practitioners, Madame d'Aulnoy, and that was the label that stuck. The French *féerie* means "enchantment," and the most accurate translation of that label would therefore be "tales of agents of enchantment," but because *fée* is a feminine noun, its use carried a tacit implication that the agents in question were female, so most fées became enchantresses or, in English translation, female "fairies," much as "*la mort*" is often represented in French personifications as female, as in two of the stories translated herein.

The problems of construing the word *fée* are, however, more fundamental than the transfigurations to which it was subjected by its typical personifications. The whole point of Madame d'Aulnoy's choice of the term is that it was ironic, but that irony was soon blurred by the fact that her stories, and imitations and plagiarisms thereof—most notably those by Charles Perrault—adapted the salon tales as children's stories, explicitly aimed at teaching morality by example. That was not their original intention, and their intrinsic rhetoric was quite different. The original versions, belonging to the oral culture of the salons, could not be preserved, and many printed versions were undoubtedly diluted or mangled, but the whole point of producing imitative *contes populaires* in an intellectualized aristocratic environment was to distort and subvert them by sarcasm and cynicism—in effect, to transform "tales of enchantment" into "tales of disenchantment." That is what the major contributors to the genre continued to do in printed works in the 18th century—when many of them were published illicitly—and in the 19th century, in a fashion that reached its eventual apogee during the heyday of the Decadent Movement.

The screw of disenchantment was relentlessly turned by self-conscious adherents of literary Decadence, initially by the prolific Catulle Mendès, who produced several collections of *contes merveilleux*, including *Les Oiseaux bleus* (1888; tr. as *Bluebirds*), and even more extravagantly by Jean Lorrain, most of whose stories in that vein were collected in *Princesses*

16

d'ivoire et d'ivresse (1902; trs. distributed in *Nightmares of an Ether-Drinker, The Soul-Drinker and Other Stories* and *Masks in the Tapestry*). Maurice Magre, who had almost certainly read both of those collections, picked up exactly where they left off, and took tales of disenchantment to an extreme beyond the limits within which Mendès and Lorrain had settled. That helps to explain why the collection, although it is a masterpiece of sorts, was not popular, and was never reprinted.

Magre's first-published *conte merveilleux*, "Le Premier amour du docteur Faust," translated herein as "Dr. Faust's First Love" helped to set the pattern for many of the stories in the 1903 collection; it was probably not included therein simply because Dr. Faust's rant was reproduced in "La Fleur de jeunesse," here translated as "The Flower of Love." The downbeat trajectory of such stories, especially as displayed in "Histoire d'un grenadier qui n'avait pas de chance," translated as "The Story of the Unlucky Grenadier" also gives them an affinity with the genre of *contes cruels*, which generally have an element of black comedy, but in Magre's work the tragic component usually outweighs the comedic component, and sometimes swamps it entirely, as in the grim "Le Marchand de jouets," translated as "The Toy Merchant," the heart-rending "Le Pauvre musicien et le petit génie" (The Poor Musician and the Little Genie") and the wry "Le Berger roi" ("The Goatherd King"). "Histoire merveilleuse de Claire d'Amour," however, strikes a more even balance, and doubtless gains therefrom, as do the ironically touching "Marinette et le vieil ondin" (Marinette and the Old Water Sprite") and "La Poupée" ("The Doll").

It is noticeable that the one story in the 1903 collections that does not undermine the happy ending conventionally attached to *contes de fées*, "Histoire de "Lili-des-Roses et du prince nègre" (The Story of Lili-des-Roses and the Black Prince") is the most awkward item in the collection, although it is not nearly as embarrassed in its manner as the one story translated herein that was explicitly framed as a moralistic story for children, presumably written to commission, "Les

trois métiers de Jeannet" ("Jeannet's Three Professions").
Magre was only fluent when following his own inclinations,
and there is cause for wonderment as well as gratitude in the
fact that his inclinations ranged so far, in such strange by-
ways, in the course of his career, and produced so many fluent
texts.

The stories in the present volume, with the exception of
"Les trois métiers de Jeannet," were all published between
1900 and 1905, and are thus separated by quite a long interval
from the author's next substantial work of fiction, *Les Colombes poignardées* (1917). In that interim there were several
significant events and developments in his circumstances, including the outbreak of the Great War, which will be dis-
cussed in the introduction to the next volume in the present
series; those events and developments changed his attitudes
considerably, and when he resumed writing prose in quantity
it was in a very different vein. He did not publish any more
contes merveilleux of the kind extensively illustrated herein,
but he did retain his strong interest fantastic motifs, and he
also preserved certain aspects of the style and narrative strate-
gy of the stories in the present volume, which never disappeared entirely from his work and made a significant return in
some of the works that he wrote in the late 1930s, not long
before his death.

Although the work featured in the present volume might
be considered atypical within the ensemble of his work, therefore, it is certainly not disconnected from it, and in one respect
at least it is absolutely crucial. Replications and variants of the
symbolic figure of Claire d'Amour continued to recur in his
work incessantly, all the way from the beginning to the end.
The flower of youth was replaced in the fullness of time by
other blooms, most prolifically by symbolic roses, but that
motif too remained perennial, in numerous variations. Philos-
ophers akin to Dr. Faust, and Bigorneau from "Histoire
Merveilleuse de Claire d'Amour," also continued to play a
central role in Magre's fiction, most of the exemplars being
more hopeful than Faust and less ridiculous than Bigorneau,

but nevertheless playing similar roles and constituting a similar sanely dampening presence. The works included here thus constituted a solid foundation, which was still in place when the author returned to writing prose after a hiatus, and provided a launching pad for ideas and images that were to undergo many future metamorphoses.

"Marcelle" first appeared in *La Revue Blanche* in May 1901. "Le Premier amour du docteur Faust" first appeared in the *Revue Hebdomadaire* for 6 September 1902. "Marinette et le vieil Ondin," first appeared in *La Nouvelle Revue* in November 1902 and was then reprinted in *Histoire merveilleuse de Claire d'Amour suivie d'autres contes merveilleux*, published by Eugène Fasquelle in 1903. "Le Berger roi" first appeared in *La Nouvelle Revue* in May 1905 and "La Dernière sirène" in the November 1905 issue of the same periodical. "Les trois métiers de Jeannet" first appeared in a small booklet, *Les trois métiers de Jeannet et Les Bon tours d'Yan*, published by Hachette in 1913. The translations of the stories from periodicals were all made from the texts reproduced on the Bibliothèque Nationale's *gallica* website. The translation of "Les trois métiers de Jeannet" was made from the version reproduced on the website *contesetlegendes.canalblog.com*. The translations of the stories that appeared in *Histoire merveilleuse de Claire d'Amour suivie d'autres contes merveilleux*, with the exception of "Marinette et le vieil ondin," were made from a copy of the Fasquelle edition.

Brian Stableford

MARCELLE

You're weeping, my love? Perhaps it's the cold wind from outside that is causing your chagrin, or my excessively monotonous amour. We're next to the fire; the curtains are trembling; there are books on the table. Just now I took your hand and I searched for sincere words. You're leaning on the arm of the chair, it seems to me that your heart is far away, and the clock is chiming between us. Oh, I know that my amour is not the one of which you've dreamed, and I sense myself that it isn't that. Those romantic desires for the unexpected, our ardors, have wandered on melancholy trams, have sat down on the benches of promenades, in little suburban cafés. Is it our own weakness that it's necessary to blame for the hovering sadness, or too poor an imagination, which doesn't know how to ornament the landscapes or, more simply, life, which is banal? Let's say that it's the sole guilty party, and that we love one another in spite of everything, Marcelle, for it's so painful to suffer ennui when one is in love that it seems then that the love is going to die. I've written poems, in order to say these things, which are in this drawer, and which I won't read to you. I content myself with asking you why you're weeping, and as you start to laugh through your tears then, and you put your arms around my neck politely, I savor profoundly the charm of not understanding.

Do you remember the evening in November when I met you? The shop windows were illuminated; a voluptuous lassitude trailed in the streets; it seemed that the same fever stirred our senses, made our words hesitant, our hands tremble. I walked with pride in being bedside you, for you had charm, without being a great beauty. We had reached a deserted spot; a pauper asked us for alms; in the distance, little girls were laughing and waving handkerchiefs, as if to salute the amour that was commencing as autumn was coming to an end.

Excitedly, you talked about your chagrins, your mother, who was dead, your Sunday afternoon, which was sad. I was astonished by the facility with which you confided yourself. The banality of my own speech afflicted me, and, not being able to tell you my own thoughts and dreams in the same sudden fashion, it seemed to me that I was far inferior to you.

We parted, and you shouted to me from a distance: "Until tomorrow!" making a sign with your umbrella. And I thought, I don't know why, of something my old maidservant had said to me the day before, pointing her finger at the rainy sky: "There'll be a lot of snow this winter."

I am twenty years-old and have a mistress called Marcelle. I love her because she has given herself to me without a hidden agenda, for the pleasure of her heart and her flesh. On Sunday afternoon we go along the avenues together, through the suburbs. Slow families wander idly, enjoying treading on grass that dust hasn't robbed of all its charm. Noisy couples sing and laugh; their gaiety, which afflicts me, gives her a sort of fever. But in order to be good to one another we go further, to where the roads are empty and sonorous, to where the soil recovers its vigor. How many correspondences that life of nature has in our being! Our sensibility is exasperated by solitude.

I remember the emotions that the passage of a diligence provoked. A passenger waved to us; we followed him with our eyes and our sympathy accompanied him for a long time in his unknown destiny. Marcelle pressed herself against me with a shiver, for all our sentiments became sensuality. The sight of lovers kissing made our knees buckle, and we experienced regret and joy. Our bodies appealed to one another ardently. We desired one another so forcefully that once, we went into an inn in order to make love in a bed scented with thyme, where rude peasants had made love before us. Another time, when night was falling and we had gone astray in the middle of fields, I possessed my lover on the bare ground. The silence was so solemn and augmented the pleasure of our bodies so much that, as we returned to the city, we wept with sadness and sensuality.

I've known evenings of intoxication. They are memorable because my soul is exalted therein and my comprehension of the universe is increased. My friend Raymond, who is a drunkard and a philosopher, knew a pleasant tavern frequented by working men and soldiers. The proximity of those noisy men didn't displease us in our hours of elevation. For from distracting our intelligence, it fortified it, and we thought, moreover, that souls like ours could only gain by hearing simple or vulgar speech. I avoided talking to my friend about Marcelle; he judged her unworthy of interest and considered my amour as a weakness of my nature. He detests that which is continuous, the material side of things, and my liaison with my mistress horrified him because of its quotidian manifestations.

Sitting in the open air, with drinks, we had conversations that embraced amour and life. We suddenly became active and generous and we were surrounded by a host of good deeds to accomplish. Then we were the most ambitious men in the world and we sensed astonishing faculties within us that would permit us all triumphs. We loved the women about whom we talked immediately. All ideas were familiar to us. Our existence appeared passionate and fecund.

A cool breeze caressed our foreheads, agitating our hair; head tilted back, we watched the passage of the stars; our heroic and fraternal reveries rose up between us like smoke.

My lover has extraordinary bouts of frankness. She wanted to tell me about all her amours. There was such a poverty of passion and such an evident trace of immoderate fantasy that I felt sorry for her. I know the names of all her lovers. There was one who followed her every morning without daring to speak to her, another who took her for excursions in a boat, another she only saw once and who left—but that one she would follow anywhere if he came back. Furthermore, she loved them all, because her greatest fault, she says, is becoming attached too quickly.

I put on an appearance of being philosophical and jovial, take an interest in her stories, and even question her about the details. I refrain from being ironic, for fear of being called mocking or malevolent, or emitting a trenchant opinion; I would be accused of not being like everybody else. I avoid, above all, remarks that are too sharp, because my lover is very sensitive. She grasps my distant thoughts when my words scarcely express them; she knows what I cannot say; she perceives with an extreme acuity the sympathies and antipathies between people. She weeps very easily. Pity, especially, causes her tears to flow. She says that it's necessary not to harm animals. One day, we found a cat in the country that children had injured mortally by stoning it. It died mewling softly. Marcelle sobbed on my shoulder for a long time, saying that she would rather have died than see that.

What I love most about Marcelle is that she is unable to put any barrier on her instincts. She doesn't hide her joy in giving herself to amour with false modesty. She states her desires, rejoices childishly in the pleasures she experiences and those she gives. Caresses are as natural to her body as leaves are to trees.

I am sitting at my table; outside, there is a blue spring afternoon. She comes in with an odor of violets. It is the bright street, the sun over the gardens and the youth and spontaneity of things that have spread through my room, over the furniture, in my thoughts. I have taken Marcelle in my arms. She goes mad at the first kiss. We both lose our minds. We are no longer in any determined place in the world. We embrace one another gently, in the landscape of our languor alone.

It's spring, the air is fine; we've passed the last houses in the suburbs. You press yourself against me and your head inclines slightly over my shoulder. Does our affection increase in the proximity of nature? We can't find any words to express what we feel, and sensuality is attenuated before the young life of things.

Lilacs in flower overflow a wall on to the road. It's a landscape of romance; it seems that we have the outdated appearance of lovers of old. You're wearing a crinoline and your name is Isabelle. Those flowers you're picking will decorate the little mansard where you live alone with your needle and your dreams...

Oh, can you, Marcelle, sometimes conform your complex soul to that ancient and naïve simplicity?

We go along a canal, beside trees. Further away there are moist vines. Fields of clover are quivering; a laborer in visible coming down a hill.

In one of those impulsive confidences typical of you, you suddenly start talking to me about your childhood.

You've always been unhappy; you don't remember your mother; your father beat you and neglected you, and still does today. There was only an old carpenter that you loved; he had a long beard; you played among the golden woodchips in his workshop and he made you toys with little pieces of wood; one day he fell ill and was taken to the hospital; you never saw him again; you don't know whether he's dead; but you often went to look at the barred windows of the poor-house, hoping to see the beard and kind eyes of the old carpenter appear there. Then there were gray days, all alike: long tedious Sundays; the returns to the workshop, the friends who taught you the art of dressing well and the poor coquetries of the street. Oh, certainly, it was necessary to admit it, you've had other lovers before me. But it wasn't your fault. You met the first one at a dance. That shouldn't matter to me anyway, since you no longer love anyone but me and you're going to love me forever.

I reply to you, Marcelle, that I'm very jealous of your past, and that I suffer greatly from the words of love you've heard, even more than those you've said. Everything I don't know about you worries me, the joy you've lavished on others is painful for me. I say these things only because it seems to me that I ought to say them and I sense that fundamentally, it's all the same to me.

Then there are silences. The grass is blue; the sun makes the water shine; a perfume rises from the fresh earth of the path. Suddenly, a bird cuts through the air, and now your soul had flown away. You're no longer the mistress that has known love in my arms, but some petty person that I've just encountered, and next to whom I'm embarrassed, as with a stranger. That's because, Marcelle, you're no longer beside me.

You're in a caleche, on a promenade full of people. You're wearing an elegant dress and pride embellishes you further. People whisper as you go by and you sense jealousy and admiration palpitating over your skin like a physic caress. You're sitting on the perron of a château; a domestic is bringing you fruits and beverages; the sun is setting over a park; adorers are leaning toward you; but you're gazing languorously at roses agitated by the wind.

Oh, I have no need for you to describe them for me to understand them, your desires for luxury. They're in your fascinated eyes before shop windows, behind your gestures, in your liking for clothes, adornment, everything beautiful and useless. But it's necessary to get rid of them, those desires; they'll give you bad advice and I know that you're weak enough to listen to them.

We come back slowly. The delicacy of things fills us. The evening makes the leaves and the grass tremble, and ripples the water. Laborers are returning from work, women are chatting on doorsteps; it seems that the community of those people shocks you.

Let's hurry, Marcelle, in order to know the sad joy of the last fires that are lit in houses in spring.

You came to tell me that day that your father was dead. I took your hands, searching vainly within myself for the spontaneous exclamation that would have consoled you, and your

26

blue eyes became so sad that I didn't know whether it was your chagrin that was causing your tears or the falsity of my compassion.

Then I followed you in the city to a house of workers in the depths of a suburb. What! It was between those walls, Marcelle, that you'd lived, that your fine soul had developed! Your father was on the bed, stiff, with taut features: a poor man, for whom it was necessary to weep, Marcelle, even though he beat you often and scarcely looked after you in our childhood. You sobbed next to the bed. Aged women who were there talked to me about your mother, whom they had known, about you, who were an orphan, about your future. They weren't astonished that I had come, since I loved the daughter of the dead man, and the simplicity of the hearts of those poor people moved me as much as the spectacle of grief.

In the early morning daylight the following day, I wanted to see the funeral pass. The form of your regrets intrigues me, and your attitude with regard to human remains. You wept a great deal, leaning on the arm of a neighbor. Oh, how can I know what importance you give to those tears? What emotion can engrave itself so forcefully that the whim of time won't erase it?

The dead don't depart with the coffins. The funeral is over and they're still in the house. They remain invisible, but they can be heard walking in other rooms. At any moment they'll open the door, sit down at the table, in accordance with the bleak habits of their life. So, Marcelle, it will take days for you to become accustomed to your solitude. It's only then that it will overwhelm you with all its weight. I know that that's painful. However, on seeing you go by behind the convoy, in the sad suburban street, I rejoice in your tears. I want the sunset to afflict you this evening, so that you'll be very unhappy, and that it will last a long time. That way, at least, I'll be sure of your heart.

I see a beggar-woman at a corner. Age weighs upon her stooped back; her miserable face is full of pain; she groans because death is passing by. Death! She understands it better than us, the poor old woman who marches toward it every day, slowly, with her crutch and her beggar's wallet.

You have a lover, Marcelle, who dresses in black to appear more serious than he is and who shows a great deal of audacity in matters of life in order to hide his timidity. The equality of his soul suits the variety of our humor marvelously. But doesn't his cheerfulness seem to you to be too systematic to be sincere? And then, he analyzes the joy of your hours of amour; he knows the meaning of decors and gestures. He summarizes their beauty too much, and there are things so sweet that one ought never to say them for fear of attenuating them.

I dread, Marcelle, that you only have for me the ephemeral affection of shared physical pleasure. That affection, everyone can attain. I'd like you to love the person that I am, outside the minutes when our kisses cease to be chaste, for you to love our true love, made of the delicacy of our rapport, of common dreams, what there is between us of sincerity and forgiveness.

Easter has arrived. I'm far away from Marcelle and I'm writing to her at length in order that her memory doesn't abandon me excessively. She scarcely responds, and I prefer that, for the qualities that constitute her charm can't affect a written form.

I'm in a country house. There's a young woman. She's fifteen years old. She's at boarding school, and during the vacations she plays croquet and performs pieces on the piano that are not without charm. Immediately, we become friends. Her name is Paule. She's one of those in whom the grace of the child becomes the sensual charm of the woman without passing through the troubled states of adolescence. Her gestures reveal a slightly unhealthy nervousness and contact with any being gives her body a voluptuous tremor. That disquiet of the senses, with the naivety of her imagination and her ignorance of things, makes her youthful soul delightful.

We walk together in the park. It seems to me that she's a younger Marcelle, who braids her hair and has a different education. I imagine what my lover would be like, rich and not knowing the necessity of working. I imagine her relationships with the geraniums in the greenhouse, the big guard dog, the fountain. My companion talks to me about dancing, which she adores, her vacations that are too short. I understand by the thoughtlessness of her speech that she has not seen many young men. She's unaware as yet of coquetry. It seems to me that she would like me to talk to her about love, just like that, right away, but I'm embarrassed by her youth and the memory of Marcelle.

We went out all afternoon in a carriage full of people and came back at dusk along the highway.

An odor of hay rises from the neighboring fields; a laborer causes a scythe to glint. Paule's gaze meets mine; in front of a farm hayricks gleam.

She says to me: "I'll give you this cornflower; bring it back to me next year and I'll know whether you've been thinking about me."

What anxiety experienced, to the sound of little bells in the quivering of the dust! Why couldn't I live with a little girl who hadn't loved anyone before me?

I know the sweetness of the awakening sympathy. The morning air is mild; I penetrate the soul of the park by way of the child who explains it to me. Then it rains; our meditations are next to windows, and the odor of damp earth embalms them. The charm of those hours. It isn't amour. It's necessary to leave before monotony sets in.

It's time to say goodbye. "I can kiss you, can't I? Don't forget me; my memory will be with you."

You reply: "Oh, no, it isn't necessary to say that. I know full well that you won't be thinking about me tomorrow. You doubtless have other amours awaiting you. How lucky you are to be free! I only know you, and I'm going back to boarding school, me, who would so like to know life…"

A cricket sings in the grass; not far away, a windmill is turning and making bread. The sun is setting; amour is drawing away to the horizon…

Little girl, that's what it is, life…

You're wearing more elegant dresses than before, Marcelle, and your frequent leisure time makes me think that you can't be working very much. I can't think about you without making a reproach; the facility of possessing you more often is like a gift that you offer me on my return.

We still make love in the closed room, but doesn't it seem to you that the air in which our kisses circulate is new? The furniture doesn't have the same benevolence, and how differently the lamp trembles! It seems that the season has changed in a few days and we no longer have the same ease in order to savor the charm of the hours. Your lips quiver, however, and you abandon yourself in my arms. I sense that your oaths are sincere and that you love me. The gaiety of our souls and the ardor of our flesh, rediscover one another. I talk to you about my hopes far from you, the desires that consumed me. I scarcely question you, by virtue of discretion. I would like you to tell me, with your habitual charming expansion, about the monotonous things of your life, which still interest me. But I believe, alas, that there's a reserve in your response, and an afterthought in your caresses.

I know that I'm telling a very banal story. I have a lover; I love her, and she deceives me. But existence is a series of very ordinary petty events, and it's that succession of which the tragedy of things is made. When I had the conviction that the insouciant Marcelle was experiencing amour in other arms than mine, the chagrin that it caused me did not take any dramatic form. Our life is too poor in fine actions for us to be able to conceive it as a novel, and there's no point in travestying the details. I experienced a great, slow and continuous sadness, and I don't know why I strove incessantly not to let it show. I took a kind of personal pride in not being moved by the course of my thoughts. I went out at the same times with my friends and I responded in an agreeable tone when they talked to me about my mistress.

I didn't ask myself whether Marcelle no longer loved me, even though it was the only thing that mattered to me. I didn't think about it for a single instant. A cruel egotism made me suffer from the pleasures that Marcelle had made known to others, as if those pleasures had been stolen from me, but I experienced that jealousy less because I felt it myself than because it seemed to me that other men would have experienced it in my situation.

Marcelle will wait for me this evening in vain. The weather is stormy, and troubled. The streets are buzzing; instruments resound, the crowd is packed around fairground booths. A carousel is turning in the light. Why did I want to chase away my sadness? Ought not all our sentiments blossom? It seems to me that my soul is like a clown who cuts ridiculous capers to please the public instead of wearing with pride and dignity the misery of his life.

I've fled into a remote street. I bemoan my fate. My mistress has betrayed me. I'll never be able to make myself loved; am I not the most unfortunate of men?

An old couple go past, arm in arm, talking in low voices. Over so many years, what misfortunes have struck them? They must have suffered the vanity of amour, fatal things. And yet, there they are. They're walking placidly and when the spring nights are arm, they must still make love and know the joy of the senses as in the days of their youth.

Oh, I know full well that I'll be consoled, but the present remains the same in spite of that...

I'm in a solitary café. Where is Marcelle now? What is she thinking? A waitress looks at me with astonishment, and I perceive that I'm weeping simply, like someone who has a chagrin.

I've written a letter to Marcelle. I say to her: *You're no longer my beloved. I believed in you. Your foolish and eccentric little soul adapted to my gravity, and we've savored all the joys of the flesh in one another's arms. You swooned over my heart as if to die of it. When we went into the country together nature quivered; we felt related to the landscapes, for amour renders us sensitive and clairvoyant to the life of things. Why have you broken that bond? You've betrayed me. You need something new, I imagine. But couldn't we have renewed our love by a continual sincerity? Oh, the beautiful evenings we've known! Do you remember them? Flowers picked in gardens, between the railings, our hopes, returning home in warm April rain, and our pity, more noble because it was common. Your caprice has therefore allowed you to weary of all that. And what a lie yours has been! You've made me believe that you would always love me and you've put enough languor into our kisses to give me the illusion of it. What was the point of that deception? Perhaps you wanted to keep me because of a habit of your senses. My pride would suffer too much in possessing you after others. Perhaps you've felt sorry for me and you've tried to accustom my self-esteem gradually to your abandonment. Women don't make those concessions to the charity of amour. A deplorable attitude of my will makes me weaken before action, and I'm writing to you, Marcelle, to tell you that we won't see one another again.*

Marcelle has no pride. Someone knocks on the door; it's her. And immediately she cries: "It's true; I've deceived you; but you had gone away. I was so bored without you and I could only think that you knew that. And then, you see, recently, I was weary of working and it was necessary to live and be beautiful. But you, but you, in spite of all that, how can you believe that I no longer loved you?"

It seems to me now, in recalling her words, that at that moment I was no longer myself, that in my mind received ideas were triumphant, theories of relatives and friends, false purity and false virtue, that current mediocrity took possession of me. A pride and an unknown jealousy stung me.

I stood up, and with a cruelty in my voice and gestures that I found I know not where, being naturally gentle, and the memory of which informs me forever what evil depths there are in my soul. I said to her: "Get out."

She went, and I remained stupefied by the unworthiness of my conduct.

What shame overwhelms me! I have killed amour, alas, by virtue of stupidity and pride. I have not been generous enough to forget. Oh, Marcelle, what did a temporary caprice matter to me, since you loved me and you delivered yourself freely to me in the fervor of your youth? I scorned you! But it's me who should have knelt down before you and begged your pardon or my unjust and suspicious heart, which had hovered like a sad black bird over the frivolity of your sentiments.

You were submissive to your flesh; your thought was ignorant and tremulous. The voice of instinct spoke in you more loudly than all other voices. You abandoned yourself to life.

And what sin have you committed? You surrendered yourself to men because you were obsessed with their desire, because you would have judged yourself cruel not to realize possible joys. You listened to nature. You loved them as they loved you, for a common hour of sensuality. No one had informed you about good and evil; no one had said to you: this is the boundary separating the fields; here is the wheat and here are the weeds; and you continued walking because the earth smelled good in spring.

You're in an arbor with a new lover and joyful company. You've forgotten me. Bright wine is flowing into glasses. The sun is making the leaves tremble and your skin quiver. The peace of things is coming to you like a voluptuous caress. Your soul is full of sweetness. In a little while, you'll hear words of love. Your lips will be burning and you'll swoon with languor and desire.

I can still see you in the mist of years. You're sitting in a room. Your hair is gray. A fire is burning. On a table there are letters, photographs, and dried flowers. One by one you are throwing all those memories in the fire, ash and smoke. Your thoughts travel into the past. You evoke all your lovers. There are some whom you confound with one another, others that have disappeared from your soul. One of them makes you pause; he was a singular individual; you loved him because he believed in life, like you, and he was young and enthusiastic. Against that one, like the others, you bear no grudge. Melancholy rises in response to these past things. Vanity of the heart, embraces are futile if nothing of them remains. No, since you created joy in offering your beauty and your amour to all comers, as another would give loaves of bread to poor people.

DOCTOR FAUST'S FIRST LOVE

Once, in a small town whose name I have forgotten, there lived a man justly renowned for his wisdom and his science, and a young student celebrated for the levity of his mind.

It is said that the knowledge of Dr. Faust was infinite. Every plant became virtuous in his hands; a cripple he had visited threw his crutches toward the heavens on the threshold of his house. Three astrologers had come from France to consult him. A rich Danish lord, mute from birth, arrived in the town one evening to the sound of trumpets, followed by a cortege of pages and halberdiers; after a short conversation with Dr. Faust he was talking like a preacher monk and haranguing the trees along the road and the birds in the sky on every subject.

Some said that such a power came from the Devil, others from God, for the judgments of men are different.

Of all the blond students who spent their time singing love songs, wooing beautiful girls under the linden trees and emptying large tankards of beer in the taverns. Fritz was certainly the most joyful, the most insouciant and the most foolish. He did not believe in either science or virtue. He had lovely blue eyes and a bold expression, and he pleased women because he desired them, without loving them in his heart. He considered that life is like a long road along which it is necessary to walk cheerfully, only pausing to pick a flower or smile at a young woman washing clothes in a stream. One friend dies, another marries; one dances and one puts on mourning. That is the course of things. God was waiting at the end of the journey, with a long pipe and yellow boots, outside the Inn of Paradise, and would judge him by the number of bottles of Rhenish wine he had been able to empty.

The student's house was opposite the scientist's. Fritz's smile and Faust's beard, wisdom and folly, were good neighbors; the world is full of such contrasts.

Now, when Fritz reached his twentieth year he fell in love. That happened on a fine Sunday in spring. That day, the skin of women was creamier than usual, and the beer on the threshold of taverns had an admirable color. Fritz was wandering through the streets, on his own. Pipe-smoke was rising up so thickly that it obscured the sun; a mild peace seemed to possess all hearts; young women were going for walks wearing new bonnets and their most beautiful dresses; audacious clerks were following them closely, and more than one kiss could be heard in the solitary pathways.

Fritz emerged from the town and reached a small wood; he saw peasants dancing under the chestnut-trees; dusk was falling gradually and the shadows rendered the trees solemn.

The music of violins resounded in the distance in the warm air; a young woman went by, and her gaze met Fritz's. Her dress had a mysterious rustle, and she disappeared around a bed in the path. But what was the student experiencing? What had that gaze cast into his soul? It seemed to him that he discovered the trees and the sky, the beauty of the world, and that his life was beginning. He ran in time to see the shadow of the young woman decreasing on the horizon, but she was a long way off. Then he retraced his steps, slowly, sat down on a bench and, perhaps for the first time, he wept.

Fritz soon learned that the young woman that he loved was the beautiful Elsbeth, the only daughter of burgomaster Frosch. Fritz had a simple nature, and in him, action always followed dreams. He therefore ran to ask for her hand in marriage.

Burgomaster Frosch had one quality and one fault: he was moral and miserly. The student Fritz, on the contrary, was reputed to have no restraint in his conduct and to throw his money out of the window. Burgomaster Frosch therefore sent the student Fritz away, and, in order to avoid the enterprises of the audacious individual, he resolved to engage the beautiful Elsbeth to one of his friends, a rich and aged lord.

The beautiful Elsbeth, like so many of her peers, hid a mediocre soul beneath the adornment of her floating hair, her brilliant skin and her pure eyes, for the ideal does not always take the most beautiful forms in nature in order to realize itself. She therefore accepted the rich and aged lord as a fiancé, deeming that she would console herself for amorous kisses with precious garments, Tibetan shawls and silks from China.

When the student Fritz learned that, he fell into a great despair, and spent the first three days getting drunk on strong wine. And as his chagrin had not eased after that time, he ran to a courtesan who was one of his female friends and spent three days with her. That time having elapsed, he was even more unhappy, because of bodily fatigue, which makes the soul wretched and weak. Then he thought that science and labor might perhaps bring a remedy to his woes. He bought books, optical instruments and poisons, and, for three further days, he studied the circulation of the blood in the human body, the transfusion of metals and the movement of the planets. His suffering only increased with his knowledge of the world. He resolved to ask Dr. Faust to cure him of the malady of amour.

On the eve of his hundredth year, Dr. Faust had a dream.

In that dream, he saw himself again as he had been in the time of his youth, not too ugly in the face, curious and good, loving nature and life. Already the flame of telescopes and the mysterious design of maps appeared to him to be more beautiful than the eyes of women.

There was a young maidservant in the neighborhood named Gretchen, who put on every morning, in his honor, a well-ironed bonnet and a pink apron, and who often went past his door, carrying water, tucking her skirt up with a gesture she knew to be pretty. She loved the student Faust because she was naïve and hard-working, but he did not want to know her, and tried to elevate his soul toward the most august thoughts.

Now, the dream that haunted Dr. Faust's mind that evening represented to him a sad winter evening vanished in the past, when Gretchen's eyes had met his for the first time. Faust was alone, snow was beating the window-panes, and someone had knocked on the door. It was little Gretchen, who, blushing and bold, had simply come to offer herself to the man she loved. And Faust, without hesitation, even though he had a good heart, had sent her away, for he was also proud and he believed that he would be able to embrace and conquer the world by means of his labor. A little sob had resounded in the snow, and he had never seen Gretchen again.

And now, after so many years, Faust heard a voice that said to him: "Weep, old man, for the child whose love you rejected; weep for the joys that you have not known, ignorant individual who did not know that the greatest wisdom is to live like all men."

Dr. Faust woke up, his forehead bathed in sweat. The yellow lamplight trembled on the walls. He looked at the dusty books, the sadly lined-up flasks, the jars, the retorts, the instruments. And then, remembering, he wept bitterly.

It was the following day that the student Fritz, introduced by the disciple Wagner, penetrated into Dr. Faust's room. A thousand strange objects were set out beneath a high ceiling: a death's-head, placed on the table, seemed ready to cry out to the visitor: "I'm the master of the house; what do you want?" At the back, sitting in his armchair, Dr. Faust was plunged in a profound reverie.

Then Fritz recounted to him his youthful folly, his unhappy amour, and how he had resolved to extinguish the flame of his desires within him. And when he had spoken, Dr. Faust stood up, prey to a great agitation, and replied to him:

"I only know my dementia, which is the equal of yours. What! Because a woman who has pretty eyes and has pleased you is going to marry an old lord, you want to renounce life? How lucky you are to have a supple body, blond hair, to love, and even to suffer! You envy my science, child? I'm the most ignorant of men, and there is no shepherd boy in the world who does not have more knowledge than me. You've come to interrogate me? But it's me who ought to have come to you, like a pilgrim with rope sandals and a cloak the color of rust. You could have informed me about the sweetness of loving a woman and thinking about her in the evening while going to sleep in a meadow. Fortunate are the amorous, fortunate are the mad! They walk like the blind, and yet they don't fall into wells, like sages. What cheerful companions fantasy and caprice are! Give me a fool's bauble and bells, young student..."

Faust started groaning, and then hid his head in his hands; and the student Fritz left, full of grief, because the truth has never consoled amour...

Several months had gone by, and one evening. Dr. Faust was meditating with even more melancholy than usual. It was winter, it was snowing, and snow gives old men sad dreams of shrouds and tombs. Then again, the bells and celebratory songs had been resounding all day, for the burgomaster's daughter was getting married. Out there, young men and young women were dancing the wedding quadrilles merrily; he was shivering by the fire. Faust's logical mind was not pleased by those contradictions.

Someone knocked several times on the door. Faust started, thinking that it might perhaps be Death that was passing by and had come to collect him. He trembled; but he was proud, and, not wanting to show any fear, he said:

"You are cruel, certainty, to come to take me away from all these good things. I was working in peace with all these dear auxiliaries of my research. But I welcome you without surprise and without fear, for I recognize your footsteps behind my door. Let me take this blue flower, this cedar stick, and I'm your companion."

Faust opened the door, and was utterly astonished to see, instead of the grimacing visage of Death, the delicate and pretty features of Gretchen, such as he had known her of old. She smiled sadly, and made him a sign to follow her. The snow was shining in the distance and Faust's mind was full of allegories. An unknown tenderness descended within him, and sweet and childish confessions hastened to his lips. "Oh, Gretchen, you whom I was unable to love, forgive me!" he cried.

Gretchen, in her white bonnet and pink apron, was still smiling, and Faust followed her through the snow. She went through the streets, emerged from the town and ran along a path. They arrived at a little wood of chestnut-trees. They stopped; the trees were beautiful and grave, and thoughts of amour were floating in the sky.

The violins that were playing at the beautiful Elsbeth's wedding were vaguely audible and, raising his eyes, Faust saw the body of the student Fritz swinging gently, hanging from a high branch. He extended his arms toward Gretchen, saying: "Look at our different follies, and how we have been punished for them."

Dr. Faust wept in the snow, and now the student Fritz, at a sign from Gretchen, descended from his tree, and a great light inundated the earth, and the landscape changed and became divinely beautiful. The trees rose up all the way to the sky, a road of blue ice descended toward a miraculous valley. Gretchen had taken Fritz's hand and Faust's hand. One had loved a great deal, the other had dreamed a great deal; there was much they had to be forgiven.

And behind the little girl with the sad smile, the young student and the old scholar entered the realm of the dead.

MARINETTE AND THE OLD WATER-SPRITE

On the bank of a canal there was a worthy man, a lock-keeper by profession, who lived in a white house with green shutters. His wife had no children, and he was very content on the day when she brought into the world a pretty little girl. He called her Marinette.

Shortly after her birth, Marinette's mother died. The worthy man continued to open and close the lock gates alone when boats went by on the canal, and he consoled himself for his monotonous life in seeing his daughter grow up and become more beautiful every day.

Marinette lived happily on the shady banks of the canal outside the house with the green shutters, with the pleasant thoughts of childhood. She collected bouquets, seized the boatmen by the hand and sometimes addressed a few words to them that brought smiles to their faces, hardened by a laborious life. She did not know anything of the pleasures of society and did not desire them.

When her fifteenth year arrived, however, she felt gripped by a new anxiety, by a delightful need for confidences and tenderness. She wept without knowing why and loved her sadness, even though its cause was hidden from her.

One day when she was out walking beside the water, some distance from the house, in a place where the trees provided a very dense shade, she sat down among the daisies and wild flowers and said: "How I'd love to know why I'm so sad."

The immobile waves quivered then and parted, and Marinette perceived in front of her the bearded and melancholy

41

face of a water-sprite.[1] She was afraid and thought about running away, but the water-sprite appeared so benevolent and so awkward that she started to laugh and listened to what he said.

"You're sad, Marinette, because you want to be loved. I'm an old water-sprite of the canal. I've known you for a long time now, having followed you from beneath these dormant waters, and loving you secretly. But even though my appearance is gross, I have a timid heart beneath these rude scales. I did not dare to speak to you; I've finally determined to do it. Would you like to marry me and live in a moist dwelling? We'll make bouquets of water-lilies. I'll show you strange fish when the moonlight floats on the water and the frogs are singing."

Marinette started to laugh heartily and only stopped because of the sadness that suddenly appeared on the water-sprite's face. She regretted having offended him and said: "I'll be your friend, old water-sprite, if you wish, but I can't marry you, not because I find you ugly or tedious, but because we're very different from one another."

Night was about to fall and she drew away, saying: "Until tomorrow."

Now, there was in the vicinity a young man who lived in idleness, although he was very poor. His name was Fortuné. He lived in a small cabin not far from the lock where Marinette was. His family had disowned him and thrown him out because he was a poet. He did, in fact, write verses about nature, the rustic life, the setting sun and the eyes of Marinette, with whom he was in love. Everything he wrote was infinitely sad. In almost all his poems he begged death to come to liber-

---

[1] The original text has the word *ondin*, which is a masculine form of *ondine* [undine]. In French, elemental spirits in the nomenclature widely popularized by a text falsely attributed to Paracelsus have two sexes, whereas in English they do not—the tacit implication of English parlance being that water elementals are essentially female—thus necessitating the substitution of a synonym.

ate him from the heavy burden of an unhappy life, and he cursed his cruel destiny. In truth his nature was open and joyful, and his character was so well made that the cares of existence left him indifferent.

One day he met Marinette in the fields and they exchanged a few words about the weather, the seasonal fruits and the number of boats that were passing along the canal. Fortuné was full of gaiety and charm, and Marinette, whose heart was sensible, went back to the house with the green shutters very troubled.

Her astonishment was great the next day when she received through the intermediary of a poor hunchback a long letter in verse from Fortuné. That letter informed her that he was wounded by an amour so great that only death could appease it.

She ran in tears in the direction of his house in order to try to stop his fatal project. She met him on a path, singing. He did not mention the letter to her and chatted with her as joyfully as could be.

However, yet another person in the surrounding area had fallen in love with Marinette. He was a very rich lord, the Marquis de Terremort, who lived in a château that resembled a fortress. He lived in a frightful melancholy because he had been born under the sign of Saturn. He had everything that a man of his condition could desire: servants, feasts, a perfumed bed, large hunting-grounds, humble neighbors that he could humiliate and women disposed to love him, but his mind was naturally chagrined because of the star that influenced him.

Having seen Marinette, he loved her; and as he judged himself to be incapable of pronouncing the light words that charm women, he resolved to use violence to abduct her. He therefore gathered his servants, made them dress as boatmen and climbed with them into a large vessel laden with barrels that was going along the canal. The worthy lock-keeper turned his handle and saluted them as they passed by.

That day, Marinette had fallen asleep sitting on the bank some distance from her house. The Marquis de Terremort saw her. The place was deserted. He made a sign to two of his men. Marinette was taken prisoner without having been able to utter a scream, and without anyone witnessing the deed.

The boat drew away to the horizon under the shade of the trees. The melancholy face of the water-sprite appeared above the water; two tears ran from his enormous eyes, like beads of glass.

The canal beside which these events unfolded ended in a river; that river ended in the sea. At its mouth there was a flourishing port, and great commercial vessels left from there for the Americas, India and China.

Marinette was very unhappy to have fallen into the hands of unknown men. As she did not know anything of life, she vaguely feared either being eaten, after having been killed and cut into pieces, or of suffering even more horrible treatments alive, which she conceived without being able to imagine them in an exact fashion.

The Marquis de Terremort was also very unhappy. As he had been born under the sign of Saturn, he could not accomplish any action without regretting it bitterly immediately afterwards. He felt remorse at having abducted Marinette, but on the other hand, his amour was too violent for him to set her free.

Seeing her melancholy, he thought that a long voyage would distract her soul and make her forget her homeland and her former life. He charted a three-master in order to depart for distance climes.

Meanwhile, Fortuné was looking for Marinette around the house with the green shutters. He loved her with all the sincerity of which a poet is capable and he waited for her that day with an extreme impatience. He was on the water's edge; he contemplated the reeds agitated by the wind, and their slight murmur made an amorous song of perfect harmony for his soul.

Then the old water-sprite appeared and spoke to him.

"Monsieur Poet," he said, "never again will you see Marinette with the soft eyes, the daughter of the worthy lock-keeper who lives in the house with the green shutters. She has been carried away on a boat by the Marquis de Terremort, a rich lord born under the sign of Saturn. I saw it, and I would have prevented it if I had had the arms and the heart of a valiant man, but I'm only a poor water-sprite, accustomed to living in marshes and dormant canals. Rescue her if you can, and if you love her enough to make the attempt."

Having heard those words, Fortuné thanked the water-sprite and started running along the bank. His entire wealth consisted of his pointed hat, a gray cloak and a hazel-wood staff.

Night fell and he lay down under an oak tree in order to sleep. A boat stopped not far away. The boatmen came ashore and lit a big fire.

In spite of his chagrin at having lost Marinette, Fortuné was joyful deep down because he detested his monotonous life and he saw in that the pretext for a long series of adventures and the subject of several poems that ought, he judged, to be admirable.

He chatted with the boatmen and gave proof of such a pleasant character that they invited him to share their meal and consented to give him a place on their boat.

He went with them all the way to the flourishing port, where the Marquis de Terremort had arrived the previous day.

He accompanied his new friends to the quayside taverns in which mariners drank, recounted their voyages and fought one another with knives.

And the first evening, as the smoke of pipes rose in thick clouds, a man who said that his name was Renaud came to asked them if they wanted to sign on with the crew of the Marquis de Terremort, who was departing for a long cruise.

All the boatmen refused, one having a fiancée, another aged parents and a third a love of his homeland. Fortuné accepted joyfully and went with Renaud.

The next day, the Marquis de Terremort's ship set sail and headed for the high seas.

Marinette occupied a cabin at the front of the ship, where she lived in a perpetual terror. The Marquis de Terremort had given her jewels and precious robes, and he hoped by means of continual respect and magnificent presents gradually to engender amour for him in her heart. He sometimes came to sit beside her and stayed there, immobile, in silence, unable to find anything to say to her. The rest of the time he remained solitary, lost in horrible thoughts, for he was naturally inclined to sadness.

On the third day, wandering at dusk on the deck of the ship, Marinette perceived the joyful face of a young mariner who bore a marvelous resemblance to Fortuné. The young mariner put a finger to his lips, and she realized that it really was the man she loved. She conceived a great joy from that, and as the sun was setting over the sea, she discovered that the appearance of things had a sublime beauty.

Meanwhile, Fortuné had conceived a heroic project.

The next day, when Marinette was strolling on the deck gain, he approached her and said to her, in a low voice: "Leave your cabin at midnight. You'll find me on the deck. We'll climb into the lifeboat; we'll cut the ropes connecting it to the ship and we'll sail away over the waves, by the grace of God.

Night fell; they were hidden by the shadow of the main mast. Fortuné took Marinette in his arms and, for the first time, he gave her a kiss on the lips, to which the shadow, the sea wind and the danger gave an inestimable price.

At the peak of happiness, Fortuné drank joyfully during the meal with the mariners, his companions. He believed in the goodness of men and his character bore him naturally to expansion. He liked his heart to be an open book to everyone's eyes.

The warmth of the wine, the approach of danger and the sympathetic faces of the mariners bore him even more to confidences. He could not help making his project known to a small group of six men, who rejoiced a great deal, giving him a thousand good wishes and swearing to keep his secret eternally. One of them, named Julius, more sensitive than the others, shed tender tears and asked Fortuné for the favor of accompanying him and sharing his perils.

And Fortuné was very emotional in his heart to have found such friends.

The hours went by rapidly; a fine rain was falling from the sky. Fortuné was alone on deck.

Suddenly, he sees Marinette's white dress shining in the distance. He cannot hold back a cry of joy, but how great is his dolor and his indignation when he is seized, knocked down and solidly bound by a group of mariners, at whose head he recognizes Julius.

"These faithful men have warned me about your treason," the Marquis of Terremort said to him then, his terrible silhouette cut out against the night sky. "Recommend your soul to God, for your death is imminent."

He leaned over the sea and saw enormous sharks, which, doubtless having understood what was happening, had grouped around the ship and were agitating their jaws with a frightful sound.

The moon suddenly appeared and cast a mysterious softness over the world. Marinette had fallen in a faint and Fortuné's eyes were filled by her gracious form.

The Marquis de Terremort made a sign. Julius and another mariner seized Fortuné and hurled him into the sea.

An hour later, the Marquis de Terremort had the ship stop and a launch put to sea, in order to save Fortuné if there was still time. He was unable to accomplish any action without having remorse for it.

The search was vain. Then he tore out his hair and fell into a melancholy even more profound than any he had known before.

At the moment when Fortuné had fallen into the water, all the sharks had precipitated themselves upon him in order to devour him. But the old water-sprite had suddenly appeared in their midst and, seizing Fortuné by his long hair, had made a sign to the redoubtable animals that he was keeping that prey for himself.

All the sharks had drawn away respectfully, for they honored water-sprites because they had human faces and were more intelligent than them.

The shore was a long way away, but the water-sprite carried Fortuné there and laid him on the sand, unconscious. Then he sat beside him.

As dawn broke, Fortuné came round and the water-sprite spoke to him in these terms:

"I've saved you from the foamy sea and the sharks with sharp teeth in order that, by means of the resources of your intelligence, you can succeed in rescuing Marinette. Don't thank me. It wouldn't have taken much for me to leave you to perish of a frightful death, in order that your white bones could be rolled by the divine waves. I love Marinette, and yesterday, in spite of the mist, I saw your lips unite at the foot of the main mast. If I shed a few tears, they're out there, in the depths of the Ocean, with the debris of shipwrecks, prodigious beasts and millenarian plants. How, though, could such a gracious daughter of men ever love such a melancholy water-sprite, whose eyes are like balls of glass? But there, I forgive you your happiness. I shall be only too happy when you have liberated her and married her, if you still come to exchange a few words in the evening beside the canal where I've built my solitary dwelling."

Having said that, and without waiting for Fortuné's response, he disappeared into the waves.

Fortuné marched along the shore for a long time. He was full of confidence in the future, but he wondered anxiously how he could find Marinette again.

As dusk was falling and he climbed a sandy hill, he perceived a city at his feet, all white in the mist that was falling.

Perhaps, he thought, the Marquis de Terremort's ship had stopped at this place.

He saw a young child wearing a multicolored mantle sitting in the heather, playing a flute. The sounds that he drew from his instrument were pleasant to hear, and Fortuné asked the boy to teach him his art.

The child cut a reed, hollowed it out with his knife and made it into a flute, which he gave to Fortuné. Then he showed him the manner in which it was necessary to blow into it at equal intervals in order to make an agreeable music emerge.

They walked to the city together, and on the way Fortuné learned that the child was called Ali, that he was a flute-player by profession, and that the country where they were walking was Turkey.

They lived together for several days, going into the houses of the rich after feasts in order to help the companions seated round the table to rejoice and to dream. Fortuné made up little stories in verse, preferably compliments to ladies, which he declaimed to the great joy of all. He acquired an infinitely rapid renown in high society; his good humor charmed everyone, especially the ladies, and more than once he could have been the object of their favors if the thought of Marinette had not occupied his soul entirely.

Someone came to look for Ali one day to ask them to go to the house of a rich French lord who lived in a marble palace near the sea, and who astonished the city with his magnificence.

The Marquis de Terremort was hosting a great feast, to which he had invited a few noble Turks.

When the feast was over the flute-players were introduced.

Marinette was sitting next to the marquis. Fortuné saw with joy that her sadness had left signs on her face. Their eyes met for a moment and Marinette recognized him. He could not master his spontaneous nature; he dropped his flute, stood up and went to take Marinette in his arms and embrace her recklessly.

The Marquis de Terremort also recognized him and uttered a frightful scream. All the servants came running. Ali tipped over a candelabrum and fled. The notable Turks did not know whether that was a French custom or whether they were witnessing an unprecedented scandal.

Renaud and Julius had seized Fortuné and dragged him outside. A terrible struggle ensued. But, being skillful in mental labor, Fortuné only had a mediocre physical strength. He was knocked down by his adversaries in an instant.

"I'll strangle him with my arms," said Renaud.

"I'll plunge my dagger into his heart," said Julius.

"No," said the Marquis de Terremort. "There's a very deep well at the bottom of the garden; throw him into it, and we'll never hear mention of him again."

This is my final hour, Fortuné thought. *My life was short but beautiful, in sum.*

And Renaud and Julius threw him into the well.

He fell into icy and salty water, but he did not feel the taste of it in his mouth. An arm sustained him above the surface and he heard a voice speaking to him. His eyes adapted to the darkness and the recognized the water-sprite.

"Thank God, it has been given to me to save you again. I've come all the way here by means of subterranean streams. Knowing that Marinette was living in the château, I was waiting for an opportunity to be of use to her. There's a profound tunnel here that will allow you to get back to the surface of the earth. Follow it, and when you find Marinette, tell her that you've seen me and that it was me who got you out of the well."

Fortuné went into the tunnel indicated to him by the water-sprite. He walked beneath the damp earth, touching salamanders, long worms and viscous animals with his hands and forehead. He finally perceived the soft light of the night.

Then he went to the city in order to go in search of Ali, the flute-player.

That day, the Marquis de Terremort took Marinette for an excursion in a carriage. He was surrounded by a dozen servants on horseback and the Turks, who are a poor and badly-dressed people, gazed with admiration at their garments covered with embroideries.

Julius, who was at the head of the cortege, was proud of that. He was sensitive to the glances of women, and sought them with his gaze. But the custom of the land was that they were veiled; and Julius was afflicted by not being able to see, in the pretty faces, the smiling sympathy that he thought he was engendering on all sides.

They arrived in a rocky valley at the far end of which there was a blue lake that was sparkling in the dusk. A light mist was floating over the water. The landscape was so tranquil and so beautiful that the Marquis de Terremort had his carriage stop, gave his servants the order to dismount, and wanted to walk with Marinette under the trees not far from the lake.

He did so, and Julius, having tethered the horses, sat down at the foot of a tree, prey to obscure thoughts. He saw a woman a short distance away, who was smiling at him.

She was extraordinarily beautiful, and her face was not veiled—a surprising circumstance in that Turkish land.

The woman gestured to him; Julius thought that his costume, combined with his personal grace, had touched her and he ran forward with an extreme urgency but scant surprise.

His astonishment commenced when he suddenly felt himself enlaced by moist arms and dragged beneath the waves of the lake without being able to utter a cry.

The servants of the Marquis de Terremort who had spread out in the vicinity also saw gracious women beckoning to them, and, victims of the same desire as Julius, were drawn beneath the surface of the water silently.

Meanwhile, Fortuné had found Ali, and followed the Marquis de Terremort. He was firmly determined, experience having taught him that it was very difficult to die, to risk everything in order to liberate Marinette.

Ali therefore advanced, playing his flute, and the Marquis de Terremort and Marinette sat down to listen to him.

Then Fortuné, dagger in hand, pounced on his rival and knocked him down.

"Help, Julius!" cried the Marquis de Terremort.

Fortuné was about to pierce the heart with his weapon when the waters opened and he saw the water-spite smiling in a melancholy fashion.

"Marinette is free," the water-sprite said to him. "The sirens of the lake, out of amity for me, have caused the servants of that unjust man to perish, while I led the waves of the sea through subterranean tunnels to his palace, which they have submerged and destroyed."

Fortuné had thrown himself into Marinette's arms and their lips had met.

The Marquis de Terremort got to his feet. He perceived, in the falling darkness, Saturn shining with an unaccustomed brightness. Then he tore his hair and his beard, ripped off his clothes and covered himself with earth, saying: "Behold the fate of a miserable Saturnian."

Then he picked up a stick and, semi-naked, like a beggar, he drew away in the direction opposite to the city.

Fortuné and Marinette slept in the open, on a bed of leaves.

The following day they went to the port and, having seen the French consul, they embarked on a ship bound for their homeland.

Ali accompanied them to the quay and wept copiously on seeing them depart, for he was attached to them. And when the ship drew away he started playing his flute to render honor to them.

During the crossing, Fortuné and Marinette surprised the other passengers and the mariners by the number of kisses they exchanged. And Fortuné said to Marinette: "I'll recount all these adventures in verse."

Having arrived in France, Marinette thought about her father, and they decided to go and live in the house with the green shutters.

They were rich now, for flute-players are well paid in Turkey and Fortuné had kept the money he had earned out there.

They bought a little boat and went up the river, and then the canal beside which they had been born.

When they arrived not far from the house with the green shutters they perceived in the distance the worthy man getting ready to turn the handle to open the lock and let a boat through. He had aged because of the chagrin he had endured.

His joy was great when he recognized his daughter and Fortuné, and he fell into their arms. He was even more content when he learned that they had a boat, which belonged to him, and that he could travel in his turn on the canal and go through the locks; for it was one of his chagrins to have seen boats going by all his life without ever having been able to travel in one himself.

That evening, they drank a bottle of old wine in the house with the green shutters and Fortuné decided that he would turn the worthy man's handle and be a lock-keeper, while continuing to write poems.

Never had such a small house enclosed such a great happiness.

When they had talked for a long time, drunk a great deal and laughed a great deal, they went to bed.

Fortuné and Marinette's room was clean and white; they looked at one another by the light of the lamp and suddenly, at the same time, they became pensive.

They thought that they had forgotten to thank the water-sprite and that they had no longer talked about him and had no longer looked for him after his last benefit was accomplished, and that they were ingrates.

That spoiled their happiness and they sat down, pensively.

Their room overlooked the canal and the window was slightly open.

Then, from outside, they heard something akin to a sigh, something long and sad, a sound that resembled a song and a lament.

And they were so impressed by it that they both went downstairs and advanced to the edge of the canal.

The night was clear and they perceived under the water the body of the poor water-sprite. He had a dolorous expression on his face, of resignation, benevolence and reproach.

Hidden in the black water, solitary and forgotten, he had heard the laughter and joyful cries of his friends escaping from the house, and he had died, for water-sprites can die of amour, as well as humans.

THE MARVELOUS STORY OF CLAIRE D'AMOUR

*I. Which names the illustrious godfather
of the hero of this story*

There was once a very pious, very noble and very poor lady. She lived in a dilapidated château surrounded by a large park, where she lived in holy meditation. Her husband had left for the war, where he died, and she had a son.

She had great difficulty finding a godfather or a god-mother, because she had ceased all communication with the noble families of the land. She therefore summoned her old maidservant Gothon and said to her: "Go to the village and try to find an honorable godfather and godmother for my son, of good morals.

Gothon went at a run, and encountered on the way a man riding a donkey who was clad in a robe and had a blond beard. Gothon liked him because he had a pleasant face, and he seemed to enter into conversation easily.

"Where are you going in such a hurry, Madame Gothon," he said to her.

Flattered to be called by her name like that, Gothon replied: "I'm looking for a godfather for the son of my mistress. She will be lucky if I can find one of your merit."

The man smiled. He was Jesus Christ, who was visiting the earth to study the mores of humans.

"I accept," he said. And there's a lady over there who is known to me, and will gladly agree to serve as godmother."

He had perceived the Holy Virgin. She had come to a neighboring field to pick a bouquet of terrestrial flowers because, being perishable, they are more charming than divine flowers, which are eternal.

All three, therefore, went together to the pious lady's château, and the baptism of the child was celebrated; he was named Maurice, because it was Saint Maurice's Day. After that, Jesus Christ and the Holy Virgin identified themselves, and the pious lady and Gothon threw themselves down and prostrated themselves.

Gothon ran to the cellar to fetch a bottle of old wine. Jesus Christ drank joyfully and in abundance, for he liked feasting and conversation at table; and the Holy Virgin accepted a bouquet of roses from the park. After that, they departed, chatting together, for Heaven. The pious lady and Gothon were both very happy that Maurice had such a godfather and godmother.

At dusk, Gothon was rocking the child by the gate of the park when an old man went by. He was dressed like a beggar, with a long beard, and was carrying a heavy sack on his back. He stopped and smiled at the child.

At the same moment, the sun disappeared over the horizon; the fir trees murmured with unaccustomed softness, and the evening dressed everything in an incomparable beauty.

Gothon ran to the kitchen and brought a glass of wine to the old man, less for the joy she had just experienced than because of her natural generosity.

Having drunk it, the old man said: "If that child has no godfather, I would gladly serve in that capacity."

Gothon laughed loudly and for a long time, and when her hilarity had calmed down she replied: "Do you think my mistress would take for a godfather a poor man who travels the roads with a sack and a staff? Know this, and you can repeat it to anyone who asks you: today, our little Maurice has had for a godfather and godmother Jesus Christ and the Holy Virgin."

Gothon looked at the man curiously in order to enjoy his astonishment and admiration, but he did not seem at all wonderstruck. He shook his head several times, looked at the child and said: "Poor child! Poor child!"

Night had now fallen completely, but the man's face was illuminated by a supernatural light; his eyes shone and radiance ran through his beard.

"That's something that doesn't promise you a joyful life exempt from cares," he said to the child. "Those who are consecrated to Jesus Christ lead a bitter life of good works, prayers and penitence. They have a rope around the body and the top of the head shaven. I'll make you a very precious gift; you'll thank me later from the bottom of your heart."

He unfastened his sack and Gothon saw, with surprise, that the sack was full of sand. He took out a handful of it; the sand sparkled like gold. He threw it over Maurice's face, saying: "I give you the gift of illusion; I am the sandman; I am the one who passes in the mist and throws that gilded dust into human eyes. I pour with it crazy imaginations, surprising dreams and winged chimeras. I show the unhappy lover the smile of his mistress; by virtue of my magic the ambitious man becomes king for a night, the beggar eats and warms himself in a palace. I dispense sleep, the marvel of life. Thanks to me, reality is transformed at the whim of the imagination, one prefers the moon to the sun, deserted woods to populous towns, silent pools to rivers full of ships. You, child, are receiving the divine illusion that will permit you never to see life as it is."

Having said that, the sandman drew away, not without throwing a little of his sand into Gothon's eyes. She dreamed that Jesus Christ summoned her to paradise and sat her down in a sparkling robe among pink angels and bearded saints.

From his infancy, Maurice was brought up in religion. The bishop of the region, having learned what an illustrious godfather he had, came to see him several times, in order to instruct him in divine matters. Gothon took him to church every day, and he spent long hours during the day praying with his mother.

In the evening, however, when he wandered in the park, alone, he forgot sacred thoughts and, because of the sandman's gift, his mind flew away to distant marvels.

Once, when he was gazing at the distant countryside, at a place where the wall surrounding the park had partly collapsed, he perceived a girl almost the same age as himself sitting in the heather. She had strange dark eyes, unkempt hair and was dressed like a pauper.

On seeing Maurice she stood up and beckoned to him imperiously. As he appeared hesitant and made his timidity visible, she burst out laughing and went away.

He often returned to the same place at the same time in the evening, and he perceived the pauper girl. She had made gestures of command and threat to him several times, but afterwards, on the contrary, she struck gracious poses, held out her clasped hands to him, and blew him a kiss.

Maurice dared not climb over the wall to go to meet her. The pauper girl's gaze troubled him. She inspired in him, at the same time, fear, attraction and repulsion. He did not mention her to Gothon, his mother or the bishop. He sometimes wondered whether she was a vision or a reality, whether she was sent by God or by the Devil.

In the afternoon, kneeling before his mother's ivory crucifix, he thought about her instead of praying; it was not the face of Christ but her image that he saw, and he associated it confusedly with forest trees, wild heather and paths descending beneath oaks. It was a similar fear and a similar hope that the pauper girl and nature engendered in his soul.

His first communion was celebrated with great pomp. Gothon put on a lacy bonnet and an embroidered shawl that day. It was the bishop who held out the host to Maurice. The child had his hands crossed over his breast and he tried to absorb himself entirely in the thought of God. The organ played, the white head-dresses of the women inclined like celestial birds; flowers, candles and incense filled the church with a divine atmosphere.

Maurice was astonished not to feel in his heart the promised joy. He watched out for the ecstasy on the faces of his little companions. He perceived Gothon and his mother on their knees, looking at him with admiration. He appealed to God with all his might, with the voices of his soul.

Suddenly, however, he ceased to hear the sound of bells and respire the perfume of garlands. It seemed to him that the candles were extinguished, that the stone walls of the church collapsed. Instead of the columns there were straight oaks whose branches split the stained glass windows and the vaults. The undulating and prostrate crowd of the witnesses was a field of large white flowers, which the wind caused to quiver. The incense-burners were birds, and the bishop had taken on the form of a rock, at the summit of which his golden miter could still be distinguished. In the place of the altar, Maurice perceived a verdant clearing, in the middle of which the pauper girl was lying, her legs and neck bare. She stretched herself out lazily in the sunlit grass, and looked at him with an ironic and brazen gaze. A flood of light inundated her and she appeared to him to be admirably beautiful.

Then he uttered a cry and tried to launch himself forward. He took two steps and fell on the flagstones. An hour later, he came round, bathed by his mother's tears, in Gothon's arms.

II. The birth and first amorous adventures of Claire d'Amour

In the village near the château in which the hero of this true story resided, there lived a drunken and coarse tavern-keeper named Samson. That man had caused his wife to die of chagrin; he spent his time drinking and quarreling with the local mariners. People were afraid of him, but he was esteemed because of his strength and evil instincts.

At about the same time that Maurice was born, he was wandering in the countryside, having drunk more than usual. He thought he perceived a white form floating in a wood that he was passing alongside. Then he heard the moans of a child. He advanced and found a tiny baby girl abandoned in the midst of the heather.

Let's take that baby, he thought, *and I'll sell her for three écus to some barren wife.*

He took the little girl under his arm and went home.

The next day he went to offer her to several neighbors, but when he had told them how he had found her, and how he had seen a white form wandering around her, no one wanted to take her, judging that she was a daughter of fays.

He thought for a moment of throwing her to the bottom of his well, and even prepared a rope and a stone for that purpose, but he reflected that when she was older she could perform the function of waitress in his inn. He kept her with him.

The child's skin was admirably white; she seemed like a ray of sunlight. For that reason, she was named Claire.

She lived in Samson's inn; she spent her time outside the door, sitting in the gutter, jostled by some and caressed by others. She had bushy hair, wild eyes and a savage expression, and was an object of both derision and pity. Every evening, when Samson had been drinking, he beat her without any reason, whatever she had done, by virtue of evil inclination.

Claire received blows both when she had worked hard for her master, fetching water, sweeping and washing, and when she had stolen from him; because of that she could never understand the difference there was between good and evil. She esteemed that all human actions were of the same nature, since they all had the inevitable consequence of insults and blows of the rope.

Once, she escaped for an entire day to run through the fields and the nearby woods. She lived the most beautiful hours of her youth. The sun was streaming; she picked wild fruits from the hedges, cut flowers and understood their beauty for the first time. She lay down on the earth and the wild grass spoke to her. They told her vague and pleasant things, which thought could not translate, but which went to her heart.

When she went back in the evening, Samson put her on her knees and attached her by her shoulders to the old table on the inn; he left her there, in spite of her groans, until an advanced hour of the night.

Claire was hated by other children of her own age; they would not admit her to their games; they insulted her and threw stones at her. Their parents had told them that she was a daughter of fays, a pagan, and they showed an aversion for her that they translated into blows when they could.

Claire, who had never known amity, was not astonished by that. She was only afflicted by not having sufficient strength to make her enemies perish. She did not even have a sentiment of injustice, supposing that all children received, in the evening, blows of the rope, and were tied to an oak table when they spent a day running through the countryside.

It required a great deal of experience and reflection in order for her to conceive that things might be otherwise.

One day when a village child had been beaten and went home in tears, Claire slipped in behind him, penetrated into the courtyard of the house and went to stick her face to a widow in order to enjoy his torture. However, she saw his mother take him in her arms, not to choke him, but to embrace him tenderly and then prepare bread and milk for him.

That day, she learned the injustice of the world, and that was her first veritable chagrin.

She did not weep, however, because there were no tears in her.

Next door to the Samson house lived a lame old mariner named Guluche. He had been around the world several times, and now he smoked his pipe, dreaming, and waiting for death. His legs and arms were almost paralyzed; he liked solitude, and his heart was full of good will.

Once, when Claire was going past his house, he called to her. Frightened, she hesitated to approach him. He went back into his house, got an apple, and held it out to her. She took it fearfully, afraid of being hit. She bit into the fruit while Guluche smiled. The fruit was excellent; she had not received any blows. The man had just given her that gift in order that he might enjoy it. She had the revelation of something new and marvelous.

She became the friend of Guluche, the lame old mariner. He gave her fruits, told her stories and poured into her soul the inestimable sweetness of amity.

Meanwhile, she grew up; her eyes softened and filled with languor; her hair, in falling over her shoulders, created a mysterious harmony; she became slender and graceful.

And one day, on the point of striking her, Samson encountered her ardent gaze and stopped, suddenly having the sentiment of beauty. He remained thoughtful, and paced back and forth for a long time in front of the fireplace.

From that day on he beat her less frequently, he gave her a greater liberty, and even gave her a few sous so that she could buy dresses and ornaments.

Claire became beautiful, and rapidly discovered the charms and dangers that accompany the precious gift of beauty.

When it was very hot she had the custom of sitting down outside the door of Samson's inn. Her unfastened corsage allowed her bare breasts to be seen; her eyes were more beautiful than usual; she dreamed about the noises of forests, the song of crickets.

At the same time every day an old lord of the region passed along the road in front of her. He leaned on a cane in order to walk, he had pale, slack cheeks and his hands were agitated by a tremor. When he perceived Claire his face went pale, his lips quivered and he became horrible to behold. He tried to speak to her several times, but he could not articulate any intelligible sound. When he arrived at the street corner he stopped and made signs to her for a long time to come and join him in a nearby wood.

Claire was very intrigued by those things, but she did not go with the lord because his ugliness frightened her.

Meanwhile, all the mariners who came to drink in Samson's tavern desired her violently. She listened with an ingenuous gaze to their coarse words, and her apparent candor augmented the desire they had for her.

Among those men there was one mariner who affected in her regard the tender manners of a man in love. He gazed at her for a long time in silence; one day, he offered her a flower. He was mild and obedient with her. One evening, when she was alone in the inn, he came in and asked her, with timid words, to go with him. She accompanied him into the countryside, embarrassed to see him so tremulous beside her. But when they had arrived at a solitary place, the man threw himself upon her and knocked her to the ground brutally, with stifled and mysterious cries, followed by sighs and shivers.

Claire discovered amour for the first time. She experienced surprise but no joy in it. But she submitted to it in the same way that she had submitted to the blows of Samson's rope, and submitted to the rain and the wind when she was caught by a storm on a road.

Having given herself once, she gave herself to all the mariners at the inn and every man who asked her, unaware of the divine sensuality she was transmitting.

Her beauty increased, and she was nicknamed Claire d'Amour because of the facility with which she allowed herself to be loved.

Her life was not joyful, however; amour did not give her any pleasure; she hated all men. The time she spent with old Guluche was the sole charm of her life.

She often fled the village and wandered through the fields. It was in the course of one of those excursions that she perceived Maurice dreaming in his park one day, and she was touched by his youth and his grace. The neat and well-dressed little boy was different from all the men she had known thus far, and she was glad to see him. She came back often at the same time, made signs to him, and a distant and pleasant friendship was established between them.

The image of Claire had taken complete possession of Maurice's heart, but he continued to be afraid of her.

One evening, as he approached the place where he was accustomed to seeing her, he found her sitting on the stones of the wall. She was staring at him with eyes full of timidity, languor and audacity.

Maurice's heart was beating very forcefully.

"Would you like to come with me?" she said.

"Where?"

"Out there." And her finger pointed at the horizon, where the sun was setting behind a wood of fir trees.

"I can't," Maurice replied. "What would my mother and Gothon say?"

Claire smiled. "Do you love them?" she said.

"Yes."

"More than me?"

"Yes, for the moment."

"Then I'm annoyed," said Claire, and, gripped by anger, she tried to go away; but Maurice retained her by the hand.

"What's your name?" he said.

"My name is Claire, but people call me Claire d'Amour."

"Why?"

Then Claire bowed her head, blushed and fell silent. They were beside one another, their cheeks were so close that Claire's hair brushed Maurice's. A cricket started singing the hymn of the evening and the earth, delightedly, and their lips came together.

After that kiss, they were ashamed, and ran away.

Having meditated, Maurice understood God's sixth commandment, the meaning of which had remained obscure to him previously. He went into the oratory where he was accustomed to pray, and fell to his knees; but he sensed that his prayer was not escaping from his heart and was not rising toward God. He had the warm taste of Claire d'Amour's kiss on his lips, and savored it in thought, deliciously.

He raised his head toward the ivory Christ and saw, distinctly, his godfather's face turn away from him.

He thought that he had sinned. He went down into the garden, went to find Gothon, who was peeling vegetables, sat down next to her, put his head on her knees and wept. And Gothon wept too, without knowing what his chagrin was, in sympathy, because he was weeping.

III. Of the abominable crime
that the innkeeper Samson committed

Claire d'Amour came back to see Maurice the next day, in vain. She sat among the crumbled stones of the wall alone, and waited until the shadow of night bathed the earth. Then she slipped into the park through the bushes. She arrived near the house and, seeing a window illuminated, she parted the vines and climbing roses and looked in.

She saw Maurice beside his mother, who was praying in front of an ivory statuette representing a man with his arms on a cross. And Maurice turned toward her, as if to implore her.

Then she thought about the stone crosses at crossroads, on which an individual similar to the one to whom Maurice was praying was crucified. She thought about the churches whose outlines the thought devoid of beauty; she thought about the sound of bells, which she had often cursed in the countryside because it drowned out the sound of the wind and the trees.

And she went away at a slow pace, saddened by having lost Maurice, with thoughts of vengeance.

In the following days, she repelled the mariners and refused to lend herself to their desires. Then she began to understand the extraordinary power that she had over men. One of them fell at her feet sobbing, another sold his boat in order to offer her the price of it, a third stabbed himself with his dagger, another, more sage, threatened to kill her. She made an exception for that one, because she was afraid of him.

Samson, seeing that she was refusing herself to all of them, thought in the simplicity of his heart that it was because of a secret love that she was nursing in her heart for him. He therefore resolved to possess Claire d'Amour. And, having drunk in extreme abundance on night, he went to the room where she slept. Claire d'Amour chased him away, because for her, Samson was an object of disgust.

Desire spoke then in Samson's soul with an imperious voice.

What, he said to himself, *that girl who has given herself to all the men in the village won't give herself to her master, who saved her from death and has nourished her. That's a truly unjust and monstrous thing.*

With that, he locked Claire d'Amour in the grain-loft of his house, telling her that he would let her die of hunger if she did not do as he wished.

Claire d'Amour remained there all day, and the disappearance caused a great distress. The mariners moaned, and they walked along the road with great strides; the old lord who went past every evening for her and now made her licentious signals from a distance, on not seeing her at the usual hour, started trembling and clicking his teeth, and his cheeks became even paler.

And Samson, who drank, and suffered mortally from the desire he had for Claire d'Amour, went to shout to her through the door that her next day, he would break her teeth and rip out her tongue.

Claire d'Amour thought then, in her heart, that it would be better to give herself to Samson a thousand times than have her tongue ripped out and her teeth broken.

When night fell, Samson, drunk, fell asleep and Guluche, leaning on his stick, came out of his house, very anxious about the fate of Claire d'Amour. He walked very slowly, because the paralysis made his body suffer.

Claire d'Amour saw him through the skylight of the grain-loft where she was a captive, and made him understand her fate by gestures. Guluche went home, got a ladder, and came back to lean it against the wall. A moment later, Claire d'Amour was free. She told Guluche what had happened, and the resolution she had made to leave Samson's inn and the country for good.

Guluche was very sad, because he had no other joy, apart from smoking his pipe, than talking to Claire d'Amour. She was his sole affection on earth.

Time was pressing. Samson might wake up. It was time to say goodbye.

Guluche tried to find the words that one says when parting, the advice and the phrases that summarize life, but he found nothing, for his mind was numbed by age.

He sensed that and was afflicted by it. He said: "Be good, pardon offenses..."

But Claire d'Amour did not understand what he meant.

"Are you sad to leave me?"

"Yes," she replied, but she was lying, for she was scarcely capable of veritable amity.

There was a thick fog; she drew away and, on looking back, saw Guluche's pipe in the distance, like little red tear.

The wind blew; the fog vanished and a storm burst. The doors of the inn moaned like human voices. Samson emerged, his eyes distraught, from a terrible dream. He groped his way upstairs, opened the door of the room where he thought he would find Claire d'Amour, and threw himself into it like a madman. The room was empty. The old clock chimed; the wind outside increased; Samson, suddenly sobered up, and tore his hair. He ran into the courtyard, saw the ladder, and understood. The rain soaked his forehead and, running down his cheeks, rendered him horrible to behold; in an infantile voice he repeated: "Claire d'Amour! Claire d'Amour!"

What weather for traveling, Guluche thought. *Virgin Mary, guide her!*

That thought absorbed him so much that he had not noticed that his pipe had gone out. He struck his briquette in order to light it again and, raising his head, he saw Samson.

"Tell me which way Claire d'Amour went," said the latter, in an imploring voice.

"It's a bad night, it's time to go to sleep," said Guluche. "Go to bed if you don't want the errant fays to take you in their round dance."

"Tell me where Claire d'Amour is!" cried Samson, opening his knife.

"Go to bed; wine counsels evil deeds."

"Where's Claire d'Amour!" howled Samson, raising his weapon.

"Go to bed, if you don't want Death to come tomorrow to pull your feet in your bed," said Guluche, staring at the shiny blade.

Then Samson seized he poor mariner by the throat and plunged the knife into his heart.

And Guluche fell, saying: "Virgin Mary, guide her..."

And he died. And as he had been honest and good on earth, he went, with his pipe and his blue jacket, to paradise...

IV. In which there is talk of nothing but amour

Maurice had turned down the lamp. He was alone in his room. He had prayed for several hours and now he was thinking about Claire d'Amour's kiss. That memory was like a very sweet enchantment, and, leaning on his window-sill, he abandoned himself to a voluptuous reverie.

The sand on the pathway creaked, and Maurice suddenly perceived Claire d'Amour, very white in the shadow, who was making signs to him to come down.

He obeyed without hesitation.

"I'm leaving forever," she said to him, "but I love you. Would you like to love me, and follow me where I'm going?"

Maurice darted a glance at the house where his mother and Gothon were in bed, in the tranquility of the night, and he replied to Claire d'Amour that he loved her too, and would follow her to the ends of the earth.

Now, the ivory Christ had descended from his cross and was listening anxiously. On hearing those words he sat down sadly, and hid his head in his hands. Then the park was animated by a joyful life. The oaks started to chat joyously; the rose bushes inclined toward one another gracefully; the frogs in the pond deployed their green robes and danced among the reeds...

Meanwhile, Maurice and Claire d'Amour walked, full of delight, along the roads of the earth, through woods and alongside meadows. They did not speak to one another, because they had nothing to say, but they kissed and hugged, and they experienced a great deal of joy. And little ladies dressed in white who were the fays of those places, smiled as they saw them go by, because fays protect lovers.

And a little later, the winds rose and embraced the world, and a storm burst.

Maurice and Claire d'Amour found a little shepherd's hut, which was empty, and where there was a bed of ferns.

They sheltered there, and lay down on the ferns, judging that bed propitious to their amours.

And all night long they changed countless kisses and knew the pleasure of amour. And Claire d'Amour swore a thousand times to Maurice that she had never loved anyone but him, had never been anyone else's before him, and that no one had even brushed her cheek with his lips. She had no need to repeat it so often, because he had believed it even before she spoke, so favorable is the illusion that one is alone in being loved welcomed by the heart of a lover.

And all night long, the winds passed under their tresses of clouds, in their misty robes, singing prodigious hymns; and all night long, the rain wandered, thin and veiled, through the fields and the forests...

And as the atmosphere paled at the approach of dawn, footsteps resonated on the damp earth near the hut in which Maurice of Claire d'Amour were lying.

It was an old man who was carrying a large sack of sand on his back. He gazed momentarily at the simultaneously unique and double form of the lovers among the ferns. Then he took some sand in his hand, threw it in their faces, and went on his way.

Dawn appeared; Claire d'Amour and Maurice were asleep. And the dream that the sandman sent them was the sweetest one they could have, for it was the prolongation of the reality. They dreamed that they were in a shepherd's hut, tenderly enlaced on ferns, to the sound of the rain and the wind.

V. The marvelous encounters that Maurice and Claire d'Amour had with a tightrope-walker, a philosopher, three brigands, and what ensued

They traveled, Maurice with a purse full of gold. In the evenings they stopped at inns, dined beneath flowery arbors, and went to sleep in unfamiliar rooms, which they populated with their kisses.

Maurice experienced an enormous pride in being the first to have possessed Claire d'Amour, and greatly enjoyed the desire she inspired in other men as they went along.

Claire d'Amour was delighted with Maurice because he knew nothing of life, he was simple, proud and charming. But she was various and changing, similar in that respect to the waves of the sea. And she soon perceived the monotony of exchanging the same words and the same caresses, and she became bored.

She did not admit it to herself at first, for that would have destroyed the new foundation of her life; but she suffered from it cruelly and desired new things.

Maurice, for his part, experienced a painful remorse when he thought about his mother and Gothon, and the amity of his godfather Jesus Christ. That thought often spoiled the pleasure that he had with Claire d'Amour.

On day, in a hostelry, they met a tightrope-walker named Pirouette. He had a leotard that was half yellow and half red, which he put on for his performances, along with a large clown's wig. He was, it was said, the most skillful tightrope-walker on earth.

He lavished a thousand gallantries on Claire d'Amour, in spite of the extreme coldness that Maurice testified to him. He was cheerful and emphatic, and Claire d'Amour declared that he was witty.

Having set up his rope in the public square of the village, he performed a thousand marvelous tricks; he swayed on it and he danced on it, to the great joy of the audience.

Maurice admired the delightful puerility of Claire d'Amour, who was filled with enthusiasm by those things, shouted and clapped her hands. He was secretly afflicted by not being able to imitate the dancer, and cursed his mother for not having made him learn that difficult art.

As the lanterns were extinguished and they returned to the hostelry, Claire d'Amour suddenly remembered that she had seen by the roadside, from the carriage that had brought them, flowers of a remarkable color. She wanted to have a bouquet immediately. Maurice represented to her in vain that there would be plenty of time to go and pick them the following day, and that the chill of the night would have added to their splendor. She was obstinate in her plan and he went to wait for her sadly beside the fire, in the company of the hotelier and a few drinkers.

Two hours went by, all the drinkers had gone to sleep, and Maurice was beginning to get very anxious, when Claire d'Amour came back. She was in an extremely bad mood, having not found the flowers for which she was searching; Maurice tried to persuade her how unimportant that was. She remained taciturn.

The rope-dancer Pirouette came back shortly afterwards and related in a joking fashion that he had been delayed in more than one inn.

He surrounded Maurice with obsequiousness and flattering words, which he mingled with eulogies to his own person, and compliments addressed to Claire d'Amour, with half-smiles and winks.

Maurice was astonished, that night, to find Claire d'Amour less expansive than usual.

He learned in the morning that the dancer had left very early without paying his bill, and he perceived that his purse had disappeared.

The two travelers paid the hotelier with some money they had on them and continued their journey on foot.

On the way they met a fat man of jovial appearance, clad in black like a priest, with whom they struck up a conversation.

"My name is Bigorneau,"[2] he said. "I'm a philosopher and I'm traveling for my pleasure, with the aim of studying men and nature. The company of lovers," he added "is more agreeable to me than that of other people, for they're the most admirable examples of human folly and I take pleasure in studying in them the extraordinary fashion in which they transform the universe."

Night fell and the road they had taken led them into the middle of a dense forest.

They were weary, and no light shone on the horizon; Bigorneau, who was pusillanimous, proposed that they retrace their steps because of the dangers of the darkness. Maurice opined that they should go forward. Claire d'Amour decided that they would camp where they were.

They sat down on the ground, therefore, and scarcely had they done so than three brigands threw themselves upon them and took them prisoner.

The three brigands were heavily armed and ferocious in appearance.

Bigorneau spoke to them in these terms:

"Lord Brigands, refrain from putting these poor and just people to death. On the contrary, wash their feet in order to resemble ancient hosts, and offer them a place at your table if, as I have no doubt, you possess a house nearby. Acting thus, you would honor greatly a beautiful young woman, a young man of good company, and a philosopher who is traveling in order to increase his knowledge of the world. Finally, you would be honoring yourselves, and what is better down here than a happy conscience?"

---

[2] *Bigorneau* is the French term for the small mollusk known in English as a winkle.

As Bigorneau spoke thus he watched the faces of the three men anxiously to see the effect of his words.

The first brigand, whose name was Chênepain, although he had an uncultivated mind, liked philosophy and poetry. The second brigand, who was called Larbalet, was tender and amorous. They persuaded the third brigand, name Tordecoeur, who was holding a naked dagger in each hand and was a violent and immoderate man, that it was necessary to spare the travelers, firstly because they were poor, and secondly because of their qualities as a philosopher and two lovers.[3]

The latter consented, grumbling, being little sensible to anything except fighting and pillage.

The brigands took Claire d'Amour, Maurice and Bigorneau to the cave where they lived, at the bottom of a mountain bristling with fir-trees, in a very wild place.

The cave was full of objects of every sort—clothes, saddles and weapons—stolen from travelers. They ornamented the walls and were strewn on the ground in disorder.

Bigorneau expressed his satisfaction on seeing those things, saying how well that habitation, which expressed human diversity, suited a sage.

They ate and drank; with the warmth of wine, a mild sympathy circulated between them. Claire d'Amour declared that she would like to live with the brigands forever, in that cave, amid that rich décor, the natural magnificence of which delighted her heart. Chênepain and Larbalet were touched by her beauty, and even Tordecoeur, who was sharpening a sword with a horrible metallic sound, darted astonished and wild glances at her on the sly.

Only Maurice remained pensive.

Bigorneau said: "Fortunate brigands! They do not recognize the arbitrary laws of the world and they live in the woods

---

[3] *Chênepain* translates literally as "oak-bread" but the name is a play on words, *chenapan* meaning rogue. Larbalet is probably a pun too, *l'arbalète* meaning "the crossbow." Tordecoeur translates as "twist-heart"

in the manner of simple men, practicing a broad hospitality. They have wines of various vintages, depending on whether the merchants who traverse their forests come from Burgundy or Champagne. They are not corrupted by luxury or riches and they become poets, because they live with the trees and they listen to the divine speech of the winds."

Chênepain was delighted by those eulogies and, desirous of educating himself, he held out a book to Bigorneau, telling him that he read it every evening with admiration; he asked him whether he had read it too, and whether its author was glorious. It was Homer's *Odyssey*.

Bigorneau replied that he knew the work, and that the man who had written it possessed a great celebrity on the earth. And as Chênepain continued questioning him, he added that the same Homer had written another book, no less beautiful, in which the Trojan War was narrated admirably, with the description of the warriors who took part in it and the battles they fought.

He concluded thus: "When you read that poem, Monsieur Chênepain, you will learn that numerous people have quit their native land and made war, and that the towers of Ilium, a prosperous city, were destroyed because Helen was beautiful, the shape of her body was harmonious and heroes fought over her. The greatest human misfortunes are always caused by the beauty of women. That ought not to cause us any astonishment, but merely inspire us to prudence in their regard. Instead of giving their actions legitimate and reasonable causes, such as personal interest, pride, sensual amour or cupidity, we see that they act almost without any apparent motive, guided by a changing whim unregulated by any law. That is, moreover, their greatest charm and what draws us recklessly toward them. That is why it is necessary to fear women. Sages are debating, heroes are sitting down dreaming of great deeds, and I see the smile of Helen shining, which will cause their doom..."

The light of the torch illuminating the cave began to flicker, close to going out.

Chênepain said, in a melancholy tone: "Women have never liked me."

Larbalet was thoughtful, looking at the portrait of his fiancée, whom he had left in a distant village, and whom he loved. Tordecoeur had fallen asleep while furbishing his sword, the hilt of which he was still holding. Claire d'Amour put her head on Maurice's shoulder. Bigorneau rolled himself up in his cloak.

Then Chênepain went to sit down at the entrance to the cave. He gazed at the forest and the stars, and, sensible to their beauty, he stayed there, his mind full of generous, confused and tender thoughts...

VI. Of the extraordinary things that Maurice saw near a spring

Claire d'Amour found a great charm in the company of the brigands. She found them likeable and handsome, but Tordecoeur, most of all, exerted a powerful attraction upon her. She accompanied them in their expeditions, helped them, stimulated them, knew the mysterious joy of stealing, and the voluptuousness of accomplishing forbidden acts punishable by death. She persuaded Maurice that the profession of thief was noble, since she exercised it, and he followed the brigands in his turn, and became a brigand like them.

He conceived a great remorse because of that. The image of his mother returned to trouble him by night. He saw her before him, silent and devoid of anger, her face tearful, and there was such a profound misery and such a resigned reproach in the expression of her gaze that he cried out in pain and woke up bathed in sweat.

But the love he had for Claire d'Amour was such that those dreams were less cruel for him than the slightest coldness on her part.

Meanwhile, Chênepain no longer read Homer, Larbalet no longer talked about his fiancée Mariette, and Tordecoeur no longer furbished his swords. All three of them were in love with Claire d'Amour.

And during their long rides through the forest, Claire d'Amour let each of them understand, in a distinct fashion, that she nurtured an irresistible penchant for him. Having made that confession in the shade of the oaks, she made each of the three swear on the sacred head of his mother to keep the secret jealously from their companions and the rest of the world.

One evening, Chênepain said to Claire d'Amour: "Claire d'Amour, you are as beautiful as the moon rising over the deserted countryside. Your eyes exert a more irresistible attraction on me than the most astonishing things one reads in books. I am giving you the work of the old poet Homer as a pledge of my love."

Another evening, Tordecoeur said to Claire d'Amour: "Claire d'Amour, you are as beautiful as the blood that flows and the sword that shines. I have made this dagger shine again for you, the hilt of which is sculpted and the blade forged in Toledo, which is the most beautiful one I possess. Take it in memory of me."

On a third evening, Larbalet said to Claire d'Amour: "Claire d'Amour, you are as beautiful as the house where I was born, where vines climb around the door. I once loved a young woman named Mariette, whose eyes were the color of violets and whose heart was virtuous and tender. You have made me forget her face and I beg you to accept her portrait, because I no longer love anyone but you."

Claire d'Amour had taken the book by Homer, the sculpted dagger and the portrait of Mariette; and she went alone into a place in the forest where there was a very deep pool. Then she tied the three tokens of love together and threw them into the middle of the still waters, among the reeds and the nenuphar lilies.

The days passed in expeditions on the roads, and the brigands came back late to the cave, where, next to the blazing fire, they rested from their fatigue. Then they listened to Bigorneau talk, smiling, about life and human passions.

That wise man said: "It's necessary to be detached. The passions are torrents that carry us away. Even amity is dangerous. The sage has no relatives, no domestic hearth, and no soil of predilection. He loves all lands, all houses and all human beings equally. He must always be ready to change his clothes for other clothes, his present existence for another. For it is necessary to be free."

One day, a young woman appeared at the entrance to the brigands' cave. She had a red headscarf, a fearful expression and eyes the color of violets. She was holding a bouquet of wild flowers in her hand. She saw Larbalet and her face lit up with a profound joy.

She cried: "Finally I've found you, my beloved. It's many days since I left the village and I've been searching for you in these forests, where I knew you were exercising the profession of bandit. But don't you recognize your fiancée, Mariette?"

She held out her arms to Larbalet.

The latter hesitated momentarily and saw Claire d'Amour smiling softly in the shadows. He said: "In truth, Mademoiselle, you are the victim of an extraordinary error. I've never had a fiancée and I don't know you."

And he turned his back on Mariette.

Mariette's eyes reflected such surprise and such great pain that Bigorneau was moved.

Mariette had fled into the forest and the philosopher followed her.

"It's necessary not to be attached," he told her. "We suffer because of our passions. Come on, dry your eyes; I'll take you out of these woods, and you can go back to your house, where your mother must be waiting for you with a great deal of anxiety."

Mariette explained, through her tears, that she was an orphan, that she loved Larbalet, and that she wanted to die.

And the philosopher said: "There is no bond so powerful that reflective thought can't break it. See how beautiful the world is. Nothing is worth the pain of being sad."

They had arrived at the place where the road whitened. Bigorneau, sitting on the grass, watched Mariette draw sway, until she was no more than a little black dot on the horizon.

And Larbalet did not regret, in the days that followed, having disdained Mariette.

The bandits' love for Claire d'Amour only increased. Maurice did not perceive anything, because he was a dreamer and did not see life as it is.

However, the bandits had acquired a dangerous celebrity by virtue of their exploits. A regiment of dragoons was sent to capture them, which started searching the forest. The brigands, therefore, sealed their cave with stones and tree branches, and resolved to live in a nearby château whose lord had left for the Court some time before.

They did that, and found it good. The dwelling was solitary, surrounded by a park and dense woods. It was an elegant frame for the amour they bore in their heart. There was a library furnished with the best books and an admirable wine-cellar. They spent a few charming days in feasting, drinking and study.

Bigorneau read Plato; Chênepain tried to compose an ode in verse in honor of Claire d'Amour, but was unhappy with the result, and discovered how difficult it is to give a written form to the sentiments of the heart.

Claire d'Amour was wandering in the forest alone when she saw a dragoon, who had descended from his horse and was about to drink from a spring. The dragoon was tall and handsome.

Claire d'Amour advanced toward him and offered him a drink in her hands.

After having drunk, the dragoon, charmed, put down his helmet and saber and kissed Claire d'Amour, and as he was young and handsome, Claire d'Amour gave herself to him in the quivering grass, to the song of the spring. Then she unfastened her hair and reposed on the unknown heart of the man, savoring the omnipotent charm of novelty.

Then she said to the dragoon: "You're looking for the brigands that are in this forest. Know that they're in the château whose towers you can see over there, and which is surrounded by a large park. If you want to capture them, you have only to come at night with your captain and your companions. You'll find them occupied in drinking, and you can easily take them prisoner."

She spoke in those terms, selling thus the companions whose bread and fortune she had shared and who loved her. And she did that out of a natural liking for treason and to see what would happen.

Now, Maurice was wandering in the forest, in the hope of encountering Claire d'Amour by chance. At a bend in a path he heard a noise, and thought he recognized the voice of the person for whom he was looking.

He listened; the voice was bizarre and halting, as if Claire d'Amour were speaking under the empire of an emotion. He was near a spring, alongside a clearing to which he knew Claire d'Amour had the custom of going.

He advanced cautiously, parted the branches in front of him, and was very surprised to see two mingled forms lying on the ground: that of Claire d'Amour, her unfastened corsage showing her bare breast, and that of a dragoon of whom he could only see the back, who was sighing and kissing the adored lips of Claire d'Amour.

That vision was so unexpected for his eyes that he did not feel any sort of emotion at first: nothing but a keen curiosity. Then his mind spun like a wounded bird. He perceived with a perfect clarity the face of his mother and that of Gothon. He noticed, in the grass, the dragoon's helmet and saber, and the exact place they occupied. And as the latter got up he counted the buttons on his uniform and made a mental note of their number.

Then the reality appeared to him in all its horror and he departed through the forest at a run.

A marvelous night fell upon the earth. The flowers stretched out languorously, the shiny greenery lit up its little torches.

Maurice was no longer experiencing anything, at present, but a great physical pain in his head. He looked to see where his footfalls had brought him. He was in front of the château where the bandits were living; he heard Bigorneau's joyful voice, followed by the sound of clinking glasses.

Claire d'Amour was in the doorway, her face full of anxiety. She was holding a shawl and Maurice's cloak over her arm

"Don't go into the château," she said, precipitately. "In an hour, any moment, the king's dragoons will be here. Come with me, let's flee."

Maurice shot her a glance full of legitimate amazement. He pushed her aside with a gesture, climbed the staircase, and went to his room, where he lay down on his bed silently. Claire d'Amour followed him, imploring him.

Meanwhile, Bigorneau and the brigands were eating and rejoicing. Tordecoeur had brought back a superb pheasant; they had cooked it and were about to slice it up.

They heard a noise outside. They looked out of the window and saw the courtyard full of dragoons carrying swords and torches. The captain hammered rudely on the door and shouted: "Surrender!"

The brigands threw themselves on their weapons, resolved to die courageously. Their hearts were united by amity and they shook hands before the battle.

Then they looked for Claire d'Amour, and she appeared in their midst, her eyes lit up, inciting them to combat.

Then Bigorneau thought: *I don't know how to handle weapons and more skillful in making use of my mind than my arms. In truth, I'll only be a hindrance to my friends; I even sense that only their extreme delicacy has prevented them from inviting me to leave. The sage is free; he must always see different people and places. The charming humor of these brigands has prolonged excessively a sojourn among them that really ought to come to an end this evening.*

He knew of a little hidden door at the back of the château. He went through it, reached open country, and fled at a run.

The dragoons hammered more forcefully on the château door in order to break it down.

Chênepain said to his companions: "It would be sad to perish in these dusty rooms. I want to strike my enemies by the uncertain light of the night, and if I fall, it will be with my face turned toward the sky..."

So saying, and followed by his two companions, he went downstairs, a sword in one hand and a dagger in the other.

Then he saw that Larbalet, completely drunk, was having difficulty staying on his feet, and that Tordecoeur was already troubled by the wine.

The château door burst into shards and the brigands suddenly hurled themselves on the dragoons. There was an indescribable tumult; swords clashed, blood stained the earth and the wind made the torchlight tremble.

Claire d'Amour, in delirium, appeared at the window and watched avidly.

At that moment, Tordecoeur, knocked down, was about to be struck by a dragoon whose saber was raised. That man was the one to whom Claire d'Amour had given herself that same day. He saw Claire d'Amour at the window and a great joy penetrated his soul—and he stopped, immobile, as if in ecstasy, before the woman whose kisses still perfumed his lips. Chênepain's sword plunged into his breast all the way to the hilt. He opened his arms as if to embrace the charming form that he could see before him, and fell down dead.

Then Claire d'Amour, full of admiration for such an exploit, began to clap her hands.

Now, Maurice, occupied by a single thought, having got up to see the cause of so much noise, went to the window and saw those things.

He seized Claire d'Amour's wrists and cried: "Wretch! How dare you applaud the death of your lover?"

Amazed, Claire d'Amour replied: "I don't know what you mean."

"Out there, in the clearing," said Maurice, "you didn't give yourself to that man?"

"You're the victim of some spell. I swear on my father's grave that I don't know that man," said Claire d'Amour, in a tone of verity.

The dragoons irrupted into the room, seized them and loaded them with chains. An hour later they were traveling along the road in the midst of the king's soldiers, with

Chênepain, Tordecoeur and Larbalet, covered in dust and blood but arrogant and glorious.

Maurice was separated from Claire d'Amour. At a bend in the road she had sent him a long glance charged with dreams and kisses. And he thought as he marched: "The sincerity of her voice was indubitable; a strange vision has deceived my eyes. Will she ever forgive me? I'm a wretch and a madman!"

VII. In which we make the acquaintance of an angel, a demon and a king

Maurice and Claire d'Amour, considered as the leaders and the most dangerous of the bandits, were locked up in deep subterranean dungeons. Chênepain, Tordecoeur and Larbalet were placed together in a high tower. Their trial was rapid; they were all condemned to death.

On the eve of the execution, Maurice felt a profound melancholy, because he regretted life. Life, for him, was Claire d'Amour, whom he had lost by virtue of his dementia.

And he wept.

And in Heaven, Jesus Christ, greatly afflicted to see his godson imprisoned like a malefactor without repenting at the moment of death, turned his thoughts once again toward sin.

He summoned one of his faithful angels, and having informed him of his will, sent him to earth.

The angel knocked on the prison door and, having gone in, sat down and drank with the jailers and the prison guards. He was dressed as a monk, and they tried to cheer themselves up in his presence by talking very freely.

The angel was very serious by nature; he did not listen to them and poured a divine beverage into their glasses that plunged them into a deep sleep. Then he took the keys to Maurice's cell and woke him up, or he was asleep.

"Sinner," he said, "I'm an angel of God, sent for your salvation by your godfather, Jesus Christ. I'm going to take you to your mother in order for you to repent, and lead an exemplary life henceforth."

Joyful to see that life would be rendered to him, Maurice prostrated himself before the angel, and, having got to his feet, marched lightly behind him.

But when they had emerged from the prison Maurice, thinking about Claire d'Amour, said to the angel: "Angel of

God, can you not liberate, as you have done for me, other sinners who will repent, and thus be brought back to the good?"

But the angel, divining his thought, looked at him with severity and remained silent. Then he took Maurice under his wing and carried him away through the air.

Maurice perceived the little bell-tower of his village and, preceded by the angel, traversed his mother's park.

On seeing them, the oaks murmured, the rose bushes inclined toward one another and the frogs sitting on the edge of the pond in their green robes spoke ironically: "What have you done, then, Monsieur Angel, to snatch this young man from amour and pleasure and return him to the ennui of prayer and the family? How can it be that, with your correct white wings and your compassed attitude, he has preferred you to life?"

An angel does not listen to the foolish things that frogs say, and this one did not turn his head. But when he saw Maurice weeping thereafter in the arms of his mother and Gothon, he thought he could permit himself a pious, appropriate and measured emotion, and cold tears ran down his divine cheeks.

Then he flew away.

Meanwhile, Chênepain, Tordecoeur and Larbalet were all saddened by the thought of being hanged the following day. And Chênepain, having reflected for a long time, said to Tordecoeur, of whose marvelous strength he was aware: "Break the bars of that skylight."

Tordecoeur did as he was asked. But the tower in which they were prisoners was surrounded by a deep lake, in which the inhabitants of the city had the custom of going to bathe at sunrise.

Then Chênepain took off his garments, exhorting his companions to do the same, and when all three were naked, he knotted the doublets and the hose together firmly and attached the whole to the window. Then he said: "May the Devil assist us!"

And he began to climb down.

Now, a demon who was passing by heard that wish, and did not want it to remain ungranted. He therefore supported

Chênepain with his black-gloved hand. The latter, having arrived at the bottom of the rope formed by the garments, threw himself into empty space, fortunately fell into the waters of the lake, and swam to the shore. Tordecoeur and Larbalet had the same good fortune.

They were glad to find themselves together because they were narrowly linked by common joys and dolors.

Daylight appeared, and they were hidden among the reeds, wondering how they could walk into the city without clothing. That would cause a scandal and be fatal to their liberty.

Chênepain remembered the subtle Ulysses, cast up on a shore by the waves of the sea and going to implore the lovely Nausicaa. He was beginning to weave a rudimentary garment out of rushes bounded together when he saw young and middle-aged men from the city who were undressing not far away and jumping into the water, having left their clothes on the bank.

They therefore mingled with the swimmers and, returning to the shore, they were suitably dressed as honorable men in an instant.

They hastened to draw away and, as they did so, they saw with surprise a man of quality wearing a long cloak and black gloves, who was making benevolent and joyful signs to them. It was the demon who had protected their escape.

They thought it was a mistake and passed on. Their pockets were garnished with a few silver coins, and they went to sit down in the nearest tavern.

Meanwhile the inhabitants of the city were heading in crowds for the main square to see the execution of the five brigands. Whole families were going, taking infirm grandparents and children, for honest people are naturally cruel.

On a high platform facing the place of execution the king had taken his place, surrounded by his court, the clergy and the army.

He was an old king, mild-mannered and weary, but to whom the spectacle of death gave a great enjoyment analogous to that of amour.

.The desperate governor of the prisoner came to announce that four of the brigands had escaped in mysterious circumstances, and a murmur of discontent ran through the crowd as that news spread.

But Claire d'Amour appeared, pale beneath her black hair, embellished by the thought of death, the rising sun and the contemplation of the people. Her arms and neck were bare; she was smiling.

The women, above all, rejoiced in the idea that a member of their own sex, whose beauty was incomparable, was about to perish. And all the pious men deemed that it was good that such an object of scandal should disappear from the world.

Claire d'Amour was thinking about Maurice, because it was the thought of her youth, and at that moment, she loved him with all her heart.

She looked at the king and recognized in him the old Lord with the pale cheeks who had once passed her door every day with manic gestures, making obscene signs to her from a distance.

It was, in fact, the man who had desired he caresses of Claire d'Amour so ardently that he had not feared to come to an obscure village every evening, with no entourage and no carriage, in order to solicit her.

He also recognized her, and stood up, prey to an extraordinary emotion; his entire body was trembling and no one understood at first what he was trying to say, so halting was his voice.

The cortege stopped. Two chamberlains came to bring Claire d'Amour down from the cart on which she was standing beside the executioner. She was free.

An astonishing tumult reigned in the square. The governor of the prison was hanged, to satisfy the people.

VII. In which the king is seen to emerge
more precipitately than he would have wished
from Claire d'Amour's palace

Claire d'Amour became the king's mistress. She had a palace with a marble perron, a garden with a lake, jewels, servants and musicians. She was famous in the city and inspired countless amours.

Every evening the king came to see her. She heard his hesitant footfalls and the noise of his cane on the stairway. On seeing her, his cheeks blanched, his entire body was seized by a tremor, inarticulate sounds emerged from his mouth, and Claire d'Amour felt the caress of his bony fingers on her body.

She soon obtained an infinite ascendancy over him, and as he inspired disgust in her she resolved to restrict her favors in order to make him pay dearly for them.

She only gave herself to him in exchange for a precious jewel or rare fabric that she desired. But the crazed king satisfied all her whims and Claire d'Amour's every wish was a command for him.

Then she became even more demanding. She gave the least of her caresses an inestimable price. It was necessary for the king to bring her a sack full of gold to obtain a kiss on the lips, twelve sacks for her to undress and appear naked before his eyes.

The king obeyed because he loved her with all his old man's senses, and riches piled up in Claire d'Amour's palace.

She soon wearied of jewels and gold. She imagined demanding from the king, in exchanged for herself, humiliating and ridiculous tasks that were a source of amusement for her.

In order to be kissed on the lips, the king had to climb a tree in the garden, or run upstairs four at a time. Once, she even wanted him to perform a grotesque solo dance, dressed as a woman, to the sound of violins. Afterwards, she laughed at him, with her maidservants, and gave herself to her musicians and lackeys.

However, she was bored to death, and ardently desired to see Maurice again.

One day, she said to the king: "I want to go back to the land of my childhood. Accompany me in your carriage."

The king did as she said, and when they arrived some distance from the village where Claire d'Amour had lived, she saw Maurice's château and said that it was there that she wanted to stop.

Maurice's mother was very glad to receive the king in her house, and Gothon ran down to the cellar to fetch the rarest wine.

Now, Maurice believed that Claire d'Amour was dead and he wept for her every day. It was a great surprise for him to see a woman who resembled her so prodigiously standing to the right of the king, and looking at him with eyes that reminded him of his sweetest hours of sensuality.

At Claire d'Amour's instigation, the king invited Maurice, in a pressing fashion to follow him immediately to court.

Maurice put on his finest costume and climbed into the king's carriage, while his mother and Gothon remained uncertain as to whether to rejoice at such an honor or be afflicted by that departure.

During the journey, Claire d'Amour did not make any sign, and remained mute.

Maurice did not know whether he was dreaming or whether he was the victim of a surprising resemblance.

They traversed the silent and deserted city by night, through which Maurice had passed some time before with chains on his hands, surrounded by soldiers.

The king stammered a few words into Claire d'Amour's ear. She said that she was tired and that she would accompany the king as far as his palace.

Maurice was now alone in the carriage with Claire d'Amour, his heart full of disorder and uncertainty. Suddenly he felt arms around his neck and burning lips on his own, and he lost consciousness of things deliciously.

He woke up in the gilded dawn, with Claire d'Amour in his arms.

Rare perfumes embalmed the bed on which they were lying; the rays of the morning sun were making the precious fabrics shone; Claire d'Amour's skin was softer than before; jewels sparkled on her hands; a fountain was singing in the garden.

And Maurice said: "Claire d'Amour, now that I've found you again, it seems to me that I love you more than in the old days, because I've wept for you as someone dead. I've had bad thoughts on your subject, but I've repented cruelly of my folly. You've forgiven me because you're good. Excuse now the insensate anxieties of a lover. Where do all these riches me from with which I see you adorned? Where does this luxury come from, which certainly suits your beauty admirably but which makes me suffer in my heart because I don't know its provenance?"

Claire d'Amour explained that she had the palace and the riches from the king, who loved her like his own daughter and that it was necessary to refrain from thinking badly of such a virtuous, good and venerable man.

And Maurice believed that, because he had received from the sandman the gift of illusion and dreams, and it is very easy to believe what a woman whom one loves says.

But on the third day after his arrival, as Maurice was in the garden, he saw the king tottering up the staircase and heading toward Claire d'Amour's bedroom.

He followed him, and was greatly surprised to see him seize Claire d'Amour in his arms and try to kiss her on the lips.

Anger took possession of him; he hurled himself upon the king, lifted him in his arms, and, as the window was open and close by, he threw him outside.

"That's the first attempt he's made on me," said Claire d'Amour, "and he's been severely punished for it. In truth, I'm equally surprised by his audacity and your violence..."

Her love for Maurice was considerably augmented in a few seconds by that brutal act, which he was already regretting bitterly.

Claire d'Amour leaned out of the window and saw the injured king being carried away, uttering cries and curses.

"Let's flee in haste," she said, "to escape his anger."

She drew Maurice toward a hidden door in the palace and they both fled through the city.

IX. In which there is mention of Bigorneau, his disciples, and the admirable life they lead

An hour later, all the king's guards were mobilized, with orders to put Maurice to death and bring Claire d'Amour back.

Meanwhile, they did not know where to hide. They had realized that they had no money. At every crossroads people were being read their description, and a large reward was promised to anyone who delivered them.

They reached the popular quarters, where, in sordid interiors, a poor population of artisans and prostitutes lived.

Night had fallen. They were going along a narrow backstreet when, on turning round, they perceived that they were being followed. A troop of guards was marching behind them, in fact.

Then they penetrated into a dark corridor, and climbed a wooden stairway with worm-eaten steps, at hazard. They opened a door and found themselves in a wretched redoubt. There, they saw by the light of a smoky lantern, a man speaking to several seated individuals.

The man was saying: "Everything has its beauty. The man who leans over a well will see all the marvels of creation in the narrow circle of water between the stones, if he looks with the eyes of a sage. But a sage is a free man. To be free, that is the essential thing. To become so, fear women above all…"

At that moment, the man who was speaking perceived Maurice and Claire d'Amour, and he threw himself into their arms, weeping with joy. It was Bigorneau.

"This is your house," he said to them, when the others had told him about the danger they were in. "You can live here as long as is necessary to develop your personality, and you can depart without fear of disobliging me when you judge that my company is infringing your liberty. These are my disciples. They're people of humble condition materially, but whose mentality is sublime and conceives the world in the most astonishing manner. They work by day and take pleasure in listening to my instruction in the evenings."

Bigorneau's disciples numbered four.

There were two prostitutes, ugly and faded, an old cobbler who worked in a poor shop in the neighborhood, and a young man of slothful appearance who was the lover of the prostitutes and did not exercise any recognized profession.

Those admirable minds welcomed Maurice and Claire d'Amour favorably, and they drank with them, while listening to the philosopher's words.

Bigorneau lived on the little presents that his friends gave him, because of his wisdom and his virtue.

Having seen a ring on Claire d'Amour's finger, he asked her for it in order to sell it, and with the price he bought wine and precious foodstuffs. For a few days he served abundant feasts in his home, to which the disciples were invited. The latter did not fail to drink excessively, and then went to sleep under the table, having broken the glasses and bottles.

After that, Maurice exchanged his clothes, which were clean and elegant in form, for the clothes of a workman, in order to obtain the price of one final meal.

Claire d'Amour had never been as happy. She amused herself with the old cobbler and the two prostitutes, and was not far from having a penchant for their friend, the young man with the slothful appearance.

One day, as no one had any money. Claire d'Amour went out, went through the city, prostituted herself to a merchant and came back with a few coins. She did it again the next day and the days that followed. Bigorneau took the money she brought back and in the evening, the meal was served with all sorts of wines, for him and his disciples.

The disciples easily became accustomed to that facile existence. They even renounced all work; the cobbler ceased to fill the street with the noise of his hammer on nails. The prostitutes no longer went to provoke passers-by at the crossroads, for they had no liking for amour and only gave themselves to it professionally. Only the idle young man did not change his existence.

They no longer made any effort, except to listen to the wise words of their master, who chatted familiarly after the meal, and their comprehension of the world increased as a result.

Meanwhile, Claire d'Amour gave herself to anyone who wanted her, for a little money, and the caresses that she lavished on Maurice in the evenings were all the more tender and passionate for it.

He once asked her where the money came from that she brought back every day. She replied that she got it from a lady she had known as a child. That lady was very rich and could not refuse her anything. And Maurice believed her willingly, because he believed anything.

However, as he had a delicate soul and had been brought up in solitude by the cares of a mother who loved him, he suffered at first from the company of people as vulgar as those with whom he lived, the sordid place they inhabited, and the acts to which he was witness.

Then, gradually, his mind became bogged down; he learned to love his lot; he had a hatred of the rich, a liking for opprobrium; he found nobility in poverty.

But that sentiment was full of bitterness.

Every evening, one of the prostitutes sang. She sang a naïve ballad from her youth, a laborers' ballad. In singing it she evoked times past, a rustic hearth, her grandmother with her chaplet, her father with his scythe and the bread of working men. Then, full of that vision, her eyes became ingenuous again.

Maurice could not listen to her without shedding tears.

Now, one evening, when she had just sung, Bigorneau said: "I want to talk to you about sobriety."

Someone knocked on the door softly. Maurice got up and went to open it; then he stepped back

A sad form appeared in the shadows.

It was Gothon.

X. The dolorous death of Maurice's mother

She had grown old; Maurice scarcely recognized her. She spoke in a trailing voice.

"God told me where you were, and the miserable life you're leading here. Your mother has reached a great age and is feeling the fatigues of old age. She didn't want to die without having seen her beloved son, and I set out to look for you. Now the poor old woman has reached her end, and she's imploring you."

Maurice hesitated, feeling remorse. But he heard the voice of Claire d'Amour calling him, and he closed the door slowly.

Uncertain footsteps, slow and light, drew away down the stairway...

Maurice went to place his head on Claire d'Amour's knees, and he went to sleep while the prostitute resumed singing.

And Jesus Christ, seeing the state into which his godson had fallen, summoned his faithful angel and said to him: "Go to Maurice and bring him back to duty."

And the angel appeared, radiant, in Bigorneau's lodgings, and said to Maurice: "Sinner, follow me in the name of God. Your mother is sick at home and would like to see her child again."

Maurice hid his head in his hands.

But Claire d'Amour appeared. She had a rose in her hair, and her eyes were so soft and naïve that the angel was moved by her grace.

She asked the angel to sit down and she offered him a drink, blushing. When he had sat down, she carelessly placed her hand on his shoulder, and then leaned over so that he could he could feel the softness of her naked skin on him.

The angel turned round, and his gaze met that of Claire d'Amour, charged with sensuality. The rose that was in Claire d'Amour's hair fell on him and shed its petals.

Then he got up, opened his white wings and flew away, terrified.

And Jesus Christ could not help smiling when he saw the most virtuous of his angels come back with rose petals on his immaculate robe...

Meanwhile, Maurice's mother was very ill, and she was calling for her son in her delirium, in a desperate voice.

And in the park, the frogs of the pond, the oaks and the rose-bushes were discussing that return. Some said: "He'll come back," and others: "He won't come back."

And time passed. Then the Holy Virgin came down from Heaven and went to find Maurice. She said to him: "Come with me." And she took him by the hand like a little child.

They both walked through the deserted streets. It was night.

When they had emerged from the city, the Virgin said: "Your mother is near death, and perhaps you won't arrive in time to receive her last kiss.

The wind of the earth, the sight of the fields and the noise of the trees dissipated the memories of his former life like smoke in Maurice's heart. It seemed to him that he was emerging from a dream. He started to run along the road.

His shadow stretched before him immeasurably; poor people asleep in the ditches woke up and wondered who that strange traveler could be. He ran, no longer having any other thought but one: to see his mother again before she died.

Out there, in the whiteness of sheets, by the light of a candle, next to Gothon, who was praying, Maurice's mother was lying, old, stiff and diminished. She knew that the Virgin had gone in search of Maurice and she tried at times to raise herself up, in order to listen, to see whether the creaking that the wind was causing the staircase to emit was not mingled with that of beloved footsteps.

Death was also there...

"One more hour, Madame Death; he'll arrive within an hour."

The time went by; he did not come. Death grumbled, for she did not like to wait.

"Another half hour, Madame Death, the time for a kiss, and you can take me."

Gothon had gone up to the highest window, and Death said: "I won't wait any longer than dawn."

"My God! My God!" said the mother, "I've always led a pious life, and it won't be just if I don't see him."

"There's a man running along the road," cried Gothon, "and a beautiful lady beside him."

"One minute more, Madame Death."

"There he is! There he is!"

Then a cock crowed; a little ray of sunlight came in, smiling, with a pink dress, through the window, open by a crack; the candlelight paled; the mysterious softness of the dawn bathed the invalid's room.

When Maurice finally appeared he was only able to kiss a hand chilled by the contact of death, eyes without a gleam and lips forever inanimate.

Death, in fact, knows no pity.[4]

---

[4] In his *Confessions,* in a chapter on the dead that return to haunt him, Magre relates that when his mother fell ill, he stayed with her for a while and then left to return to Paris; when he was summoned by telegram to return he arrived to find that she had just died. Desperate races against the clock to reach someone on the brink of death, which fall frustratingly short, are featured in several of Magre's works, including *Priscilla d'Alexandrie* (tr. as *Priscilla of Alexandria*), *La Luxure de Grenade* (tr. as *The Angel of Lust*) and—again featuring a mother—*Les Frères de l'or vierge* (tr. as *The Brothers of the Virgin Gold*).

*XI. Of the extraordinary good fortune that Bigorneau
and Claire d'Amour had in the Roman clergy*

Drunk with grief, Maurice entered the convent of the red penitents the next day, not to emerge again.

That convent was situated some distance from his château, in the depths of a desolate valley. It was like a tomb. Those who entered it made a vow to remain there until they died. There was hardly anyone there except repentant criminals. The bell of the chapel had a particular harmony, which poured sadness and despair into the hearts of those who listened to it. The monks slept on bare stone and the light of day only reached their cells attenuated and distantly.

Deprived of Maurice, Claire d'Amour soon felt an immense ennui. Because of his nonchalant attitude, she took Bigorneau's young disciple as a lover, but she wearied of him very quickly.

She therefore decided to get Maurice back at any price, and one morning she declared to Bigorneau that she was leaving.

"I'll go with you," said Bigorneau. "I sense that I'm getting attached to the places and people that surround us, and that my liberty is thus going to be impeded. My disciples, in any case, have learned the fundamental principles of life from me and my voice is no longer indispensable to them. Let's go see new things.

They left; they went to the Maurice's château, and then to the convent of the red penitents.

A porter with shining eyes and a thin face replied that it would be necessary to be the Pope to get into the convent.

Claire d'Amour and Bigorneau set out for Rome.

When they arrived there, after a long journey and various adventures that do not merit description, the Pope had just died; the election of his successor was about to be held.

In those days, the candidates for the papacy met on the appointed day in the Basilica of Saint Peter, and the Pope was named by the vote of twelve cardinals chosen because of their age, their spirit of justice and their sanctity.

Claire d'Amour arrived in Rome twelve days before the election.

The first evening, she bought medallions and chaplets, and disguised herself as a seller of religious objects. She went to see one of the twelve cardinals and asked to see him, saying that she had brought relics that had belonged to a French saint.

When she was alone with him, she let him know that she was a woman and that the relics she was carrying were no less precious for being profane. She remained with him all night, employing in order to charm him the science of caresses, in which she was very expert.

Meanwhile, Bigorneau, who knew her plans and judged them to be sublime, waited for her in taverns and instructed boatmen and water-carriers in the truth.

On the second evening Claire d'Amour went to see a second cardinal, and she did the same on twelve evenings for the twelve cardinals.

Now, her power was so marvelous that all those who had enjoyed her body desired ardently to do it again. Claire d'Amour promised to yield herself to them again if they appointed as Pope a young monk who was her brother, and whom they would recognize by virtue of his extraordinary resemblance to her.

On the thirteenth day, the day of the election, she put on a monk's robe and mingled with the candidates for the Papacy.

There were very illustrious men there, who had been plotting for years to attain the highest ecclesiastical dignity. There were saints who had come with souls as white as lilies, thinking that the purest are the foremost. There were very rich men who had bought the votes of cardinals with gold. There were priests of all lands, and even a monk of short stature who had come from Lapland with a fur robe because of the icy climate of that region.

And Claire d'Amour was named Pope, because the warmth of her bare skin and the ardor of her kiss were more powerful than glory, gold and virtue.

There are solemn ceremonies at which the clergy of the entire world is represented. Claire d'Amour made a tour of Rome under a solid gold awning, over a road of rose petals, and she extended her white hands, skilled in the sensuality of amour, over the prostrated people in order to bless them.

The cardinals never saw the Pope's sister again, who had appeared to them one evening dressed as a seller of religious objects. Three of them died of chagrin.

Bigorneau became an archbishop.

*XII. Which tells the story of the Pope's visit
to the convent of the red penitents*

Throughout the land there was no talk of anything but the passage of the Pope. He was visiting the convents, accompanied by a fat and jovial archbishop. He was young and handsome, it was said, and more than one young woman was troubled in kissing his hand.

There was even an old gentleman, a libertine and a heretic, who related one evening in the tavern that the young pope was not insensible to the beauty of a charming chatelaine who was smitten with him. He had stayed overnight in her house, and she had gone to find him in his bedroom during the night. The old gentleman added that she had only emerged again in the morning, with an expression full of lassitude.

But can one add faith to the words of a libertine and heretic? Can one believe in the misconduct of a Pope?

There was a knock on the door of the convent of the red penitents.

The thin porter darted a glittering gaze outside, and then opened the door and prostrated himself. The Pope had come to visit the convent.

The superior came running, the melancholy bell rang. Followed by the fat jovial archbishop and a few prelates, the Pope marched behind the superior, who took him to the chapel and the cells.

He saw all the monks and allowed them to kiss his sacred ring. Then he said to the superior: "Is there no other?"

"There is also Brother Maurice," said the superior, "but as he cannot forget a woman that he loved and has lost, he has locked himself in a subterranean cell in order to be unable to evoke her image."

"Go and fetch him," said the Pope.

Maurice came, sad and changed.

"I've chosen you among all," the Pope told him, "in order that for your salvation you leave this convent and accompany me in my journey."

Then the fat archbishop stated laughing, and all the red penitents envied Maurice such an honor.

There was also a young red penitent, gracious of face, whom the Pope had noticed and was also tempted to take with him, but he contented himself with caressing his cheek with his hand.

They left the convent under the fulgurant gaze of the porter. They traversed the valley, and the Pope told the archbishop, then, to go and wait for him in the village with the prelates. He took Maurice into a little wood.

The grass underfoot was thick; the foliage sang around them. Maurice saw that the Pope was Claire d'Amour. But he did not have time to be astonished by that; she hid her face in her hands, moaning, and gave all the signs of an extreme dolor.

She accused Maurice of no longer loving her, since he had locked himself in a subterranean cell in order to forget her image.

That unexpected dolor was only partly feigned.

They lay down on the grass; Maurice did his best to console her, and to the delirium of amour was added for him, the voluptuousness of an irremediable sin.

The hours passed, and she made him a thousand other reproaches between her kisses.

And Maurice knew thereafter that, with her tears, she had once again knotted around his neck an imperishable chain.

XIII. Which concerns a crime, a sea voyage,
a battle, a shipwreck and a dream

They changed clothes and resolved to go overseas; they made Bigorneau party to that project.

The latter replied: "This is working out marvelously. I had resolved to quit the ecclesiastical habit today myself, and I was going to tell you. Our life ought to be different every day if we want to elevate our spirit.

They went to see the captain of a ship departing for Constantinople, who consented to take them with him. The ship was to set sail the following day at dawn.

Claire d'Amour wanted to revisit the places where she had spent her childhood, and Maurice went with her.

On the way she was still reproaching him for not loving her, and she told him that she would not believe him if he did not give her undeniable proof of that love.

They arrived thus at Samson's inn, where Claire d'Amour had awoken to life under the blows of that cruel master.

They went in; Samson was alone, but Claire d'Amour had difficulty recognizing him.

He was an old man now, so greatly was his face ravaged and so much was his body stooped. He was staring, with obstinacy and terror, at an empty armchair facing him. One might have thought that his eyes were contemplating a frightful vision.

Since the distant time when Samson had murdered Guluche, the same scene was renewed every day at the same hour in the inn. When dusk descended over the earth, Samson heard several raps on the door of the inn. Then it opened quietly and Guluche came in slowly, dragging his paralyzed leg. He had a slightly sad expression, and he gazed at Samson benevolently. He came to sit down facing him, put down his stick, lit his pipe, and sometimes murmured between two puffs: "Virgin Mary, guide her!"

Samson had tried in vain to flee. Wherever he was, at the same hour, the phantom appeared. If Samson was walking, he walked too; if he ran, he still followed him, maintaining on his face the same expression of sadness and benevolence.

Nowadays, Samson was considered in the village to be mad; his inn had been deserted and he remained there, solitary and resigned, waiting during the day for the evening apparition, the thought of which chilled him with terror.

In seeing him, Claire d'Amour felt her past hatred reawakening in her heart. She turned to Maurice and said to him: "The moment has come for you to prove your love to me. If you love me, you'll avenge me on that man, who has made me suffer cruelly, and you'll kill him."

So saying, she took a knife hanging on the wall and she held it out to Maurice.

Samson had turned round, and he perceived Claire d'Amour. An extraordinary joy illuminated his face tortured by remorse; he held out his arms.

Maurice plunged the knife into his breast; he fell to the ground, face down. The phantom of Guluche put his hands together, and dissipated.

Then Claire d'Amour took Maurice in her arms and kissed him recklessly. For her, he had become a criminal, and because of that, it seemed to her that she loved him less than she had before.

The next day, in the first rays of the sun, they were sitting in the bow of a three-master with Bigorneau, sailing over a foamy sea.

Gazing at the horizon, which was the color of blood, Maurice thought about the blood he had shed the day before and was astonished not to feel any remorse. It seemed to him that the frame of his mind had enlarged, that he had reached the ultimate limit of forbidden things; now he considered favorably everything that was crime and sin, prohibited by laws and religions, and he found an unexpected and powerful beauty therein.

Meanwhile, Bigorneau had befriended the mariners; he lavished the advice of wisdom upon them, and they were proud to be living in the intimacy of a man of such great merit. They were all troubled by the beauty of Claire d'Amour, and they dreamed about her at night.

But there was one young passenger who never looked at her, and whom she left insensible. He was due to disembark at Cadiz. No one knew him; he was traveling for his pleasure. He walked alone on the deck of the ship; he gave the impression of being free, indifferent and joyful.

Claire d'Amour employed all her artistry to move him. He chatted to her gladly, but did not show her any sign of amour.

The ship stopped in the harbor of Cadiz. The stranger disembarked there, having paid the captain, and having saluted the other travelers and the mariners with great politeness. He had no luggage.

Claire d'Amour followed him on to the quay among the pomegranate sellers and the castanet players. She would have liked to give herself to him in a tavern near the sea, to the sound of guitars, while the vessel that had brought them swayed in the harbor.

But he said: "What's the point? I don't love you and can't love you. Your memory would spoil the dream that I make of life. I've taken the best of you and I'm carrying it away with me. I've written a little poem about your beauty, the salty air of the sea, the whiteness of sails and the sounds of the port of Cadiz, which will rejoice my heart more than the bitter taste of your kisses. I brush joy, but I don't touch it. I'll take the flower from your hair, but nothing more. If I took the more precious flower of your heart, I'd no longer be able to love the roses of the earth tomorrow. Then again, only a desire that one doesn't realize is sweet. Adieu; when I sit down as the day declines on a hill or before the sea, your image, as light as the evening mist, will float around me, with a favorable smile."

Having said that, he drew away, twirling a little laurel cane that he was holding in his hand, and Claire d'Amour went back to the ship, thoughtfully.

Maurice asked her where she had been; she replied that she had gone to breathe under the lemon-trees in flowers, and he believed it, because of the gift of illusion that he had received at birth.

The ship departed again and reached the open sea. They had been sailing for a few days when the man on watch signaled a ship in the distance that was carrying no flag and had to be a pirate ship. That vessel approached with great speed and they soon saw that it was full of men wearing turbans, who had terrible faces and were redoubtably armed.

The captain put his crew under arms and exhorted them to a heroic defense. Maurice and Claire d'Amour also armed themselves, and she was joyful to be able to make blood flow and kill in a legitimate cause.

The two ships came together, and immediately, a host of pirates leapt on to the deck. As they were far superior in number they rapidly massacred the captain and the crew.

Maurice, Claire d'Amour, Bigorneau and a little cabin boy named Yvon, having taken refuge at the stern, were about to perish in their turn when the man who appeared to be the leader of the pirates uttered a loud cry and stopped his companions. He took off his turban; Maurice and Claire d'Amour recognized Chênepain.

Tordecoeur and Larbalet were with him, and a few minutes later, they were in one another's arms.

They traveled in company, therefore. Chênepain narrated a series of adventures that, although marvelous, do not merit being reported, by which he and his companions had been led to undertake brigandage on the seas. And he was delighted to be both a warrior and a mariner, because he compared himself in the secrecy of his heart to the divine Ulysses wandering over the seas.

Bigorneau harangued the pirates and praised them because of their vagabond life, which was the image of liberty, and told them that the greatest danger they were running was not being locked up in the depths of a hold with a cannonball attached to the feet, or being hanged from some yardarm, but being bound by the chain that a woman's arms comprise.

A frightful tempest burst and broke the masts of the ship, which, having collided with a rock, began to take on water in all parts.

The pirates leap into the launch and drew away from the vessel. The launch was also overturned by the wind; all the pirates fell into the sea and were eaten by the sharks that were very abundant and very redoubtable in that region.

Maurice, Claire d'Amour and Bigorneau had stayed on the ship, along with the cabin boy Yvon, Chênepain and his two companions. They constructed a raft in haste with barrels, planks and fragments of the masts. They put it to sea and climbed on to it just at the moment when the ship was engulfed in the waves.

The wind calmed down and the raft became motionless on the sea.

The victims of the shipwreck suffered cruelly from thirst and hunger. Night succeeded day without them seeing land on the horizon.

Claire d'Amour lamented no longer being able to see her face, except in the ever-motionless water that only reflected it imperfectly.

Bigorneau was in despair, feeling himself to be the slave of the sea. But the little cabin boy Yvon was the saddest of all, because he reflected that he was the youngest, and he remembered an old song that he had once sung, whose cruel verity he had not previously understood.[5]

---

[5] There are several macabre songs about post-shipwreck cannibalism, in which the cabin boy is invariably the one who gets eaten, but the one best known in French is "Il était un

On the third day, Maurice extended his face toward the heavens and had a dream.

He dreamed that Claire d'Amour was identified with the sea. Like her, it was innumerable and changing, by turns green, blue, pink or black, full of reflections and mirages. It extended from one continent to another, over a bed of sand, immense and voluptuous, with its tresses of algae, its smile of foam and its vast arms open to all desired. In order to possess it, he threw himself into its waves and he swam with all his might, recklessly, until death, in order to embrace it all. But no matter how hard he swam, new waves always unfurled before him, and he sensed with despair that he would never be able to embrace its immensity.

He woke up; joyful cries resounded. The wind had risen and was pushing the raft toward a coast, the design of whose contours they could already see.

---

petit navire," often sung to children, in which the boy is saved in the nick of time by the Virgin Mary.

XIV. How, having spoken of their amours, three heroes died beside the sea

They were cast up on a sandy beach at the foot of a high cliff. Chênepain, in a resounding voice, thanked the winds and the waves that had preserved them from death.

They scaled the cliff and discovered a horizon of forests, lakes and rocks. In the far distance, there was blue sea again, which made them think that they were on an island.

They built a house with tree branches, and Tordecoeur, who was industrious, fabricated bows for hunting, with flexible lianas.

And they lived there for many days, during which they told one another all the stories they knew. Bigorneau explained a thousand times the dangers of passion and ennui visited them.

The monotony of life made Claire d'Amour suffer most of all. One day they were attacked by a huge savage ape, and having seen it she went into the forest alone, dreaming of astonishing amours with that beast. She only came back three days later, haggard and exhausted by fatigue, and she took her friends to the lair where the ape slept, where Tordecoeur struck it dead.

Out of boredom, Claire d'Amour gave herself in turn to each of the three brigands, and she made them swear again the terrible oath not to reveal to anyone the signal favor of which they were the object.

Now, as everybody knows, an invincible force obliges men to talk.

One day, Bigorneau and Maurice were fishing for shellfish, Claire d'Amour and the cabin boy Yvon were watching the sunset from the top of the cliff, and the three heroes, sitting on the shore, were exchanging the words that the hazard of the conversation, amity and the cool evening breeze inspired in them.

Larbalet, who was loquacious and sentimental, and whose heart was overflowing with tenderness, by virtue of an impulse of joyful expansion, felt the need to confide his good fortune to his friends. He leaned toward them and made the revelation in a low voice.

Chênepain and Tordecoeur immediately stood up, full of wrath, exhorting their companion to take back his lying words. As he refused to do so, each of them swore that he alone was loved by Claire d'Amour, and that what Larbalet had said was vanity and calumny.

An extreme confusion ensued. All three swore that they had possessed Claire d'Amour, and sought to give one another proofs of it. They soon saw that all three of them were right. Then the anger of having been deceived, pitiless jealousy, blind violence and the natural instinct that drives men to throw themselves upon one another for amorous causes, placed a blindfold over their eyes and their hearts.

They drew their daggers and they struck one another with all their might. Their blood stained the sand of the beach red and they fell, pierced by thrusts, still trying to strike one another.

Suddenly, their raised arms remained motionless, leaving death in suspense, and their faces froze in amazement.

Up above, on the cliff, standing in the blue evening air, allowing her adored hair to float in the wind, they had just perceived Claire d'Amour, who was holding the cabin boy Yvon in her arms, lavishing on him the precious kisses for which they had just shed one another's blood.

They saw that, and they understood. They understood that for a heart devoid of fidelity, they had forgotten their long communal life of travels and wars, and bread shared, and had misunderstood divine amity...

Then, sensing death coming, they embraced one another, weeping.

When Bigorneau and Maurice arrived, Tordecoeur and Larbalet were already deprived of life. Chênepain's eyes were veiled by dream.

He saw Claire d'Amour in the distance, who was descending towards him amid stones. He got up, and when she was close by and he had contemplated her one last time, he took the hand of the philosopher, smiled sadly, and said:

"Greetings, Helen, daughter of the gods!"

And he expired.

Bigorneau dug a grave for the three friends with his own hands, and went to dream alone on the shore in order to compose an epitaph for them.

And Maurice could not explain their death, because of the sandman's admirable gift.

The next day, Maurice and Claire d'Amour had disappeared. Bigorneau and the cabin boy Yvon searched the island in all directions, in vain; they could not find the slightest trace of them. Nine days went by, and they were obliged to admit that they would probably never see their friends again.

Then something strange happened; the philosopher tore out his hair, ran like a madman along the shore, fell to his knees, got up again, and ran again, imploring the forest, the sky, the sea and God, in whom he did not believe, to return Claire d'Amour to him.

A French ship had just passed by and had seen the signals that the cabin boy Yvon was making. The captain put a boat to sea and, thinking that he was collecting castaways, came to the coast with a few sailors.

Bigorneau went toward him and spoke to him in these terms:

"You have before you the slave, the miserable slave, of a frenzied passion. I only had to put out my hand to satisfy it, and I did not do it, out of pure folly. Believe me, Captain, and you, sailors whose faces reflect sentiments of honesty and compassion, never become attached. You can see where a deadly passion has led a sage and a free man. Under that mound in the sand over there like three heroes with the great hearts of the Trojan War. Take this cabin boy with you, whose soul is charming and prompt to forget. Leave the poor slave on the foreign soil and sail joyfully toward our fatherland."

"This man's speech is devoid of sense," said the Captain. "Doubtless his misfortunes have caused him to lose his reason."

He took the cabin boy Yvon with him, and both of them, while the ship drew away, gazed for a long time at the silhouette of the philosopher, who remained alone, his head in his hands, sitting on a high rock.

XV. The end of this marvelous story

In an almost inaccessible place on the island, in the midst of rocks, there was a profound cavern. That cavern opened to a subterranean tunnel that connected Hell with the earth.

Wandering in that direction, Claire d'Amour had encountered a passing demon. The demon had looked at her curiously and sympathetically, and had said to her: "You're beautiful and you please me. Are you a daughter on the earth, and of what father are you?"

Claire d'Amour had replied: "I don't know who put me in the world, but I heard it said in my childhood that I was a daughter of fays. I was beaten because of that. I have suffered and I have caused suffering, and I have loved, and here I am."

And the demon said: "I recognize you; you are of my race. This is the road to Hell; come back to it with me; you'll live in flames with your peers."

Then Claire had gone back to Maurice and she had said to him: "I'm bored on earth. I no longer love you. I no longer loved you from the day when you committed murder to please me, and I sensed that you belonged to me completely. Adieu. I've discovered a road that leads to Hell; it's there that I'm going, in order to know new joys there."

And she drew away—but Maurice followed her.

On the way, he showed her with his hand the forests with their centenarian oaks, the mists wandering through the valleys, and the lakes blue in the moonlight, in order move her by means of the aspect of terrestrial beauties.

But she was no longer sensible to them.

Having arrived at the cavern that was the entrance to Hell, Claire d'Amour turned toward Maurice and said to him again: "Adieu. This is my native land."

And she went into the darkness with a resolute tread.

In Heaven, Jesus Christ, who had been afflicted for a long time by the bad and impious life that his godson was leading, seeing him on the point of going into Hell, launched himself down to earth and seized Maurice's arm at the moment when he was about to follow Claire d'Amour.

He spoke to him with a great tenderness, for he was extremely generous, and even his reproaches had a perfume of benevolence.

"Do you think that I carried you in my arms on the day of your baptism to see you come to such a miserable end? Do you know that you're penetrating into the blazing abode of Hell? And you're going to do it deliberately, without a backward glance, without any repentance for the wretched life of vulgar lust and sin that you've led on earth. Anyone else would be damned forever, but you're my godson, and one is unjust for one's own. Come back to your senses, and I'll forgive you."

And Maurice replied: "I prefer Hell to Paradise, crime to virtue. All I regret of my life is the time I spent praying. I've loved, and if that was in opprobrium, at last I've participated in the misery and joy of human beings. What would I do among your lilies, with your virtuous angels? I can't sing canticles. I prefer eternal flames in the arms of Claire d'Amour.

And Jesus Christ said, not without regret, or he did not like to inflict pain: "You shall know the truth, since it's for your own good."

And he told Maurice the entire life of Claire d'Amour, her lies, her treasons and her innumerable lovers.

But Maurice did not appear touched by that at all.

"How dare you lie like that, my godfather, you who are God and wear an aureole of light around your forehead? I shall not allow myself to be caught in such a primitive trap. I love Claire d'Amour, she loves me, and I'm going to join her."

Jesus Christ took his head in his hands. "But she told you just now that she didn't love you."

Maurice smiled. "She's deceiving herself, or wanted to deceive me. But I know the true sentiments of her heart."

And with that, leaving Jesus Christ stupefied, he went into Hell with a joyful step.

Such is the great power of women...

THE TOY MERCHANT

*I. Which features a ruined temple and the reflections
of two somewhat philosophical old crows*

In those days, every spring was inhabited by a very beautiful lady, whose green robe could be seen gliding over the water in the evening; in those days, the population of joyful and sage dwarfs lived and labored in the profound realms of the earth; the traveler gone astray in the forest was exposed to a thousand enchantments; sirens sang on the shores of seas; an old woman carrying a faggot whom one encountered at the bottom of a hill was almost always a powerful fay; the animals talked as well as, and often better than, humans; in those days, the women who spun outside their doors told marvelous and endless stories, like the threads of their spindles.

Now, in a village whose name I have forgotten, there was a small boy named Lubin and a little girl named Colette, who loved one another with all their hearts. They spent their days together on the roads, counting white pebbles, playing, and gazing at the astonishing images that clouds make in the sky. They embraced one another, weeping, when the shadows of the forest extended over the earth, because they believed that the night would last forever and that they would never see one another again.

Colette was the daughter of a barber named Lafarie; Lubin was the son of Sinus, the bell-ringer at the church. That man lived in great poverty and was reputed to be simple-minded. The only things in the world that he loved were his son and the voice of bells; no one else in the land knew how to make bronze speak as marvelously as he did; the angelus spread a strange speech over the vibrant countryside; women

117

shed tears when vespers sounded. Sinus emerged from the old tower where the bells were with his eyes shining, his expression exalted. He was feared and hated because of that.

The barber Lafarie had a big pipe, and was a jovial man. He told stories and loved literature; he gave medical advice, talked about astronomy and knew the names of distant cities.

Colette was likeable and pretty. Lubin was strong and brave. Colette had blonde hair, Lubin had black hair.

One fine day in spring, the day of their thirteenth birthday—for I forget to say that they were born on the same day—they went for a walk in fields more distant than usual. The countryside was deserted, and a breeze agitated the gorse.

"How beautiful and big the world is," said Colette.

Lubin made no reply, but he looked covertly at Colette's eyes, and found them more beautiful than the rest of the world.

A little spirit that lived in an old oak saw them and shouted: "*Bonjour! Bonjour*, children!"

"I didn't know trees could talk," said Colette.

"They talk very often and very well," said Lubin, who did not like to seem ignorant of anything.

As they went along they picked flowers and made a crown of them. Then they met an old lady who was leading a donkey.

"What are you doing here at this hour, naughty children," she said to them. "Night is going to fall; go back to the house quickly."

But the children laughed and continued on their way. They passed close to a spring and went into a little wood. Dusk was gradually falling; an inexpressible charm filled the earth. Traces of extraordinarily tiny feet could be seen on the ground. They were the footprints of fays who lived in the wood.

They arrived thus at a place where they suddenly discovered ruined walls, fallen columns, statues and porticos. The place was considered to be dangerous and accursed by all the local inhabitants. The ruins to be seen there were the vestiges of a temple once raised to unknown and evil divinities. For centuries, a thick ivy had covered all the stones. Alone in the midst of all those forgotten things, a single statue of a woman stood forth intact from the wild grass, like the graceful goddess of the past...

It was on her head that the two children came to place their crown of flowers. And when they had done that, they both felt troubled; their gaiety disappeared and they sat down on the ground, prey to a great emotion. A fresh wind blew, and as the first star lit up in the sky, two little tears shone in the children's eyes and trickled slowly down their cheeks. They looked at one another and they saw that their tears had the same color as the star.

"Will you love me forever?" said Lubin.

"Forever," replied Colette.

"Until death?"

"Until death."

"And afterwards?"

"Afterwards, we'll be in that star up there, and I'll continue loving you."

For the first time, they gave one another an amorous kiss.

Then the statue of the goddess smiled ironically; faces of men with horns on their forehead, which were sculpted on the columns, opened their eyes of stone, and two old crows that were somewhat philosophical exchanged the following words:

"Did you hear them talking about love?"

"'We'll be in that star!' That's ridiculous."

"How insensate these humans are!"

"In truth, nothing exists except the cool wind of the woods, the joy of flying freely, the odor of firs..."

II. In which the barber Lafarie purchases
some strange toys

Lubin and Colette loved one another and were happy.
They met in the evenings in the barber Lafarie's house. That
pleasant and literate man told them marvelous things about the
history of peoples, their mores, and their wars. The children
listened, full of admiration, while Sinus the bell-ringer seemed
to be following the harmonies of an inaudible carillon in
space. A pressure of the hand, a furtive kiss behind a door: all
their happiness was in that, and it was very great.

At that time, an ambulant merchant passed through the
village. He had a multicolored cloak and boots of yellow
leather. He sold toys, toiletries, portraits of kings and also
magic potions that, it was said, made children grow taller,
effaced wrinkles from faces and cured maladies. Although the
man was reputed to be something of a sorcerer, Lafarie bought
a doll and a Polichinelle puppet from him, of which he made
gifts to Lubin and Colette.

The doll was pink and blonde with alert and malicious
eyes; the puppet was red and particularly ugly.

"You'll see that these toys will amuse your children," the
ambulant merchant had said, when he sold them to the barber.
And to express his contentment, he had made a singular grimace, which would have frightened Lafarie had he seen it.

Colette was very pleased to own the doll; she installed it
in her bedroom on a blue cushion, in such a way that she could
see it from her bed. And on the first evening, when Colette
came to kiss it before going to bed, the doll's eyes became
animate, and it spoke in these terms:

"You know nothing of life, little girl, and that's why I
want to give you some advice. Look: I have porcelain eyes
and cardboard breasts, and if I make a gesture expressing joy
or pain, it's because of the spring that governs me. I don't feel
anything; I have no heart; and yet I'm loved; I'm loved be-

cause of that, for my insensible beauty. If you want to be loved, child, be like me. Give birth to dreams and love without dreaming or loving. Cause suffering, and watch suffering with eyes that do not know tears..."

From that moment on, everything changed in the life of Lubin and Colette. She spent entire hours with her doll, consulting it as to the best way to do her hair, the pleats of her bodice, and the flower that she ought to put in her hair.

"Be coquettish," the doll said. And Colette became a little more coquettish every day. She took pleasure in making fun of Lubin, she no longer wanted to go for walks with him, and she no longer told him that she loved him. She even simulated a great amity for a boy of the same age as Lubin, but taller and better looking than him.

Lubin fell into a profound sadness. He was seen wandering on his own in the countryside, leaning over solitary wells, lying down on the bare ground. And one day, when he came back to his room sadder than usual in order to think about Colette, he saw the puppet that Lafarie had given to him and he said to it: "Why am I not free of all cares, in order to amuse myself in your company, Polichinelle? But see what great dolor oppresses me."

The puppet smiled, shrugged its shoulders and replied: "Nothing is worth the trouble of a veritable chagrin. Go as far as the nearest tavern, ask for a bottle of wine, and a magical power will change your irritations into bursts of laughter. If Colette doesn't love you, laugh and drink. Above all, drink, wine being divine in nature. Fortunate is he who can spend his life in a multicolored costume, under the arbor of an inn, with a glass in hand and laughter on his lips."

In the same way that Colette's doll was a brazen coquette, Lubin's puppet was an arrant drunkard. And as they were enchanted toys, the two children had to follow their advice.

III. Our hero's touching adieux and the wise words of a windmill

Colette was picking roses in her father's garden. Her doll was on a bench, and she sometimes turned round in order to smile at it. The sun was on the horizon, about to set; the voices of laborers returning home from work were audible on the road; the night spirits were waking up in the bushes, adjusting their blue hoods, and preparing their lanterns and holly staffs.

Lubin appeared in the garden,

"I've come to say adieu, Colette; I'm leaving."

He stood still, watching out for an emotion on his friend's face.

Colette's heat beat faster, but the doll tugged her dress urgently, and it was with indifference that she replied, while continuing to pick roses: "Where are you going?"

"I'm going to Paris to seek my fortune."

Paris! How mysterious and far away that was, full of temptations and dangers! Colette shivered and even thought that a tear was about to moisten her yes.

She leaned over in the middle of a bouquet, devoting all her attention to cutting a rose larger than the rest, and her voice did not tremble when she said: "You'll see beautiful landscapes on the way. That's annoying; this rose has pricked me."

"I'm going away for a long time, perhaps forever," said Lubin.

The first star lit up in the sky. Colette looked at Lubin. Forever, he had said! But no, it was necessary to retain him, to tell him that she still loved him.

She saw the doll making signs to her. She had finished her bouquet; she took a piece of thread out of her pocket and began tying up the rose stems carefully,

"My God," she said, "how good these roses smell!"

"You don't have anything to say to me, then?"

Nothing to say to him! But yes, she had a host of things to say to him, which were crowding her heart and shivering on her lips.

"Be coquettish; never let your sentiments show," murmured the doll beside her.

"I wish you *bon voyage*, truly, a good and fortunate journey."

She was standing at her door, respiring her bouquet, distracted and bored.

Lubin despaired then, and fled, at a run, along the road. And when his silhouette had disappeared in the distance, and Colette felt quite alone in her garden, she took her roses in her nervous hands, tore them up, scattered their petals on the path and then fell on to the bench and burst into sobs.

Thus are the hearts of women made.

Lubin fled, running, into the descending dusk. He no longer wanted to think, no longer wanted to remember, but to quit that accursed place rapidly. He left the village and climbed the hill; then, as he was weary, he stopped for a moment. Blue mists floated in the depths of the valley; in front of him, in the distance, extended the admirable earth with its rocks, its wild lilies and its fir woods...

The road he was following was bordered by windmills; the wind was blowing and the windmills were turning joyfully in the air. They too were amorous, the handsome lovers and the great musicians of nature.

There was one of them whose sails were broken, whose door was demolished, and which had been abandoned because of its old age. It was no longer turning in the light; that one had ceased to love.

Near the old mill, behind a bush, a being that Lubin could not see was singing; its voice was drawling and unhappy, and this in approximately what it said:

"Listen to the abandoned mill, child. It was young once, like you, it was a friend of the sun, it sheltered the village musicians. See how it is suffering for having loved. Believe it, stop on the slope; the wind breaks the sails of those who rise up in audacious flight. Stop at the first kisses, the first tears..."

Lubin resumed his route and walked for a long time. His village was already lost in the mists when he was astonished to hear in the distance an angelus more melancholy than usual. And he thought that it was his father who was ringing it...

*IV. In which the strangeness of the hearts of women
is observed once again*

After long days of walking, Lubin arrived in Paris. In those days that city was less beautiful and less prosperous than it is now, but it nevertheless inspired a great deal of astonishment and admiration in Lubin.

He had brought with him, as a puerile souvenir of his amour, the Polichinelle that Colette's father had given him. He had gradually become attached to it, and had made it his traveling companion and confidant. It was to the puppet that he spoke about his chagrin in the evening.

"Forget, make merry, drink," the puppet repeated.

And in order to follow its advice, Lubin willingly got drunk in taverns. He had sworn to himself not to think about Colette any longer, but when night came and his mind filled with chimeras under the influence of wine, the image of Colette always smiled alongside him. He emptied glass after glass in vain; he could not chase away the ironic gaze of her blue eyes.

Lubin was ambitious; he told himself that in order to reach a high position in the realm it was necessary to get close to those who distributed placements, decorations and honors. So he went to the king's palace, and as he had a certain knowledge of flowers and their growth in accordance with the seasons, he was employed as a gardener.

He worked every day, therefore, in the great royal park, writing the name of Colette on the sand of pathways and giving particular care to the flowers that she loved. Still advised by the puppet that he carried with him, he drank to forget, and sometimes, in the evening, he went to sleep in an arbor under the stars, to wake up with a weary body and an exhausted spirit in the morning dew.

One day when he had drunk more than usual and he was in a very bad mood, he saw a young woman of great beauty coming toward him along a path in the park.

Loving Colette had rendered him so unhappy that he had conceived a hatred for all women. He turned away when she went past him and made a semblance of examining attentively a toad that was wandering nonchalantly over a flower-bed a few feet away.

Now, that young woman was Aude, the king's daughter, justly renowned for her coquetry and her grace. She was accustomed to troubling the hearts of all the men she saw and leaving an immortal memory in them. Three princes had already killed themselves for love of her, the king's jester had been hanged and an aged lord, the father of a family, had fallen into dementia. But she had an insensible heart; she said that she never wanted to love anyone.

There is no humble homage for women. She expected the silent admiration of that gardener, and her astonishment was extreme when she saw him turn away and look at a toad.

She stopped, touched Lubin's shoulder with her finger and said: "Insensate! How dare you look at that filthy animal when the most charming princess on earth passes nearby?"

She was before him in a pink dress, her hair undone, more beautiful than she had ever been. Lubin thought how deceptive women's eyes were; he looked at her angrily and said: "What do you want with me? You horrify me. I'd a thousand times rather sleep next to that toad than next to you. If it's ugly, I can at least turn away from it, and thus its ugliness is diminished by the knowledge I have of it. But you have eyes that reflect divine things and a horrible soul. Go on, get away from me, hypocrite and liar!"

Lubin raised a menacing fist and Aude, the king's daughter, fled in tears, already knowing in her heart an immense amour for the first man who had ever dared to insult her, and had nearly hit her.

V. The amour of Lubin and the king's daughter

The apartments of the king's daughter overlooked the gardens where Lubin worked, and the day after his encounter with her, he perceived the princess at her window, her hair undone, beautiful and pensive.

It was night; a soft shadow veiled the contours of things, the flowers in the flower beds embalmed it. And as soon as Aude saw Lubin, she made extravagant signs to him to invite him to join her.

Lubin expected to receive death for his conduct the previous day. He told himself that if the princess was summoning him, it was doubtless to make him perish before her eyes and to enjoy his torture. He thought about fleeing, but then thought that he would be caught rapidly, and that it was better to look the danger in the face.

And then, after all, one cannot see a beautiful princess making signs to you by night to come to her apartment without being strongly tempted to obey her orders.

He therefore placed the ladder that he used to climb trees against the wall, and he went up, recommending his soul to God.

When he had reached the last step and had penetrated into the room, the light went out and he felt the body of the princess against him and burning lips pressing upon his.

And he discovered, that evening, that the heart of a woman is a well of darkness.

Lubin came back every evening to meet Aude; she waited for him when night fell, and he did not leave until the morning song of the nightingale. But Lubin did not love the king's daughter, because he could not banish the memory of Colette from his mind. After the fugitive pleasure of caresses, the rapid sensuality, he experienced beside the princess an immense ennui, which he could not disguise, and which made her cherish him more.

He pleased himself then by evolving the image of Colette, the days of childhood, holding hands, and chaste kisses. And it was always when those pleasant scenes unfolded before him, and the exact moment when he was most desirous of solitude, that Aude took him in her arms again and talked to him about her love.

There were harsh words for her then; he pushed her away; he made her cry. Aude sensed than she did not possess her lover and she loved him all the more for it.

Then they rested, heart to heart, narrowly united in appearance, but as far apart as if seas and high mountains separated them.

One day, as dawn was about to appear and they were about to part, Aude said to Lubin: "I want us to be united forever. I'm going to confess everything to my father; you'll marry me and you'll be king."

"The sun is already gilding the trees in the park," Lubin replied. "We'll talk about these things again this evening."

He ran through the gardens, left the palace, and traversed the city with great strides. He reached the open country, cut himself a holly staff and, for the first time in a long time, he felt his heart full of delight.

The idea of living permanently with the beautiful princess caused him an infinite terror. It was Colette that he loved, it was Colette that he wanted to see again at any price.

As he went past a spring he undressed and bathed, in order to purify himself of Aude's kisses, which he sensed on his body like burns.

That evening and the following day, the princess, vibrant with amour, waited in vain for the man she loved beside the lowered lamp.

The day after that, there was a great reception at the court. A Norwegian prince was being received there, who had crossed the sea in order to see Aude. The king, his host, and all the lords waited for the princess to emerge from her apartments. And as the orchestra played a solemn march by way of a prelude, she appeared, her hair undone and her clothes in disorder, singing a barrack-room song.

The king fainted, the courtiers covered their faces, and the Norwegian prince left, believing that he had been insulted.

Alas, Lubin, as he left, had forgotten the enchanted puppet in the princess's apartment, and such were the results of its perfidious advice.

VI. Lubin Encounters Death

Lubin was treading the road of return joyfully. The sun had just set; he reached the edge of a profound forest and perceived an old woman who was sitting on the ground lamenting.

She seemed to have attained an extraordinary age; she had a huge scythe beside her, and Lubin saw her try in vain, several, times, to put a large sack over her shoulder.

"Would you help me, Monsieur Traveler," she said to Lubin, "to put this sack on my back. I can't succeed in doing it, even though that back is very stooped and not far from the ground."

Lubin helped the old woman, and when the sack was solidly placed on her shoulders, she picked up her scythe, started to laugh, and said to Lubin: "I'm Death, child; you've just helped me to lift a sack that contains a terrible plague, which I'm going to unleash over a country a long way from this one, because I'm weary of seeing robust individuals arrive at an advanced age there. Then again, I like seeing the grimace that the disease in question imprints of the human faces it has touched. But you've rendered me a service and I want to give you a recompense. Take this little bone; it will be able to save you once from the terrible destiny that lays humans in the tomb. Leave it with a relative or a friend at the moment of your death and tell him to come and touch your forehead with it twelve hours after you've been laid in the benevolent earth."

Having said that, Death made a grand gesture of farewell, and flew away through the air.

Lubin took the little bone and continued on his way, very pensively.

When he arrived in his village, he was initially astonished to see it full of soldiers with fine uniforms. He learned that a regiment of blue grenadiers had been installed in the region and had populated it with songs and heroic dreams. All the girls were in love with grenadiers, and Colette was going to marry the general.

That was a great event, about which there was much talk. The barber Lafarie had conceived an extreme pride in consequence. His loquacity had never been as great. He told his clients the history of the regiment of blue grenadiers, all the wars in which it had taken part since the remotest antiquity, its campaign and its victories.

Lubin went to fall into his father's arms and tell him his dolor. But Sinus the bell-ringer replied: "My son, nothing on this earth is worth the trouble of living through. Come with me to the tower of the church; you'll see with what marvelous spirit bronze is animated. Only that which gives life to bells can know a divine joy. You see that when Sunday is sunny, and when, having rung the bells for mass, I lean out of the tower and I see in the distance the peasants in their velvet garments, the young women with their lace, the good wives with their hoods and chaplets, and I think that it's at my signal that they're all heading toward the church, I'm gripped by such a pride that the other joys of the earth no longer have any value in my eyes."

Lubin saw clearly that his father could not understand him; he resolved to go find Colette, to speak to her, and to try to win her back.

As on the day of his departure, he pushed the wooden gate that gave access to her garden and he perceived her beside another young woman, gracious and pale, among the roses.

Colette recognized Lubin perfectly, about whom she had often thought. She put her hand on her heart, which was beating very rapidly, and murmured: "I don't know you! What do you want?"

Then she turned to her companion and said: "Who is that man? He has a nasty expression; let's go inside."

VII. The Regiment of Blue Grenadiers

The marriage of Colette and General Labride was celebrated with an extreme pomp. Lafarie appeared there with a brand new green coat, and he was more jovial and more knowledgeable than usual. There was a great feast, in which all the soldiers of the blue grenadiers took part and all the young women of the region.

That evening, Lubin wandered through the country along the same roads where he had once strolled with Colette. A little spirit that lived in an old oak and knew him well called out to him: "*Bonjour, bonjour*, Lubin."

He arrived in the middle of the ruins where he had once exchanged his first amorous kiss with Colette. The stone goddess was still smiling ironically, the faces of men with horns of the forehead sculpted on the columns grimaced when they saw him. Lubing sat down on the ground and he heard two somewhat philosophical old crows, who said:

"In truth, nothing exists except the cool wind in the woods, the joy of flying freely and the odor of firs..."

A few days later, Lubin enlisted in the regiment of blue grenadiers, reckoning that it was impossible for him to live far from Colette. He distinguished himself rapidly by his intelligence and skill in military exercises, and General Labride selected him as an aide-de-camp. He was thus required to see Colette every day. He sometimes followed her on horseback during her rides with the general; he ate at her table; he saw her chatting familiarly with her husband, caressing him and kissing him. He still preferred the spectacle of those things to being distanced, even though it gave him infinite pain. Once, he even got up at night and went to stick his ear to the keyhole of the door behind which Colette was lying in the general's arms.

Colette had kept the doll once bought by her father; she still amused herself with it and listened to its advice. And as before, the enchanted doll taught her coquetry and deception.

Lubin, whom Colette still seemed not to recognize as her childhood friend, had made the decision to simulate a great indifference in her regard. In vain she lavished the most tender words upon her husband in front of him, deliberately, in vain she swore that she had never loved anyone but him; Lubin's face never reflected the slightest emotion, although his mind was struck by a very profound amazement.

Once, they were in the general's garden at dusk when someone came to fetch the general; they found themselves alone for the first time since Lubin's departure. The air was humid and heavy, impregnated with a storm. The perfume of the flowers rose up around them and intoxicated them; in the distance, a cricket began to sing.

Crazy images crossed Lubin's mind. He dreamed that General Labride had just fallen down, struck by lightning, that he saved Colette from a terrible fire at the peril of his life and carried her away on horseback by night into a valley of dreams.

And certainly, if he had taken her in his arms at that moment, she would have pressed herself against him, fainting, and saying that she loved him. For she did love him, in truth, with all her heart, and only the bad advice of the enchanted doll prevented her from telling him so.

But Lubin was staring with great attention at a point in space and seemed to be taking a great interest in the flight of a bee.

"How shiny the wings of that insect are," he said.

"Do bees interest you, Monsieur Lubin?"

"I love them, because they're frivolous and capricious, similar in that to women, but unlike them, they do not harm to the flowers on which they alight."

"Have women made you suffer a great deal Monsieur Lubin?"

"I'm only repeating what I've heard said; for myself, I've never loved anyone."

There was a silence, during which Colette wanted to see Lubin expire in the most frightful tortures."

General Labride reappeared in the garden and said: "Get your thickest fur coat, Colette. War has been declared with Norway and we're going to fight in that country."

*VIII. In which the war between France and Norway
is recounted*

The Prince of Norway, in fact, indignant at the insult that
Princess Aude had offered him, had just declared war on her
father, the king. The regiment of blue grenadiers, therefore,
embarked in a ship that set sail for that country.

Colette had gone with her husband, the general, taking
the enchanted doll with her. She believed that she detested
Lubin because of the coldness he showed her. Sitting in the
bow of the ship, she wept with amour for him, and would often have gone to throw herself in his arms if the doll had not
tugged her dress at those times.

Lubin, who sat with his head in his hands in the stern of
the ship every evening, wept with amour on thinking about
Colette, affected an indifference before her that increased every day.

Such are the singularities of amour.

As the winds were not favorable and the vessel sailed
very slowly toward Norway, Lubin, desirous of covering himself in any glory whatsoever in Colette's eyes, began recount-
ing stories to his companions in order to relieve the tedium of
the voyage. The desire to be noticed gave his wit such verve,
and he invented things so pleasant and so tragic, that everyone
listened to him with admiration; the crew abandoned their
maneuvers to listen to him, and General Labride himself came
to sit beside him. Colette therefore remained alone while
Lubin was talking, and as that annoyed her greatly she finally
came to listen to Lubin's stories. But then her anger against
him became even greater.

During the crossing, Lubin linked himself in amity with
an old soldier who was something of a poet, named Poignard.
The old soldier liked wine, reverie and battles. He carried on
his person the portrait of a fiancée that he had once loved, and
who had died without their lips ever having been united. He

was sentimental, and wrote very simple songs about his amour. Lubin took him for a companion.

When the regiment of blue grenadiers had disembarked in Norway and it was necessary to deliver battle, General Labride fell into a great embarrassment. He was very cowardly and did not dare to put himself at the head of his troops in order to attack a terrible fortress in which the Norwegian army was contained.

Then Poignard said to Lubin: "Would you like to win the victory for yourself alone? Me, I no longer care about glory and I'd be glad to see you made illustrious by some great deed. You must have a fiancée somewhere who would be delighted to her your name cited with eulogies. Mine is dead; it's since that time that I no longer desire celebrity."

"I do indeed have a fiancée; I'd like to win the battle, but how?"

"I once campaigned in this country; I know a tunnel that leads to the fortress. Go find General Labride; tell him that the King of Norway will be his prisoner tomorrow and that the fortress will be in flames."

Lubin did so, and General Labride burst out laughing, thinking that he had gone mad.

"I'll promote you to colonel if you succeed," he said, "but if you're lying, you'll be shot."

"And if you come back victorious," said Colette, "I'll give you this ring."

When he drew away he was very embarrassed in his heart, because he did not know whether he ought to wish for his death or his triumph, desiring either one equally.

Lubin and Poignard quit the camp by night, and went to the tunnel, some distance away. The entire country was covered in ice, and a terrible cold reigned over the earth.

They marched in darkness for a long time and Poignard held Lubin's hand. The tunnel ended in a secret stairway that spiraled upwards inside a thick column and opened into the finest bedroom in the castle, that of the King of Norway.

The warrior prince, after having conferred with his prime minister, said his prayers and went to bed, to have a dream that night of a battle in which he saw all the blue grenadiers of France lying dead in the snow.

He was very surprised when he saw two blue grenadiers beside his bed, and found himself solidly tied up and carried away in robust arms. And the most painful sensation for him was not knowing whether he was dreaming, or whether those things were happening in reality.

Having seized the King of Norway, Poignard struck his briquette, lit a torch and held it against a large bookcase full of dry volumes. The books, which were the writings of the poets of the country, rapidly caught fire, and shortly thereafter the whole castle was in flames.

As dawn appeared, Lubin brought General Labride the captive King of Norway, who was beginning to understand that his dream was over. The entire regiment of blue grenadiers, who had shivered all night in the intense cold, ran to warm themselves up a little in front of the burning fortress.

The Norwegian army surrendered; the victory was assured. Lubin, acclaimed by the soldiers, was promoted to colonel, and General Labride embraced him in front of the whole army.

That evening, Colette sent for him; she was alone in her tent, so wrapped in furs that the expression on her face was invisible, and Lubin did not know whether it reflected anger or admiration. She did not say a word; she put the ring that she had promised him the day before on his finger. As he was about to withdraw, she called him back and handed him the lace handkerchief that she had been holding until then over her lips. In offering it to him she had a movement full of grace and abandonment, and, in the light of the evening, as she leaned toward him, Lubin saw that her eyes were full of tears.

She still loves me, he said to himself.

And he ran to hug the modest Poignard in his arms effusively, who was just finishing a poem about the great victory won by the blue grenadiers in Norway.

IX. In which Poignard gets drunk and Lubin is shot

The regiment of blue grenadiers returned to France, covered in great glory, and returned to Lubin and Colette's homeland.

The barber Lafarie did not hold back his joy in being able to relate, before a numerous audience mute with admiration, all the details of the campaign that he obtained from his daughter. He exaggerated them and embellished them, adding his personal observations on Norway, its climate and its customs. Thanks to him, people in the village knew that the curious people in question had trained for war in a great number of exceedingly savage polar bears, which Lubin, General Labride and also his daughter Colette had destroyed after a bitter struggle.

Meanwhile, in the church tower, Sinus rang joyful carillons, and even funeral knells took on an air of gaiety.

Colette loves me! Lubin thought. His heart was burning with an infinite love for her. He loved her as of old, perhaps with an even greater ardor. However, he continued not to let anything show, and every day she conceived indignation and wrath in consequence. She resolved, in the end, to doom him, and fell into accord in that regard with her husband, who was importuned by Lubin's military glory.

Colette loves me! thought Lubin. And as he went out one morning, repeating her name to the trees on his route, four blue grenadiers came to arrest him and take him to prison.

He was accused of having stolen Colette's ring and lace handkerchief, and she had accused him of it herself.

"It's true, I stole the objects," Lubin responded the next morning to an old judge and the stupefied General Labride.

He was therefore sentenced to be shot.

He desired death ardently, and when he learned of the sentence that condemned him he thought at first, with joy, that he was about to be delivered from a burdensome life and the henceforth-odious memory of Colette.

Having returned to his prison, however, he perceived between the bars of the window a little patch of blue sky. And, either because the sky that evening was a more admirable color than usual it because the thought of seeing it for the last time embellished it with a new charm in his eyes, it seemed to him that he discovered the beauty of the heavens, and he regretted bitterly not having looked at them more often.

As he leaned forward he perceived in the distance the form of a tree on a hill. That tree was marvelously harmonious and lovely; Lubin had never contemplated its like; it was undoubtedly the most extraordinary tree that had ever grown in the soil. Perhaps all the trees that existed were also as lovely as that one, except that he had never considered them attentively enough to understand their beauty. If only he had another few days of existence to enjoy all those good things!

With that, Poignard came into his prison, with glasses and a bottle of very old wine.

"Oh, my dear companion, what will become of me now?" he said. "You are the only being that I loved down here, except for my fiancée, who has been dead for many years. Perhaps you'll encounter her among the dead. Tell her that I carry her dear portrait over my heart and that I think of her under the cold tents of camps. Wait for me together in the misty abode; I shan't be long in joining you. But this evening, let's drink, if you like, in order that this wine, whose aroma is sweet, will put a taste for the things of this earth on your lips one last time..."

They drank. And Lubin thought then about the little bone that an old woman had once given him, and which he still carried on his person. He had little confidence in that talisman; however, he said to Poignard: "Take this bone and, twelve hours after my death, lift up the heavy stone that covers me and place it on my forehead. Perhaps then I shall get up and return among the living...."

They continued drinking, and Poignard said: "I've composed such a touching epitaph on your death that all those who read it will shed tears.

They spent the night in meditation and conversation. Dawn was blanching the countryside and giving the slopes of the valleys a divine softness when they came to fetch Lubin for his execution.

Then Poignard fled, at a run, all the way to the nearest inn. He drew his sword and threatened to cut off the innkeeper's head if he did not take him to his cellar and open his largest cask of wine for him. So the man did that. Poignard put his head under the tap of the cask and drank until he lost consciousness.

Meanwhile, Lubin was taken to a deserted field; there was a fir-wood alongside it, and a perfume of moist branches reached him. Light vapors were floating in the distance. Two crows were chatting not far away. Lubin recognized them as the ones that haunted the ruined temple where he had alternately loved and wept, and he heard them say once again, as they looked at him pityingly:

"In truth, nothing exists except the cool wind in the woods, the joy of flying freely, and the odor of firs..."

Twelve blue grenadiers were lined up; Lubin heard the dry sound of muskets being loaded. At that moment, the first ray of sunlight gilded the hill, and the eyes of the condemned man were blindfolded.

Then, suddenly, with the eyes of his soul, Lubin perceived, very far away, Colette smiling at him sweetly: the infantile and charming Colette of old. She was in her garden; he recognized the bench, the familiar flower beds, the rosebushes; she had interrupted her embroidery and, pink with emotion under her blonde hair, she beckoned to him...

How glad she seemed to be to see him, how she loved him!

A detonation resounded, and he fell, dead.

And when the smoke of the muskets had flown into the sky with the two philosophical crows, when General Lubin had gone back to his house rubbing his hands, a death-knell descended upon the country from the tower of the church such as no human ear had ever heard: a knell so terrible that all the inhabitants made the sign of the cross and fell to their knees, and General Labride, trembling with terror, had all the doors of his house closed in order not to hear it. But he covered his ears with his hands in vain, in vain he summoned three blue grenadiers, who played drums alongside him; the knell traversed all the walls, drowned out all other sounds, and resounded prodigiously.

It lasted three hours, and after that time a frightful din was heard in the tower. And when the curé and the beadle dared to cross the threshold, they found the bells, shattered into a thousand pieces, on the flagstones of the church. They had fallen from the top of the tower, dragging Sinus the bell-ringer with them.

X. In which Lubin is resuscitated and
meets an old acquaintance

Poignard woke up in the shadow of the cellar; the cask beside him was empty; wine stained his clothing and covered the floor. He thought about the bone that Lubin had given him before dying and what he had said to him. He hastened to emerge from the inn; he must have slept through an entire day, for night had fallen.

But Poignard, who did not fear the living, was afraid of the dead and he was full of terror at the idea of reopening Lubin's tomb. Even so, he went to the gravedigger's house and invited him to accompany him to the cemetery.

"Renounce that project, Seigneur Grenadier," the man cried. "You doubtless don't know that at this hour, the phantoms of the dead emerge from the earth, and the mere sight of them, under the cypresses, is sufficient to make you fall into dementia..."

"Your death is imminent if you don't come with me," replied Poignard, threatening him with his sword.

And they both went to the little cemetery that reposed silently beneath the nocturnal mists. At the noise they made reclosing the iron gate, the shades of two old men that were chatting familiarly on a stone fled in terror, for, contrary to popular belief, the dead are more timid than the living.

The gravedigger took Poignard to Lubin's tomb, and they both trembled and crossed themselves on seeing a black form kneeling on the freshly moved earth, which took flight at their appearance.

"I recognized a vampire," said the gravedigger. "It comes to disinter the dead in order to drink their blood, and if we went to sleep in this place, it would make an invisible puncture in our neck through which it would aspire all our blood."

"God preserve us from ever reposing here!" replied Poignard.

Actually, it was Colette; she had been weeping since the morning. Not until Lubin's death had she understood that she had never loved anyone but him; and, when evening came, she had carried roses from her garden and her belated tears to his grave.

The gravedigger then set about digging the ground, and when he had reached Lubin's coffin he broke it with his implement. Whiter than a sheet, Poignard advanced and touched his forehead with the magic bone. Then Lubin stood up, stretched himself and asked in a loud voice where he was.

But Poignard and the gravedigger, mad with terror, ran through the tombs, reached the wall, scaled it with an extraordinary agility and launched themselves into the open country, crying.

Lubin understood by what marvelous circumstance he had been returned to life, and, glad to feel the nocturnal breeze agitating his hair, he emerged from the cemetery and set off delightedly along the road.

He traveled; he slept in forests in the moonlight, intoxicated by the passing wind and the perfume of foliage. Life had recovered all its sweetness for him; the dust of the road, the water of the river and the color of the sky gradually made him forget Colette.

He had been marching thus for several days when he encountered an ambulant merchant in an inn. He was sitting at a table by the fire. Lubin had just asked for a piece of bread and a large glass of water. The ambulant merchant considered him for a moment with astonishment, and then burst out laughing.

"Don't you prefer wine to water, friend?" he said to him.

"There was a time, in fact," Lubin replied, "when I preferred wine to water."

"It's really for you and one of your little friends that I once sold a barber a Polichinelle and a doll?"

"It's quite possible, and it seems to me, in fact, that I've seen your multicolored cloak and yellow leather boots somewhere."

The merchant started to laugh again—a long, silent laugh—and when Lubin asked him the reason, he replied: "Your eyes are soft and full of sadness; I like you, and that's why I want to tell you my secret. I'm a very skillful magician, child, and I employ my art to deceive people. I have a thousand things in my pack dangerous in their application, evil in themselves, which are disputed everywhere at a high price, for people always cherish that which leads them to their doom. I sell poisoned manuscripts, the reading of which makes the purest heart an abyss of perversity; jewels and necklaces that render young women vain; powders and paints that corrupt their skin and give them a precocious old age; in sum, toys that are the human passions. People think they are amusing themselves, whereas it is the toys that are moving the springs of their lives. I once sold for you a puppet that was to infuse you with a taste for drunkenness, and a doll that was coquetry; if your life has been agitated and unhappy, it's to those toys that you owe it."

Having said that, the merchant got up and left the inn, and Lubin saw that in the village square, young women, wives and old men were running after him and surrounding him, in order to buy the perfumes, the ornaments and the talismans that were to cause their misery.

He was plunged into a profound reverie by the announcement made by a public crier in a resounding voice. The king was making it known that he promised a large recompense to the physician that could cure his daughter of the deadly passion for wine that possessed her. He promised to grant whatever was asked of him, but if the physician did not succeed in curing his daughter after having attempted to do so, he promised to put him to death.

On hearing that, Lubin conceived a grand plan, and immediately headed for Paris. He bought a wig, a false beard and a physician's robe. He put them on and, having become un-recognizable, he went to the king's palace.

There, everything had changed since Lubin's departure. There were no more splendid feasts; all the courtiers wore the mask of dolor; the king lamented and wept all day long; the clowns had been expelled, for their gaiety had become untime-ly. No one had yet been able to put an end to the abominable scandal made by Princes Aude, who spent every evening shut up in her apartments singing at the top of her voice and drink-ing wine.

"I've come to cure the princess," Lubin told the king, and asked to be left alone with her.

Since Lubin's departure, Aude had not ceased weeping and bitterly regretting the nights of amour that had come to an end. She had found the puppet forgotten by her lover and had kept it preciously as a souvenir both pleasant and dear. And it was the magic toy that had advised her to drown her sorrow in wine.

That evening, she was dreaming in a melancholy fashion of the time when Lubin had climbed up nimbly to the window and come to place his lips on hers, when, suddenly, the door opened and she perceived him, young and handsome, as in times past. She uttered a loud cry and stood up, trembling.

But Lubin stopped her with a gesture and spoke in these terms: "Aude, my beloved, it is not a living man who is speak-ing to you. I am dead. This form that you see before you is only a vain shadow. I have been killed during the war in Nor-way, and my body reposes out there, under the gentle snow. It is necessary not to think about me any longer, and not to be unhappy any longer; that is what I want. I have come to give you my last amorous kiss."

By that stratagem, Lubin wanted to prevent Aude from continuing to love him.

She held out her ardent arms to him; her marvelous flesh gleamed within her partly open robe. That last kiss should have been as light as a breath. Lubin was firmly resolved scarcely to brush Aude's forehead; he did not love her; he had only come in order that she would forget him.

But the kiss he gave her was so soft and so punctuated with sighs that the nocturnal moths outside the window panes, alarmed, hid their eyes with their gauzy wings, and it was so long that the lamp paled while it was still enduring.

Aude had lost consciousness from surprise and happiness. Then Lubin looked round, discovered the magic Polichinelle, took it, left the room, and, having put on his physician's disguise again, went to tell the king that his daughter was cured.

XI. The great review of the blue grenadiers
and the death of Colette

A few days later, Lubin was appointed Maréchal by the grateful king. He therefore put on a marvelous uniform and departed for his homeland, where the blue grenadiers were garrisoned, followed by a numerous escort of officers. He had General Labride informed, on the evening of his arrival, that he would carry out a great review the following day.

The entire region was in great emotion. It was the first time that a Maréchal has been seen there. The houses were decorated with flags, the doors were ornamented with flowers. Many people went to Lafarie to hear what that talkative and literate man had to say about the event.

Since the death of Lubin and his old friend Sinus the bell-ringer, however, the poor barber had lost his former verve. His speech no longer had the same admirable grandeur and his eyes were sometimes so obscured by tears that he was obliged to interrupt himself while shaving his clients, for fear of cutting their throats.

So he scarcely affirmed that the Maréchal who had just arrived was a very noble and very illustrious man and that he had once known him well.

When night fell, however, Lubin went out in the uniform of a simple soldier. He would have liked to find his companion Poignard, but he searched in vain in the taverns and the barracks. Then he slipped as far as General Labride's house and climbed over the garden wall. He walked silently through the trees and bushes and soon perceived General Labride and Colette sitting on a bench in front of the perron, talking.

It was a sad conversation, interrupted by silences, as if an afterthought had retained the words on their lips.

At one moment, General Labride struck the iron table with his fist to summon his aide-de-camp. Then Lubin, who was wearing the uniform of a simple soldier in the blue grenadiers and was exactly as he had been before, ran forward and came to place himself four paces away from the general, making the military salute, motionless and rigid, seemingly awaiting his orders.

General Labride's eyes widened immeasurably; terror and remorse froze his blood. He ran away into the garden, followed by Colette. That was what Lubin wanted. He went into the house and went to Colette's room. He soon discovered, in a cupboard, the doll that was the cause of all his woes, and he seized it.

Lubin knew of an exceedingly deep well at the extremity of a pathway shaded by a little clump of trees. Having emerged from the general's house he ran there. He had brought with him the puppet stolen from Princess Aude, as well as a thick rope. He tied the puppet and the doll to a stone and threw them into the well. He watched for a long time until the water, in which the moon was reflected, has resumed its immobility above the two toys. Then he went away, while a toad, a local inhabitant, troubled in its reveries, cast its ironic and dolorous lamentation into the night.

At sunrise, the drums rolled, the uniforms of the blue grenadiers sparkled, and Lubin, followed by General Labride, passed the regiment in review.

"General," he said, "Isn't one of your soldiers missing?"

"No," replied Labride.

"Veritably, one is missing."

"He's a bad soldier named Poignard. He's perpetually drunk and has become an object of scandal for everyone. I've had him put in prison."

"Send someone to fetch him," said Lubin.

Poignard arrived, his eyes vague, a residue of intoxication in his heart.

"Soldier Poignard, I'm making you a captain," said Lubin. Then he went on: "General, isn't there still one of your soldiers missing?"

"No," replied Labride.

"Veritably, one is missing."

"You mean a bad soldier named Lubin. I had him shot because he was a thief."

"You're lying, wretch," said Lubin. "And with that, he took off his wig and his false beard and had himself recognized by the blue grenadiers, who were very glad to see him again. He was cheered, and twelve men took General Labride some distance away, where he was shot in his turn.

Then Lubin summoned Poignard; he made him a sign to follow him, and they both hastened toward Colette's house.

On the way, he told him the sad and marvelous story of the enchanted toys. But now the doll was dead and Lubin was going to find his Colette as amorous and tender as of old. A great hope lifted him up.

They knocked in vain on the door of the general's house. They went in; they went through the deserted rooms. A neighbor came to tell them that she had seen Colette go out and head for the cemetery.

They went there at a run; they went through the narrow pathways; the tombstones were glistening in the sunlight; flowers were budding.

They saw Colette, in a black cloak, her hair undone, lying on the spot where Lubin had once been laid to rest.

On seeing her, Lubin shouted: "I forgive you for the harm you've done me. I want to forget that you've betrayed me, that you've slept beside another man and have made him the gift of yourself spite of your oath. I still love you. I loved you when you made me suffer by caprice, I loved you when you betrayed me, I loved you when you caused my death. I knew that a destiny stronger than your lies would bring us together and that it was to me that you one belong one day. You spoke with the voices of the evening, you were the wind passing by, my shadow in the sunlight. Now the enchantment is destroyed, the rose-bushes are embalmed as in days past; our youth is recommencing; get up, therefore, and come with him, my beloved...

He spoke thus, but Colette remained extended on the ground.

Deprived of the perfidious advice of her doll, Colette had understood the magnitude of her folly, and she had come to kill herself on Lubin's grave, whom she had always loved and whom she believed to be dead.

Lubin saw that Colette's black cloak was stained with blood in the place of the heart. He fell down beside her and embraced her, weeping, while Poignard thought:

Happy is the man who has never encountered the toy merchant, with his multicolored cloak and his boots of yellow leather.

THE STORY OF LILI-DES-ROSES AND THE BLACK PRINCE

For Mademoiselle Amélie de Pouzols[6]

I

She was known as Lili-des-Roses because when she was small she liked nothing better than the roses in her garden. In the company of her flowers, with her red apron and her blonde hair, she had become similar to a rose herself.

"Bonjour, little sister!" said the joyful roses when they saw her appear in the morning.

And a large yellow rose, which flowered alone along a wall, even said in a familiar and maternal tone: "Bonjour, little daughter!"

Lili-des-Roses did not pick the roses, because she knew that flowers suffer and die like humans.

Lili-des-Roses was the daughter of a poor widow. As she grew older, she became so pretty that her beauty made her famous throughout the land, and shepherds who had seen her once brought her presents of little baskets, which they had woven themselves on the mountain.

There was an old actor in the village named Juste, who had retired from the stage. He wore a long threadbare blue coat, a flowery waistcoat, spectacles and a wing that was always askew. He conceived an amity for Lili-des-Roses; he taught her to declaim verses, to sing and to play the harp.

---

[6] Amélie de Pouzols, later Pouzols de Saint-Phar, was an actress on stage and in silent movies, who was at the height of her career between 1900 and 1918.

Lili-des-Roses gradually became highly skilled in those arts. The admiration that she engendered was further augmented. People came in search of her at fêtes. She was the glory of the country. Her mother wept with joy on seeing her so beautiful and so beloved.

A young pastor known as Jean-des-Bois, who passed for a simple soul, had a limitless love for her. Desirous of distinguishing himself, he hollowed out a flute in a reed and he invented tunes that were sublime, because it was his heart that dictated them to him.

One day, he went to find Lili-des-Roses and played her a tune on his instrument. But Lili-des-Roses started laughing and made fun of him, for, not having known amour, she was still ignorant of veritable beauty.

Jean-des-Bois was greatly pained to see his naïve composition disdained. He fell to his knees and confessed his amour to Lili-des-Roses; but she mocked him all the more and said to him: "You'd do better to go and guard your sheep in the hollows of valleys, amid the wild broom.

Jean-des-Bois returned to his sheep, weeping. He sat down in the heather and composed other admirable tunes, in which he expressed his dolor. In what he invented there was the aroma of the earth, the voice of the wind in the trees, and the bells of the flocks. Afterwards, he went to sleep on the ground, thinking about Lili-des-Roses.

Now, there was in the land a black prince who was extremely ugly, but who possessed an incalculable fortune. He lived in a château in the depths of a dark forest

One day when he was hunting he went past Lili-des-Roses' house; he saw her and he fell in love with her. The next day, followed by a numerous cortege of black servants, he came to ask for her hand in marriage.

"Lili-des-Roses," he said, "my skin is black but I have jewels that are as clear as the water of river and the light of day. I am very ugly, but my château is very beautiful and the dresses that I shall have prepared for you are in marvelous fabrics. Incline toward me with a benevolent heart, as the palm tree in the desert shelters the weary camel with its shade."

He spoke thus, and gave her three days to reflect.

And Lili-des-Roses said: "I shall marry that black prince because he is rich."

And her old mother put her hands together and replied: "My God! My God!"

When it was known in the village that Lili-des-Roses wanted to marry the black prince, everyone was grief-stricken.

Juste, the old actor, went to see Lili-des-Roses He knew from experience that women, especially harp-players and those who know how to mime and dance, often sell themselves for gold and precious objects, but he could not believe it.

"Alas," he said, "I will have taught you the secrets of the art, I will have developed in you the science of rhythm and beauty for the joy of a vulgar black man! True wealth, everyone bears in the heart. Renounce this black man, I implore you."

Lili-des-Roses' neighbors lamented, saying: "She is the one who taught us to dream. The music of our life will fall silent. How can nature unite the lily with the toad, the serpent with the rose?"

And the roses in the garden leaned toward Lili-des-Roses and murmured: "What are you doing, little sister? In truth, you will no longer be able to love us when you are the wife of a wicked black man. For is it plausible that one can love at the same time a wicked black man and the amiable roses that we are?"

Lili-des-Roses' mother said: "My God! My God!"

On the third day, Lil-des-Roses remained unshakable in her resolution, and when the black prince came to find her she was waiting for him on her doorstep, smiling, and she held out her little white hand to him.

The black prince made a frightful grimace of joy, and a large tear ran over the old actor Juste's flowery waistcoat.

"My God! My God!" repeated the mother.

"Is it possible? It's a great misfortune! Such a thing has never been seen!" said the neighbors.

And the roses uttered a thousand sighs, which the wind carried away. And in the distance, in the hollows of the valleys, amid the wild broom, Jean-des-Bois played on his flute a tune so melancholy that even the nocturnal owls were saddened, and opened their round eyes immeasurably.

II

The little spirits of the morning were very surprised, on entering a bedroom in the château at dawn, on seeing Lili-des-Roses, very white, sleeping in the arms of the black prince. She was sleeping with her hair undone, gracious and inclined, while the black prince was looking at her with eyes that desire rendered horrible, and holding her neck in his large hand.

And the little spirits of the morning were very troubled, and they hid their faces in their gilded robes.

A little later, when Lili-des-Roses was combing her hair in front of her mirror, three roses that were blooming on the balcony spoke in these terms, severely:

"Oh, Lili-des-Roses, what have you done?" said the first.

"How have you been able to deliver your body, made of an essence similar to ours, to that indecent and ugly black man?" said the second.

"You deserve, in truth, to become black yourself," said the third.

Then Lili-des-Roses, irritated, cut the roses and plucked off their petals.

She went down into the park and heard a whispering amid the foliage. It was the roses who were murmuring reproaches as she passed by.

She started to tear them away and trample the underfoot, and as she was not sufficient to the task, she summoned several servants to help her. She cut all the roses in the park like that, and when she had finished, she was very sad.

She went back into the château and she began to stir gold and jewels, thinking that she would obtain some consolation from that, but her sadness increased and only grew from that day on.

She asked the black prince for permission to go to see her village and her friends, but he refused, for he was very jealous by nature.

She asked the black prince to acquire a harp in order that she could play tunes, but he refused, because he detested music.

She asked the black prince to acquire books, but he refused because he did not know how to read.

The she began to hate the black prince; he soon understood that, and he suffered cruelly in consequence, because he loved Lili-des-Roses with a prodigious amour in his black heart.

One day, he said to her: "Why do you detest me, Lili-des-Roses?"

And Lili-des-Roses replied: "I hate you because of the black color of your face and your body."

That cause of hatred inspired a limitless dolor and wrath in the black prince, because it seemed to him to be irremediable.

He went into his château at a run, lit a great fire and had an iron bar heated. Then he called to Lili-des-Roses through the window.

When she had come, he kissed her on the lips and held her in his embrace for a long time. He said a thousand loving things to her, he wept, and he asked her: "Tell me, Lili-des-Roses, whether I horrify you."

And Lili-des-Roses replied, from the bottom of her heart: "You truly horrify me, my husband."

Then he seized her by the neck, tipped her backwards and, having seized the red hot iron, he put out her eyes.

After which he had his great horse saddled, and he went hunting in the forest.

III

Lili-des-Roses wandered henceforth in the great park of the château; she could neither contemplate the light of day nor weep, since she no longer had eyes, and was thus deprived of the consolation of the woeful.

She could not run away because the black prince had her closely watched and because the walls that enclosed the park were very high. She could not converse with the roses because she had killed them all with her hands, and she experienced a great regret for that.

But one evening, when Lili-des-Roses was wandering alone along the walls of the park, she heard an invisible music. She recognized Jean-des-Bois' flute. It was, in fact, him, who had come to play for Lili-des-Roses.

Jean-des-Bois voiced the sadness of solitude, nights of reverie under the moon, and misunderstood amour...

Then Lili-des-Roses, full of gratitude, shouted: "Thank you, Jean-des-Bois!"

Jean-des-Bois came back every evening to play the flute behind the wall; he did not see Lili-des-Roses, but he heard her voice thanking him.

However, the black prince noticed that Lili-des-Roses went every evening to listen to an invisible flute. His love had only increased since he had put out Lili-des-Roses' eyes. He conceived a new jealousy.

In order to be liberated from it he set out with Lili-des-Roses in a carriage, reached the sea and embarked on a ship bound for Africa.

After a long and perilous crossing they arrived in a land burned by the sun, where they were welcomed joyfully by the black people.

Lili-des-Roses excited a great admiration among those men, and, as they had simple minds, many of them tried to steal her from the prince. The latter knew the joy of satisfied pride, and he cut off the heads of his rivals.

Then he put an iron collar around the neck of Lili-des-Roses and he started traveling with her in order to show her to a great many black men as his wife and excite astonishment and envy.

Lili-des-Roses walked behind him, no longer having any thought but one. She now loved Jean-des-Bois for the sweetness of the tunes that he had found and the love that he had testified to her. And it was not so much the blue sky and the landscapes of her homeland as the shepherd's face that she regretted being unable to contemplate with her closed eyes.

One evening, they were crossing a desert strewn with rocks when an enormous lion loomed up before them. The black prince drew his curved sword and put himself on the defensive.

The lion considered the two travelers momentarily, and, seeing a woman as beautiful as Lili-des-Roses enchained by an iron collar, he became both saddened and angry.

Lili-des-Roses, who could not see the lion but who could hear him, fell to her knees and cried: "Lord Lion, deliver me from the cruelest prince on earth, who has put out my eyes and is making me lead an ignominious life."

The lion's heart was filled with indignation on learning these things. He threw himself upon the black prince, crushed his head between his teeth and then ate him. Then he said to Lili-des-Roses: "Princess, the color of your skin is marvelous to behold, and I would love you amorously if God had not made me a lion. What can I do for you?"

Lili-des-Roses was sitting on a rock; the sun was setting on the horizon and the lion was licking her feet. She replied: "I would like to see once again my singing-master, my mother and Jean-des-Bois, who plays the flute in the midst of his flock."

And the lion was afflicted, for lions are full of conceit, like men, and he had hoped to seduce Lili-des-Roses with his first words.

"Where are the people of whom you speak, and who seem to be so dear to you?" it replied, not without bitterness.

"Very far away, alas, beyond the foamy sea, in a little village, in the shadow of a gray steeple. How kind you would be, Lord Lion, to take me as far as the shore."

If she has no amour for me, the lion thought, *it's because she cannot see me with my gilded mane.*

He told Lili-des-Roses to climb on to his back, and they would travel together.

They became linked by amity on the way. The lion brought Lili-des-Roses her daily nourishment, and in the evening he lay at her feet. The lion loved Lili-des-Roses tenderly and, as his heart was pained by the thought of being separated from her, he did not hurry in bringing her to the shore, and when his knowledge of the country allowed him to sense the presence of the sea, he made a great detour and drew away from it.

Meanwhile the people who saw the blind young woman, remarkable for her beauty, passing by sitting on the back of a lion, thought that she was a divinity. There were some who fled, others who rejoiced by dancing, others who made human sacrifices, and others who brought presents of all sorts to the feet of Lili-des-Roses.

Lili-des-Roses told the lion to continue on his route without stopping. She was horrified by all the men because, without seeing them, she understood that they were black. Nor was she touched by their presents. The only present that would have been agreeable to her, no one gave her: that was roses, and roses did not flourish in that country.

One evening, when the lion was asleep and the heat was overwhelming, Lili-des-Roses took a few steps over the burning sand. She heard the sound of water, and walked in that direction. There was, indeed, a spring that as gushing from a rock. Lil-des-Roses drank from it, and she felt a little rose brushing her cheek.

Lili-des-Roses was overjoyed, but she did not pick the rose and contented herself with caressing it and speaking to it.

And the rose replied: "Since you have not killed me, I want to save you in my turn. You will never reach the sea and will never see your homeland again if you stay with the lion. He loves you and he is deliberately taking you away from the shore because he does not want to abandon you. Nothing is more dangerous than an excessively faithful friend. Take advantage of his slumber; walk straight ahead, following the water of this spring. You will hear the sea singing in the nascent dawn and you will find skillful and joyful mariners who will take you back to your homeland."

Thus spoke the desert rose. Lili-des-Roses hastened to obey it, and she walked all night, even though she was very weary and her feet were lacerated. Dawn was breaking when she heard the sea singing. Then she ran straight ahead, until the waves wet her feet. Then, putting her hands to her lips, she tasted the salt.

There was a company of mariners on the shore who were about to embark. They called to Lili-des-Roses and she heard with joy that they spoke the same language as her. She told them her story and they were moved by pity.

"Come with us," said the captain. "We're going to Brest and we'll take you back to your homeland."

She therefore followed the mariners on to their ship, and they lifted anchor and extended their sails. Lili-des-Roses sat down at the stern of the ship.

At the same moment, the lion appeared on the shore and saw Lili-des-Roses in the distance, at sea.

He was haggard, covered with sweat, his mane bristling, unhappy and pitiful. His eyes were full of an infinite kindness and sadness.

Her face turned toward him, Lili-de-Roses could not see him. He uttered a long roar. What he wanted from his friend was a sign of amity, an adieu; after that he would be glad to see her happy.

But the sound of the rising waves drowned out his voice.

He roared again in a desperate fashion. The ship drew away toward the horizon. Lili-des-Roses, not having heard anything, remained motionless, leaning over the sea, and her image was effaced in the morning mist.

Then the poor lion returned to the desert at a slow pace.

IV

Lili-des-Roses traveled for many days, and after that time, the ship that carried her arrived in Brest. There, an old mariner who had taken her in amity, served as her guide to return her to her homeland.

"You'll see in the distance a gray steeple and a little white house under rose-bushes," Lili-des-Roses said to the old mariner.

They were walking together. The old mariner lit his pipe and told her about the adventures he had had in Lapland and under the equator. Lili-des-Roses respired the air of her home-land joyfully. And when the old mariner said to her: "In fact, I can see a gray steeple over there...," she felt her heart break-ing.

It was known in the region that the black prince had put out Lili-des-Roses' eyes and had taken her to Africa.

"My God! My God!" said the old mother, when Lili-des-Roses came into the house. "I shall see my child again before dying, then!"

And she gave a large glass of wine to the old mariner, who was very thirsty.

Juste came running; his flowery waistcoat was very fad-ed, having received so many tears, and he said: "If your eyes are dead, at least your heart is alive."

Lili-des-Roses went out into the garden to salute her old friends the roses.

Then she heard a voice that said to her: "You have al-ways loved roses, my child, and I, the fay of the roses, want to recompense you for that love. Come with me and you'll re-cover your sight."

A hand took hers, and Lili-des-Roses walked behind the fay of the roses. The latter led her to a spring that was flowing, white and hidden, in a forest.

They fay took water in her hand, rubbed Lili-des-Roses' eyes with it, and vanished like a breath of air.

Lili-des-Roses could see. She saw the water of the spring, the ferns, the tree trunks and the sky. That landscape had a divine beauty for her.

Jean-des-Bois was coming down the hill, followed by his flock. He thought that he would never see Lili-des-Roses again, since she was wandering the lands of Africa with the black prince.

Then Lili-des-Roses appeared at a bend in the road, she looked at him with eyes full of light, recognized him, and took him in her arms.

They went back to the house together, and Juste, the actor, the old mariner and the poor mother started dancing around the table with joy, raising their hands, laughing and weeping, when they saw that Lili-des-Roses was no longer blind.

Lili-des-Roses married Jean-des-Bois and there was a great feast to which all the local inhabitants were invited. People danced for three days and drank several barrels of wine and cider.

The old mariner amused himself so much that he declared that he was weary of navigation and had resolved to live in the village with his friends.

Lili-des-Roses and Jean-de-Bois loved one another and were very happy. Every evening, the old mariner came to smoke his pipe with them; there were long evenings by the fire. Everyone wanted to know the marvelous story of Lili-des-Roses; and Juste the actor, told it in choice language, in order to tell everyone what great misfortunes befall a young woman when she marries a black man for his money.

THE POOR MUSICIAN AND THE LITTLE GENIE

For Pierre Rameil.[7]

There was once in Paris a poor musician who lived in a mansard in an old house. From his window he could see the Louvre ad Notre-Dame, and the Seine flowed at his feet. He possessed a violin and extracted divine music from it. When he played his instrument it seemed to him that he was floating amid the clouds. Then, a thousand unexpected and marvelous visions appeared on the bare walls of his room, of kings with their retinues, lovers enlaced in the fog, and beautiful young women with long blonde hair. His concierge, whose name was Gudule, came upstairs to listen in silence outside his door, and the birds passing by in the air said: "What extraordinary music!" and stopped to listen.

That was because a little genie lived in the violin and sang when the bow glided over the strings.

The little genie knew a great many songs; he never got tired and sometime, when the musician was asleep, he emerged from the violin and walked around the room humming tunes that he invented. He loved the poor musician with all his heart and lived with him happily.

---

[7] Pierre Rameil (1878-1936) was an advocate from Perpignan who subsequently—long after the publication of the present story—became a Senator responsible for the Arts budget and secretary of state for education. In the early 1900s he was in Paris, dabbling in poetry, and he also adapted a Catalan drama for the French stage.

The musician sometimes went out with his violin to play in concert halls full of beautiful ladies and handsome gentlemen. On a stage, other ladies, with sequins in their hair, played castanets and danced foreign dances, but he did not notice either the color of their skin, their grace or their sidelong glances; he was only occupied with the voice of the little genie that he heard singing in the violin.

He earned his modest living thus. However, either by virtue of bad luck or because they found his music too beautiful, the directors of the concert halls dismissed him, one after another. In the meantime, winter came, with its white robe, and its faggot of dead wood.

Floc! Floc! went the snowflakes against the poor musician's window-panes. And the genie, who had a child-like heart, was very content and clapped his hands on seeing all those tiny white individuals falling from the sky in thousands. A genie who lives in a violin knows nothing of life and has no idea how harsh winter is for the poor.

Then the musician went to a second-hand dealer who lived in the neighborhood and asked him to come to his apartment to estimate the value of his furniture.

So Monsieur Zacharie—that was the merchant's name—came to the musician's home. He was avaricious, old and ugly. And the little genie, who had a joyful nature and was given to irony, and did not know how to hide his sentiments, burst out laughing on seeing him, and cried: "How ugly you are, Monsieur Zacharie!"

And Zacharie, who hated little genies, made a grimace and swore to get his revenge.

He bought all the musician's furniture for a few écus, and had it carried away, and said as he left the mansard: "Whenever you like, I'll give you five gold pieces for your violin."

But the musician sent him way, indignantly.

The écus were quickly spent and poverty and cold returned to the mansard. The poor musician played the violin in order to forget his woes, but he was sometimes very hungry.

Gudule, the concierge, who was astonished that such a great artist was so poor, brought him bread and butter and wine from time to time, but she did it without his knowledge, for the poor musician was proud. Only the little genie saw her, and he thought within himself: "How good people are, and love to help one another!"

However, Gudule fell ill. The poor musician went two days without eating and he had become as white as snow the snow in the sky. In the evenings he strode back and forth in his room and murmured, prey to fever: "Five gold pieces! Five gold pieces!"

"Damn! Damn!" said the little genie.

In the night, the poor musician woke up. A soft light was floating around his violin, illuminating the room vaguely, and the little genie hidden in the depths of the instrument sang, in an emotional voice:

"I can see your misfortune, but I beg you not to get rid of me, my companion! I could no longer sing in other hands than yours and your heart would break far away from me. All people are good, I'd like to believe, but they don't all have a taste for divine things, and there are ugly ones that a little genie like me can't see without horror. Let's die together, if necessary, but let's never part."

The poor musician swore then, weeping, never to be parted from his violin.

The next day, he played all day long, and the little genie had never sung so marvelously; but when evening came, the artist shut the violin in its case, put it under his arm and ran to Zacharie's shop.

"Five gold pieces, Monsieur Zacharie," he said. "Give me five gold pieces. Here's my violin."

And Zacharie, laughing in his beard, counted out the five gold pieces for the poor musician.

Zacharie's shop was gloomy and terrible. There were pieces of old furniture, clothes, ancient weapons, a clock that no longer worked, a stuffed stork and, at the back, a large crucifix from which the Christ had been detached and was lying face down on the floor.

At first the little genie was pleased to see all those singular things, because he loved novelty; but, perceiving Zacharie, he understood his fate and tried to flee. The second-hand dealer seized him by the midriff and snatched him out of the violin.

"Don't hurt me, Monsieur Zacharie," said the little genie, weeping. "I said that you were ugly because, in truth, you are, but if you want, I'll say that you're as beautiful as all the angels."

Zacharie dragged the little genie to the back of his shop and, taking a hammer and nails, he crucified him on the big cross devoid of a Christ.

Then he went to have his evening meal with his family.

Before expiring, the little genie cast a glace around him, searching for some pity. But all the items of furniture were like judges sculpted in wood, and the clock said, in its own language: "It's just that that little genie should be crucified."

Only the stuffed stork, when the shadow of night had descended and the little genie was dead, came to wipe up his blood fraternally with her white wing. She too liked songs and clouds. She knew, herself...

Meanwhile the poor musician ran along the street, and in his pocket, the gold pieces sang. The first piece said: "I am the succession of tasty and perfumed dishes, the well-served table..."

The second gold piece said: "I am the old bottle of Burgundy wine that a silent waiter will bring in a basket and will procure you dreams of a divine quality..."

The third gold piece said: "I am the warm and luxurious restaurant, the smile of the venerable host behind his counter, the consideration of the students at table..."

The fourth gold piece said: "I am a fine hat of gray felt and a colored neckerchief that will make people say of you: 'There's an elegant young man!'"

The fifth gold piece said: "I am a woman with a silk corsage, make-up and perfume, who will give you amour during a long night..."

The poor musician went into an expensive restaurant where there were students at table, smoking pipes alongside young women with painted faces, bourgeois who were playing cards, clean-shaven waiters gliding like shadows and, behind the counter, in the smoke, a fat and red-faced proprietor, like a god. He ordered tasty and perfumed dishes and Burgundy wine.

When he had drunk the contents of an old bottle to the last drop, his eyes were witness to something extraordinary.

The fat and red-faced man who was behind the counter put a crown on his head, seized a scepter in his right hand and, getting up, seemed to be of superhuman stature. The lights of the restaurant were resplendent with an unaccustomed glare, and a gypsy orchestra made a discordant music resound. The students, the women and the bourgeois who were playing cards rose to their feet tumultuously. They gave great signs of joy, grimacing and dancing. They surrounded the poor musician; one shook his hand, another kissed his forehead, a third called him "My brother!"

Meanwhile, the clean-shaven and mute waiters had gathered around the crowned man as if for a ceremony. They drew the poor musician to the counter and the king touched his forehead and his heart with his scepter, amid the acclamations of everyone. Then an old man, whom the poor musician had not noticed until then, emerged from the crowd and advanced toward him. He had long hair, and his expression was severe and sorrowful.

"You are not an artist," he said. "If you had been a veritable artist, you would have died of starvation rather than sell your violin."

The poor musician could not respond; the witnesses had thrown themselves upon the old man and had hurled him outside. The music redoubled, glasses shattered into shards, and the poor musician was drawn into a dance in which the impassive waiters took part, and the king himself, behind his counter.

Suddenly, everyone prostrated themselves, their hands joined; an invisible force curbed the poor musician toward the ground. When he raised his head to see what everyone was worshiping, he saw at the back of the room, illuminated and tall, Zacharie the second-hand dealer, raising a great black cross over the kneeling audience. And on that cross he saw the little genie, his friend, bloody and crucified, who was looking at him with his divine eyes charged with affection and reproach.

He made a supreme effort, stood up, flung his five gold pieces in the face of the stupefied king, and fled into the street, filled with terror. He went back to his mansard and fell into a deep sleep there.

The next day, Gudule knocked on his door loudly and introduced into his room a man dressed in black with a white cravat, whom he remembered having seen once before, doubtless the previous evening, in the fine restaurant where he had dined and sent part of the night.

The man dressed in black said: "I'm a notary, Monsieur Musician, and I've come to tell you that you're the inheritor of a considerable fortune. One of your uncles once left to seek his fortune in America. He discovered large gold mines and exploited them cleverly. Now he has died and left you an inheritance of several millions. I'm bringing you on account this bag full of gold, and I apologize for having disturbed your sleep at such an early hour."

The notary placed a bag of gold and a thick wad of banknotes on the bed, because there was no other furniture, and left.

The poor musician, who had now become a rich musician, got dressed in haste and ran to Zacharie's shop.

"I'll sell your violin back to you for ten gold pieces," said Zacharie, "because, in truth, it's a very poor violin."

The rich musician paid and left, joyful at having recovered his cherished instrument. Alas, it was in vain that he tried

167

to play it as before. The little genie was dead and the violin no longer knew how to charm and draw tears. Believing himself to be the victim of an illusion, the rich musician called Gudule.

"That piece doesn't go to the heart," said that simple woman.

He played another, and then another, which were unable to touch Gudule.

Then he sent her away, calling her ignorant and nasty.

He bought a fine house; he had servants, mistresses and friends. He gave great feasts at which there were many guests, well-known musicians, great poets and famous actresses. There was dancing, sorbets were served and delicious wines. He sometimes played the violin, and when he had finished, everyone surrounded him and congratulated him, and everyone seemed to feel a great emotion. Those of his friends who wanted to borrow money even shed tears and begged him to play again.

But he knew very well, in the depths of his heart, that the voice of the little genie had not sung in the violin, and that it was Gudule who was right and not the flatterers.

He became very unhappy. He summoned to his house the masters most knowledgeable in the art of playing the violin, but nothing, neither their instruction nor his assiduous work, rendered him his genius of old.

One evening in winter, a year later, he was wandering alone not far from the house in which he had lived in the time of his poverty. The cold was very intense, snow was falling from the sky in abundance, and the evening was exactly similar to the accursed evening when he had sold his violin.

He crossed a deserted square; lights were shining in the windows, confusedly, through the snow. He was surprised to hear melodious music. He advanced and saw an old man playing a violin. The man resembled, unmistakably, the one who, a year before, had appeared to him in a dream and had said: "You are not an artist!"

168

He was dressed like a beggar and seemed to be playing without the hope of alms, for the square was deserted.

But—O marvel!—the rich musician recognized that the beggar's violin had a sublime tone, a soft and heartbreaking voice such as he had never heard since the abandonment and death of the little genie.

His joy was great, because he knew what power wealth gives men.

"Why are you playing, beggar," he said, "since no one can throw you a sou."

The old man smiled and replied: "I'm not playing for the alms that might be given to me, but for myself and for those who understand me. In these closed houses there are families sitting in the lamplight whose members are chatting and dreaming. My distant music reaches them. Perhaps it will give birth to a beautiful thought in the soul of a young woman, a new image in that of a poet. That's sufficient for me..."

"I understand very well," said the rich musician, "and I'll buy your violin.

He took a handful of gold out of his pocket and held it out to the beggar. But the other shook his head.

"I don't want to sell my violin."

Then the rich musician took the rest of the gold and the banknotes that he had on him and offered them to the beggar in exchange for the violin, but the other still refused.

"Do you know the power of these bills on which two women holding hands are designed, and other symbolic figures."

"Certainly I know it."

"You're rich, then?"

"It's now more than three days," said he beggar, "that I haven't eaten, because no one has thought of throwing me a few sous. But that's of no importance to me. And if death were to come to take me soon I would get up joyfully when I heard her footsteps making the snow crackle, and I would say to her: 'The old musician is ready to go with you, but permit him to carry among the dead this cherished instrument clasped to his heart..."'"

Then the rich musician drew away and, as wealth had made him wicked, he did not give any alms to the beggar.

THE FLOWER OF YOUTH

To Mademoiselle Paulette Sarraut.[8]

I

There was once in the land of Guirec a very beautiful and very cruel princess named Raphaële. She lived in a château overlooking the sea. In the evening she liked to walk along the shore accompanied by a single hunchbacked servant who was frightful to behold. She loosened her long hair in order that it could be moistened by the perfumed wind coming from the islands. Sometimes, she played the harp on the terrace, and she took pleasure in seeing the moonlight wandering over her robe and her hands.

In the city there was a naïve and dreamy student named Joël. He was very poor, wore a torn doublet, and lived in modest lodgings in company with a dove, a dog and an old woman, who cherished him equally. The Dove, named Douce, sang love songs to him in the morning; the dog, named Ombre, went with him on his walks and caressed him with amity. The old woman, whose name was Silence, prepared his nourishment every day and taught him that in order to direct himself in life he must be sincere, courageous and good. But one evening, on the strand, Joël encountered Princess Raphaële, and he fell in love with her with all his heart.

His book no longer had any charm for him; he neglected the room in which he was accustomed to dream to the songs of the friendly dove; he consumed his days writing long elegies

---

on the roads florid with broom and reciting them to the clouds and the sea.

In vain old Silence, who saw him growing thin and pale, enquired anxiously as to the cause of his melancholy. He remained taciturn and, at nightfall, he returned to the place on the strand where Princes Raphaële had previously appeared to him.

One evening, he was sitting, as was his custom, amid the seashells and the pebbles.

The sun had just disappeared; red flames were shining in the windows of the château that was visible on the high cliff. The tamarinds of the shore were rustling softly; a pale light trailed over the waves, and a thousand tiny benevolent faces could be seen smiling in the foam.

Joël's heart began to beat faster, for the simplicity of his soul was such that he sensed the events of his life before they happened.

In the distance, on the sand, the robe of Princes Raphaële made a sky-blue patch. She advanced, letting her hair float; her hunchbacked servant was following her.

When she was close to Joël, the latter fell to his knees and cried: "Madame, I love you more than the sea, more than the freshness of the morning and more than the verses I write in your honor. Since I have seen you, thoughts have been born in me as innumerable as the stars in the sky, and each of those thoughts speaks to me of you. Would you like to love me as I love you and to be my companion in life?"

Princess Raphaële started to laugh and looked the student up and down. But as the naivety of his eyes pleased her she said: "I forgive you, because your words are those of a child. Perhaps you do not know that I am Princess Raphaële and that I have in my service three astrologers who examine the planets in order to read my destiny therein. I know that my beauty troubles the hearts of men to the point of causing their death and I have conceived a vast ambition in consequence. I shall only love the King of France, the Devil, or the man who brings me the flower of youth."

Having said that, she drew away, and her servant gave Joël such an ugly grimace that two seabirds in the process of making love amid the algae fled in a clatter of wings.

II

Joël remained all alone on the shore. The stars were shining in the sky; their soft light illuminated tiny gleams in the blond sand. He sat down facing the waves, feeling a great pain. He saw mist trailing over the horizon, and counted the ships passing by.

Then, in the silence of the night, he wept. And when he had wept a great deal, he placed his head on a stone and went to sleep.

Then the waves parted and a little siren appeared in the midst of the foam. Her eyes were as green as the sea when the moon is reflected in it; his skin had the whiteness of the sand; her face had the charm of candor.

She had seen the student Joël weeping and had felt pity for him. Among the sirens, as among women, pity is the sister of amour. The little siren Genofa gazed at the student Joël asleep, his eyes red and his hands joined, and she fell in love with the student Joël.

When she had watched him for some time, she took a little flower from her hair, which was pinned there, and placed it over the student's heart; then she started singing to wake him up. Her voice was musical and her words resonated softly along the cliffs.

And the powerful spirits that live in the rocks said to one another: "That's the little siren Genofa, who loves the student Joël; what will come of it?"

Joël rubbed his eyes, thinking that he was dreaming, and the little siren said to him: "You're weeping, student Joël, you must be chagrined. Look, I am beautiful, I am smiling at you, I love you. I am the sister of the sirens of the sea. Navigators sitting at the foot of their mast in the evening throw themselves into the water when they have heard us. It was to flee our enchantments that Ulysses, the wily mariner, poured wax into the ears of his companion. We are immortal; we live in damp and profound grottoes, and the delights we make known to men are infinite. Come with me to our submarine palaces. You will contemplate unknown beauties and share my eternity."

But the student Joël, putting the flower that Genofa had given him into his doublet, replied: "Certainly, O siren, your songs are agreeable and sweet to hear, but I don't desire so many marvels. My mortal eyes would be wounded by your eternal clarities. I'm human, and I prefer the temporary joy that, among humans, is accompanied by the fear of misfortune, to your cold and all too sure sensualities, which would last forever..."

At those words the little siren hid her face in a cluster of wrack and disappeared, allowing little white and very pure pearls to fall behind her, which were her tears.

III

The little siren Genofa cleaved through the blue waves of the sea. Several of her companions called to her in vain; a starfish spread its futile light for her. In vain, three marine monsters smiled at her graciously. She descended ever more deeply into a region where marine flora no longer grew. She finally stopped; she had reached the entrance to the sacred grottoes where the queen of the sirens lived.

She penetrated beneath an immense vault of rocks; a sad light reigned there and sometimes caused innumerable stalactites to sparkle. There dwelt the spirits of navigators whom the sirens had charmed and caused to perish, and had rejected after having enjoyed their dead bodies. A vast groan dragged on incessantly beneath that vault; supplicant hands were raised toward the cold stone walls. A host of shades surrounded Genofa on all sides, but she had no fear of them because she knew that those forms were vain and fugitive.

There were men of every sort there.

There were mariners made illustrious by their voyages; they had seen all the lands bathed by the foamy sea; they had been returning to port on ships abundantly charged with weapons and wealth; they had already been able to see the familiar towers of their city sketched in the mist and their hearts were joyful. But they had dreamed near the sculpted prow as dusk fell. Out there, in their home, a big fire had been lit as a sign of joy; their wife was preparing the most precious wine and the most beautiful cups; their bed was ready; their servants were at the door. And for the beauty of a song, they had thrown themselves into the waves.

There were also humble fishermen. They let themselves drift into great reveries when the nights were clear; they saw luminous fish in their nets; all the protective stars were floating above their masts; every wave was a woman and, quietly, they went toward those mirages.

There were also poets that the sirens had seduced on the shore; there were men who were assumed to have lost their reason by their fellows; there were several kings, and even a mountain shepherd with his gourd and his crook, who was thinking about his goats wandering through the ferns.

They were all dreamers, and they were there because they had dreamed of the ideal on earth, and were suffering bitterly...

Genofa slid through the midst of all those phantoms, toward a more distant dwelling. The waves were resplendent; she had reached a blue pearl grotto that was filled by a divine music. The queen of the sirens was there, admirable for her wisdom, her power and her beauty.

Genofa said to her: "O venerated queen, welcome with benevolence the humblest of your daughters, I love a mortal, with an amour so great that it makes me hate the splendor of the seas. My heart refuses to bring him to our grottoes with the aid of our enchantments. He will only love a daughter of women of temporary beauty, but whose design would be similar to his own. Permit me, therefore, O queen, to become a woman subject to death and let me go to seek, in the light of the sun, a rapid happiness during counted days..."

"Imprudent and feeble child," replied the queen, "the equitable laws that regulate us do not permit me to refuse what you request, but know that, once you quit the empire of the seas, you can never again return among your sisters. Know that if you go to the world of humans you will submissive, like them, to disease and old age, and your beautiful form will subsequently become white bones and dust."

"I am determined to make those sacrifices, wise queen," said Genofa. "Old age will be sweet to me beside my beloved. I shall bless death, if it comes to strike me one evening when we are holding hands and my eyes are contemplating the sunset."

The queen made a sign to Genofa to follow her, and took her outside the grotto with her, while the plaint of the dead deprived of light resounded, lamentable and infinite.

IV

The student Joël had returned to his house, his heart moved by dolor. He sat down sadly beside the fire.

Douce, the dove, alighted on his shoulder and caressed his cheek with her white plumage. Ombre, the dog, lay down at his feet and licked his hands. Old Silence put a bowl of steaming soup in front of him. But he did not want to eat and said: "Do you, Silence, whose years have rendered you knowledgeable, know the flower of youth? Do you know its color, its virtue and where it can be found?"

"Certainly," the old woman replied. "It has been mentioned to me as the most precious product of nature. If I can believe what my ears have heard, its virtue is more powerful than that of all the wines matured by the sun during fecund autumns. Its gleam is as gray and dull as the evening mist, but its perfume gives those who respire it eternal youth and eternal beauty. I cannot tell you in what place on the vast earth it flowers, but it surely flowers somewhere; otherwise, its story would not occupy the evenings of human beings, for every-thing has a reason for being.

Instead of sleeping, Joël nourished a great project in his mind, and when the first cock sang he took his cloak and his staff and went downstairs silently.

He saw dawn break; a soft light bathed the fields and the woods, and then a vapor that trailed over the roofs and the bushes dissipated; the white road extended toward the horizon. He thought that his dove might die of solitude, that his dog might howl desperately at the sky, that the old woman would shed bitter tears in the ashes.

He closed the door firmly and drew away with long strides without looking back.

At the same time, the little siren Genofa emerged, timid and beautiful, from the blue waters. She was a woman, she was treading the fine sand joyfully, and she was going to see the man she loved.

Happy, with her moist hands, she saluted the sun...

V

Joël marched along the road, and his memories rose up and fell with the dust. On the evening of the third day he met a soldier at a crossroads who was coming back from the war. He had a large feather in his cap and a long sword with a shiny hilt by his side. His stride had a proud and pleasing elegance.

"Where are you going, friend?" said the soldier to Joël. "Your clothes are covered in dust, but you seem likeable and well-informed. Night is falling, let's travel together."

"Tell me who you are and where you're going," the student replied, "in order that I know whether my route will be yours."

"My name is Glorifer and I follow the profession of arms. I've served under the King of France and I've lost more blood than I've acquired wealth. But only glory impels me; poverty is agreeable to the man who has the treasure of cour-age. Now I've been dismissed because there are no more wars;

humankind will deteriorate from day to day. I've forgotten the place where I was born, and I'm traveling in quest of adventures."

"Come with me, then," exclaimed Joël. "I'm searching the world for the flower of youth for Princess Raphaële. When I've found it I shall marry that princess; I shall have a great kingdom and I'll appoint you as general-in-chief of my armies."

Glorifer was ambitious and that promise made him smile. He was even happier to find a companion for his route and a goal for his life. He therefore followed the student Joël.

Night had entirely fallen and they perceived the horizon of the sea. They went along a deserted strand and reached a beach in the depths of a bay. They lay down on the sand and shared a generous wine and black bread, which the soldier's gourd and knapsack contained. The Glorifer went to sleep.

He dreamed that he was in command of armies without number, that he stimulated the anger of all peoples and took rapid possession by force of arms of the empire of the earth.

The student Joël listened for a long time to the plaint of the waves; then he saw birds on a rock that were mingling their song with that of the waves. Afterwards, a crow with damp plumage arrived from the direction of the sea. It spoke in its own language to the other birds, and this is what Joël heard:

"Birds, welcome me into your flock; I am your exiled sister. My body reposes out there beneath foreign soil and I can only contemplate by night these shores dear to my heart. Oh, sing, birds; you are not dead, far from Brittany."

Then Joël wept, sensing the sadness of quitting his homeland.

VI

The timid dawn appeared over the world and the travelers set off on the march. They arrived at the entrance to an oak wood and saw a milk-white ewe lying on the moss. Joël went to her and stroked her, because he found her beautiful. Then, as a stream was flowing not far away, he collected water in the hollow of his hand and gave it to the ewe to drink. Scarcely had she drunk than her fleece fell away, her animal body became a human body and Joël had a pale and svelte fay before him.

Glorifer, whose soul was romantic and sensible to beauty, was moved.

The fay floated momentarily above the grass and said to Joël: "You have come, traveler, to the entrance to the ancient forest of Broceliande. My name in Viviane and you have freed me from a baneful enchantment that retained me captive in the fleece of a ewe. My story is sad and marvelous. Perhaps you have heard how I was once loved by the illustrious Merlin, and how I enchained him beside me thanks to the science he had revealed to me. We were enlaced beneath a rose-bush for eternity. Alas, my amour ceased to be sufficient for him and my caresses importuned him. He succeeded in breaking the charm that retained him and he changed me into a bleating animal. I have been wandering in the woods ever since, biting in vain the bark of oaks and weeping amorous kisses. I had to remain thus until a man with a pure and loving heart offered me water in his hands. All those I have seen have thrown stones at me or tried to take me to their sheep-folds. You have come, stranger, and your kindness has rendered me beauty. But tell me what your homeland is and the goal of your journey."

"I love Princess Raphaële," replied the student, "and I'm searching for the flower of youth for her. Can you tell me who possesses it?"

"I believe that at this moment it is still in the hands of the illustrious Merlin, who has respired it and is handsome and immortal. Plunge into these forests; perhaps you will find him there, prey to meditation. You'll recognize him by the nobility of his face. Speak to him without fear, imploring him. He is good, even though he has made me suffer; he will listen to you and grant your plea."

Joël thanked the fay, and was getting ready to leave, joyfully, followed by Glorifer, when Viviane called him back and said to him, blushing: "If you see him out there, tell him that I have recovered my form as a woman, and if you have found charm in my eyes, tell him that too. You can add that I still love him, that I am waiting for him, my hair undone, under the willows, and that I am singing his praises to the birds of the forest and the broom of the heath."

Joël and Glorifer wandered for several days through the clearings and the thickets. They nourished themselves on wild fruits and slept in the hollows of oaks. They arrived in a place where the bushes were so dense that Glorifer was obliged to separate them with his sword. They saw a spring flowing in a clearing; they ran to it. Near the water, a man was dreaming, with his head in his hands. He was tall and venerable, and the travelers recognized Merlin.

Joël prostrated himself at his feet and told him about his journey and how he had come to seek the flower of youth. Then Merlin, after having heard him, raised his arms toward the vault of verdure, agitated his beard and exclaimed:

"Insensate traveler! You are preparing the worst of your woes. Look at me: I am suffering and nothing can console me. Once my youthful desire embraced the universe; I led, joyfully, the career of life and the solitude of my mind stimulated my ardor. But I fell in love! I respired the flower of youth in order that time would not erode the beautiful white marble of our amour. I have known the monotonous joy of endless dreams. The amour that lasts forever is the greatest of tortures, Child! Old age and death are the great friends that console our soul."

"O Merlin, under these profound forests, in the shade of these bushes, among the myrtle and the broom, you have loved in the manner of humans. I also love; understand my heart and grant my plea."

"I will not go against your destiny," replied Merlin. "Can one ever have only oneself to blame for one's misfortune? The flower of youth was stolen from me once by Moch, the spirit of the sands. He took it to Dehut, the daughter of Gradlon, King of Ys, who offered her kisses at that price. But the anger of the heavens prevented that union. The waves of the sea engulfed the city of Ys one evening, for Dehut's impurity wearied God. Go to the nearest shore; when you see a rock that has the form of a sleeping crow, stop. There dwells Moch, the spirit of the sands. Perhaps he has kept the flower of youth. I can do nothing more for you; I no longer know anything. I have lost my power, amour has corroded my mind like a wound."

Having said that, Merlin fell back into his meditations; but Joël, as he was about to draw away, remembered Viviane and said to him: "O Merlin, listen to me again. I have liberated a fay hidden in the body of a white ewe. She is marvelously beautiful. She told me that her name is Viviane, and that she loves you."

Scarcely had he spoke those words than Merlin's face expressed a horrible terror. He got up and cried: "Viviane is free! Accursed be the beauty that has caused my eyes to dream, accursed be the flesh that has given pleasure to my flesh! If I encounter her under these trees she will enchain me in the prison of her arms. To the sterile sensuality of amour I prefer the unconsciousness of stone!"

Marlin cut an oak branch and drew a circle around himself. In the place where he had been standing, his eyes sparkling with light, there was no longer anything but a great melancholy rock. For all eternity, Merlin had returned to the bosom of his august mother, the earth, of whom he was the most illustrious son. He still reposes out there, invisible for our mortal eyes, amid the rosemary, under the gray fogs of Armorica...

Joël and Glorifer saluted the silent rock with a long adieu, and then they drew away through the forest.

VII

After having reached the sea, they went along the shore for some time, and they stopped in the house of an old mariner.

There they made the acquaintance of Tinah, the gatherer of seaweed, whose eyes were as blue as the horizon. She was still a child; she lived alone on the shore, awaiting the return of her father, who had departed three years before. Every evening, when the tide went out, she shed tears, because she thought that he was dead. Every evening, however, she lit the fire and set another place for him at the wooden table.

She linked herself in amity with the travelers; she told them the story of her petty life, her chagrins, and her great hope of seeing her father's sail appear on the sea.

Joël and Glorifer stayed there for several days. While Joël dreamed about Princess Raphaële, Glorifer accompanied Tinah over the shingle and told her the story of his adventures. Once, he had cut a bridge with a single stroke of his sword; another time, like Samson, he had broken the columns of a temple in order to crush his enemies.

Tinah pretended to take a great interest in such exploits, but she often questioned the soldier about the cares of his friend. Joël intimidated her, even though he was almost the same age as her. She could not speak to him without blushing, and fearfully.

One evening, while he was sitting down and gazing at the stars, she took his hand gently in hers and said: "It's not necessary to be chagrined, student Joël..." But then she turned away and hid her face.

That evening, the travelers decided that it was time to leave, and that they would set forth again at dawn.

When dawn came, Tinah walked with them along the shore. She told them that a rock similar to a sleeping crow was situated a short distance away. Moch, the spirit of the sands, lived in a deep cavern; he was a cruel and strong old man who challenged fishermen to wrestle and put them to death when he had defeated them.

"Have courage," she said, when she quit them. "I shall pray for you, and you will be illustrious heroes. I shall wait for my father on the beach, and the sound of the waves will remind me of you."

In the distance, she extended her small white hand toward them. Glorifer waved his long arms and his big feather so many times that the birds passing by were frightened. And when, on turning round, they could no longer see Tinah's dress, he pulled his hat down over his eyes in order that the student Joël would not be witness to his weakness.

They found the spirit of the sands asleep in his cave. Joël approached him and woke him up by tugging gently on his bead. Then Moch got up, prey to a great anger, and challenged them to fight.

Having put down his sword, Glorifer exhorted Joël to stay by the cave entrance, and he took the old man in his arms.

Their struggle lasted for several hours; after that time, Glorifer had the spirit of the sands under his knee; the latter asked for mercy and promised to realize the travelers' desire. Glorifer help his adversary to his feet and wiped away the dust covering his body.

When Joël had explained why he had come, Moch replied, weeping:

"I've been defeated in wrestling, and I certainly experience a great dolor because of it, but that dolor is nothing compared to the one that your words reanimate in my soul. I loved the daughter of the King of Ys, but my lips never touched hers. She was the most beautiful of all the women whose eyes have contemplated the sea. She surrendered her flesh to those who desired it but my amour was all the more ardent for that. Her sins are illustrious throughout these shores.

"I stole the flower of youth for her, but the waves invaded the city of Ys just as I arrived there to offer it to her. I saw her, voluptuous until death when the waves carried her away. Then I threw the flower of youth away, and I fled weeping.

"It's in thinking of her that I immolate my victims. I see her eyes in the stars, her hair in the wrack, and her heart in the sun. You're fortunate, stranger, to love a woman; amour alone is beautiful!"

His eyes were full of tears and he let long moans escape. However, he added: "I remember that a traveler captive in my cave mentioned the flower of youth to me. He told me that the waves had cast it up on a shore where an astrologer named Asmodius had found it. That astrologer departed for the palace of King Louis XI, who, fearing death more than life, has promised immense treasures and great honors in exchange for the flower of youth."

Joël and Glorifer had heard enough; they left Moch, the spirit of the sands, to continue his lamentations. They emerged from his abode, glad to see the light of the sky again.

The sun had just disappeared over the horizon; a blue mist floated over the water; it was the time when the powerful spirits who inhabit the rocks exchange solemn words between themselves like the sounds of the wind. The first star made its light tremble; the travelers gazed at the sea.

Under the transparent waves they perceived great ruined towers and the phantoms of palaces, the shade of a city. It was Ys, the melancholy and misfortunate city asleep on the ocean bed.

And slowly, in the religious silence of the falling night, one by one, bells rang with a distant, mysterious and beautiful sound. Their voice resonated over the cliffs and the distant islands, like human sobbing.

Joël and Glorifer saw errant forms trailing over the sea, twisting their arms; they advanced toward them and could already hear their sighs; but they fled, frightened, in the direction of the land.

VIII

They marched for several days toward the capital of the kingdom of France. On the way, they encountered a dwarf who was fighting with an eagle. The dwarf was little and old; the eagle was powerful, and was holding the dwarf's hood in its beak, trying to lift him into the air.

Moved by pity, Joël ran forward and struck the eagle with his staff. Glorifer thrust at it with his sword and the eagle fled, staining the treetops with its blood.

The dwarf that Joël had saved was jovial and benevolent; he was a forest dwarf. He made several pirouettes and picked several daisies as a sign of joy, for dwarfs have simple and puerile souls. Then he said to Joël:

"I live in the profound earth and I am a friend of the oaks. My name is Mus. Take this whistle; if you're ever in danger, call me, and you'll see that dwarfs are not ingrates."

And he went away, singing.

The next day, Joël and Glorifer saw towers appear in the distance in large numbers, and they understood that they had reached Paris, the city of King Louis XI. They stopped in a meadow to get a little rest and brighten up their garments.

Glorifer went to sleep, and while he slept, Joël perceived some distance away an orchard full of blonde apples. The fruits tempted him and he ran to the trees to pick some. The apples had an admirable taste and he ate several. He was about to go and wake his friend, but six of the king's archers who were passing by threw themselves upon him; he had been eating apples from the royal orchard.

Joël tried to struggle, but the archers were very strong; he cried out, but Glorifer's slumber was very profound. Joël therefore entered Paris as a captive, as a thief.

When they arrived in the city the leader of the archers asked him whether he knew a minister, a bishop or a noble of the court, in which case he could be released. Joël replied that he was a student and had come from Brittany. Then he was taken to prison and was assured that he would be hanged in three days' time.

Joël believed in his lucky star. On the first evening he searched the sky through the bars of his dungeon for its friendly light. There was one that was brighter and softer than all the rest; he thought that it was his, and went to sleep dreaming about Raphaële.

On the second evening he remembered the whistle given to him by the dwarf Mus. He put his head to the narrow sky-light from which he could still see a corner of the word. The Seine curved silently at the foot of his prison; the somber city reposed in the distance. He inflated his cheeks and blew with all his might. The walls did not crumble; the footsteps of a jailer resonated in the corridor. Joël threw the whistle into the water and a great anxiety entered his heart.

On the third evening, thinking that he only had a few more hours to live, he wept. He saw again the house in his homeland, the woman he loved and his companion Glorifer.

Then he heard a rattle of keys, and the jailer who was accustomed to bring him bread and water at that hour came in. He seemed to Joël to be shorter than usual; he raised his lantern Joël recognized the jovial face of the dwarf Mus.

The latter took him by the hand and drew him through the somber corridors and stairways of the prison. Joël noticed that the sentinels they passed were all little bearded men who made comical grimaces of amity at Mus. They arrived in the courtyard and there Joël perceived the bodies of men bound and gagged. Instead of the archers of the guard post there were dwarfs who were playing games. The gate was wide open; Joël ran outside; he was free. Before he had recovered from his astonishment, the prison closed again; the dwarf Mus had disappeared.

The student perceived a church. He lay down under the porch and went to sleep, for he was very tired. At dawn a doorkeeper and a cruel priest woke him up brutally and drove him away. In those days, the priests readily deemed that it was only necessary to be good to the rich.

Joël moved on, and as he went he asked an artisan where Louis XI lived; it was in the king's abode that he counted on finding the flower of youth.

He was told that the King's residence was in a place called Plessis and that the people were waiting impatiently for him to die, for the sovereign feared death for himself but lavished it on his subjects. He lived in prayer, surrounded by holy images, while honest men rendered their souls at Montfaucon on his orders, while cursing God.

Joël set forth to walk to Plessis and arrived there after several days as the sun was setting. He wandered in the city for some time and perceived that an extraordinary joy reigned there. The taverns were resounding with songs and young students like him were going through the streets arm in arm.

King Louis XI must have respired the flower of youth, Joël thought, *and wants the people to rejoice*.

He arrived at the royal dwelling. It was a crenellated fortress surrounded by a broad moat. The drawbridge was lowered; nearby, soldiers were drinking and playing cards; many were drunk. Night had fallen.

Joël went into the courtyard without being noticed, climbed a staircase, and went through a few halls, taking advantage of the general disorder. There were people running hither and yon, others banqueting at tables; others were groaning, but their laments had something discordant and false about them.

Several times, Joël heard cries of "Vive le dauphin!" and he thought that the King was dead.[9] The cries of a weeping woman resounded; that was perhaps the most sincere grief.

Then there were the sounds of instruments; musicians and shepherds were playing lutes and flutes. The king had sent for them in order that their music would keep him awake for as long as possible as the great sleep approached. Now they were creating joyful sounds for the ears of the living; then they would return home to recount the death of the king and the large salary they had received.

Joël perceived a lamp at the end of a corridor. The lamp in question was flickering in a narrow room with thick walls. There was a door studded with iron nails and bolts. The window was barred; a star was smiling there. And at the back, on

---

[9] Louis XI died on 30 August 1483.

the bed, gray, ugly, humble, solitary and shrunken, the king was lying.

He had done everything he could, the poor king. She had come, the one he feared more than the Duc de Bretagne or Charles le Téméraire. The doors were firmly shut; the halberdiers were watching on the towers; how had she got in? What somber wrath animated her, in order that in squeezing the temples, she had spread so much horror over that visage?

Joël fled, full of dolor and terror.

IX

He went back to Paris with the hope of finding his companion Glorifer and learning what had become of the flower of youth. He wandered for some time from one crossroads to another and one hostelry to another. He could see that the change of sovereign had not transformed the State. Beggars continued to be hungry, bourgeois to die in abundance in their houses, and priests to honor God at the expense of men. And he was greatly astonished by that.

One evening, as he was going along a dark street, he saw an old man sitting on a stone, who was weeping. As his soul was charitable, he went to him and asked him the cause of his tears.

The old man had child-like eyes and was making the gestures of a madman. He cried: "I'm a dreamer, Monsieur. You see before you the most unfortunate of astrologers. I have spent my days reading the secrets of the world in the stars. I can say that I have lived in the sky. At the end of my life I loved a woman; she was beautiful and loved me for the beauty of my dreams. She understood that the ideal must be detached from all material preoccupation, and I always found in her home a table ornamented by light, sought-after dishes and virtuous bottles. I loved her, Monsieur, and she betrayed me for a soldier."

Joël consoled him with soft words and asked him how it had happened.

"My marriage," the astrologer replied, "was already arranged with Simone, the beautiful proprietress of the Cheval Rouge. A couple so united had never been seen. I dreamed and she worked. But one day, when we were in the large room of the hostelry, a soldier came in. He seemed to be poor, but had the arrogance of a Maréchal. He told her to bring him all the wine in our casks, for he had a great sorrow to drown, and then he wept. Aided by one of Simone's soldiers I tried to put him outside gently; he drew his sword and threatened to kill us all. It was at that moment that Simone commenced to love him. He had the coarse beauty of men of war. We served him drinks, he put Simone on his knees and kissed her in front of me, and as I was gripped by a just indignation he threw me out violently. God knows what he has eaten and drunk since! Simone loves him and is going to marry him. The hostelry has become a subject of scandal; the soldier is perpetually drunk and invites passers-by to drink with him. The table is open to all the paupers of the street and Simone, once so orderly, opens the oldest vintages herself. I've gone there disguised as a beggar and have been treated like a king without opening my purse. Is that not shameful?"

Joël was on the track of his companion. He begged the old man urgently to take him to the hostelry of the Cheval Rouge; he might be able to soothe his woes. The latter agreed readily, and on the way he said:

"My names is Asmodius and the greatest destiny was promised to me. I nearly became as powerful as the King of France, for I nearly saved him from death. I had found the flower of youth and I was taking it to him attached to my staff, in order that it should seem devoid of value and that no one would steal it from me; but the bird Orock, who lives in the Caucasus Mountains, passed by and stole it from me. What has become of it now"

When they reached the hostelry Joël's heart was full of joy. The old man's dolor became indignation; a flame of wrath was shining in his eyes. The joyous sound of songs and clinking glasses was audible; the scene of the feast was visible through the windows.

There were a large number of guests of all sorts: bourgeois whom the abundance of wine caused to forget their dignity; drunkards made illustrious by their prowess; a gallant abbé who was talking amorously to a young woman with a naïve gaze; avid paupers taking advantage with all their might of such a windfall; and two young lovers who were affecting to drink from the same glass. In the middle, under her admirably white coiffure, the beautiful Simone was radiant. And Joël perceived beside her the worthy Glorifer, in person, drinking, his face serene, and displaying in his attitudes the grandeur of his martial and sentimental soul.

The beautiful Simone was standing up, she had a cup full of golden wine and was about to drink to the health of her lover, and all the guests were attentive.

But the astrologer could stand it no longer. He opened the door abruptly, irrupted into the room and launched himself toward the woman who had betrayed him. He cried:

"Oh, thrice ingrate who has snatched me from sacred dreams for fleeting lusts. The planets have spoken to me this evening in a puerile language that does my old age good. In the woods or before the sea I understood them and I was happy. Render me all the beautiful things that you have made me hate. You have destroyed my high prestige and have rendered me an object of derision. I demand your body and your house in exchange for my lost dreams..."

A great stupor was painted on all faces; one of the paupers hid a ham under his doublet; the two young lovers, holding one another tightly, gazed at human misfortunes with indifference. All eyes turned to Glorifer.

But at that moment the table collapsed, the candles went out and the guests were knocked down. Glorifer had perceived Joël on the threshold of the house, had bounded forward and fallen into his arms.

An indescribable tumult reigned in the darkness; there were cries, and the sound of shattering glass and breaking porcelain; the lovers hugged one another more ardently; the bourgeois invoked reason; the abbé groped for his neighbor; the paupers set forth in pursuit of the food; the beautiful Simone was heard sobbing.

Glorifer closed the door behind him and drew his companion through the streets in haste.

X

Joël and Glorifer had resumed their journey and were wandering the world again in search of the redoubtable bird Orock. They slept in fields or under trees; sometimes they received kind hospitality in houses, and Glorifer caused astonishment by the facility he had in eating and drinking.

They had left the land of France a long time ago when they arrived in a city where the men drank beer of an admirable color and almost all the women were pretty.

It was Sunday; the taverns were full of joyful drunkards; the smoke of pipes rose so thickly that it obscured the light of the sun. A mild peace seemed to possess all hearts. Young women were strolling on the promenades wearing new bonnets and their finest dresses. Audacious clerks were following close behind them, and more than one kiss was audible in the solitary pathways.

Joël saw peasants dancing in the shade of linden trees and he thought about his homeland. How sweet it must be to love with simplicity like that, on Sundays, to the sound of violins, and then resume quotidian labors!

A man laden with years had just passed by. Everyone saluted him respectfully, even the most beautiful women, who usually had no thought of anything but amour.

Joël asked who the old man was and was told that he was the illustrious Dr. Faust, renowned for his wisdom and his science. Joël resolved to go and interrogate him about the flower of youth, in the hope of obtaining some precious indication. When dusk fell he went to his dwelling, while Glorifer waited for him in front of a large tankard of beer.

Conducted by the disciple Wagner, Joël went into a room with a high ceiling. A lamp made its yellow light tremble over the dusty leather of books, and sad rows of bottles, jars and instruments. A death's-head posed on the table seemed ready to cry to the visitor: *I'm the master of the house. What do you want?*

At the back, in his armchair, Dr. Faust was dreaming.

Then Joël told him about his travels and why he was undertaking them.

Faust said to him: "You envy my science, child! I am the most ignorant of men, and there is no rude manual laborer on earth who does not have more science than me. You've come to interrogate me! But I am the one who should have come to you like a pilgrim with a hazel-wood staff and a cloak the color of the road; you could have taught me the sweetness of loving a woman and thinking about her in the evening, while going to sleep in a meadow. Alas, during all the nights of my youth, I searched in the depths of books for the light of verity. It filtered over my table with the moon's rays, as it does today, but I did not understand it. Now I've attained the arid kingdom of wisdom and I remember with bitter regret the beautiful domain of the foolish. Happy are the fools! They march like blind men, and yet they do not fall into wells, like sages. What gay companions fantasy and caprice are! Sleep under the dust, excessively veridical books! Cease laughing, O death's-head! Give me a fool's bauble and bells, and also your heart, young student!"

Faust began to groan, and then fell into a somber reverie, while Joël went away silently.

XI

The two travelers wandered in lands without number. They traversed great rivers bordered with palm trees, climbed mountains devoid of flowers, contemplated luminous cities. They saw people made ugly and short by a rigorous climate, and other to whom a propitious sunlight gave harmonious forms. There were some who worshiped the moon, others who worshiped fire and the wind, others who worshiped animals, others who worshiped an invisible and abstract God, and others who did not worship any God at all. Among all of them they found the same passions and the same dreams; all were obliged to seek their nourishment on the land and all feared death.

Three years had passed since Joël and Glorifer had left the city of the savant Faust when they reached the sea of a thousand waves. On the somber shores they found an honest and peaceful seafaring people. They were welcomed joyfully, and then elected kings by those men expert in manipulating oars. Their reign lasted nine days, and at the end of that time they chartered a ship and departed over the waves, guided by skillful pilots.

A violent tempest soon rose; the wind carried away the sails. The stars were the color of blood. The vessel broke up on reefs and was engulfed, but Joël and Glorifer clung on to a mast and confided themselves to the impetuous winds. In the rain and the darkness, they were cast on to an isolated rock, similar to a God.

There they found a man sitting alone in the midst of the foam. A similar misfortune united them and they embraced, full of love for one another.

"Doubtless you've been saved, like us, from some terrible shipwreck?" said the student.

"I'm accustomed to these adventures," the stranger replied. "I love the proximity of death. I've escaped the Old Man of the Sea, the Trembling Island, and the giants that only have one eye in the forehead. I have riches that twenty ships couldn't carry; in India I've found the largest diamonds that exist; I would even possess the flower of youth, which I stole from the bird Orock seven years ago, if I hadn't let it fall into the sea. I'm illustrious in Bagdad for my voyages, and my name is Sinbad."

Having said that, he stood up, showed his companions a tremulous light that had just appeared in the distance and had to be the beacon of a ship, and, having exhorted Joël and Glorifer to follow him, he launched himself into the waves.

They saw him struggling momentarily against the tempest, but the darkness was intense; they could no longer hear anything but a long cry that was lost in the roar of the wind and the plaint of the sea.

Joël perceived then that Glorifer's head, which had collided with the rocks, was bleeding abundantly. And the latter, sensing that his hour had come, said:

"Student Joël, you'll appoint another man than me as general of your armies. I shall not have known glory among men, but I believe that God will give me a large troop to command in Paradise. If you pass the hostelry of the Cheval Rouge again, tell the beautiful Simone that I was thinking about her as I died. And you, my dear companion, who love me, remain joyful in dolor, good in prosperity and always march through life heroically..."

Glorifer opened his arms, made a comical and resigned grimace, looked at the sky and died.

The sea had calmed down and the student Joël's tears fell one by one into the quiet waves. The darkness dissipated, and when morning appeared, passing sailors came to take the student Joël off the rock where his friend was sleeping forever.

He stayed at the stern of the ship, overwhelmed by grief, his eyes staring at the fatal rock.

In the distance he could see the brave Glorifer extended, motionless and stiff, as if on parade, amid the blue wrack and the gentle foam. And he, therefore, was going to resume the course of the endless journey alone. For the first time, his heart failed.

Dawn illuminated the world and the song of the pilot rang out. Every tear shed was a little benevolent spirit that was to follow him over the luminous sea and then over the obscure land, for the tears of friendship are the only ones that never perish...

XII

Joël had been set down by the mariners on an unknown shore. Inhospitable men lived there, who did not welcome travelers in their houses, and Joël marched in the direction opposed to the sea. The land seemed disinherited and misfortunate; an eternal mist enveloped it; there were arid valleys and mountains planted with fir trees. The stars that floated over those landscapes were yellow or red, and their light sowed terror and desolation. There were pools of glaucous water and the divinities of those marshes were ugly and groaning.

Leaning on his staff, Joël advanced through that country. His heart was so sad that he was inaccessible to fear; he understood that he was about to reach the limits of the world and only his curiosity guided him. He climbed terrible summits where the rocks and the clouds were confounded; he went past lakes as profound as the earth, where green beings lived, which gazed at him with a single enormous eye and were not endowed with movement. He no longer saw birds overhead. He descended precipitate slopes and traversed mysterious plains. Several times, he thought he saw white phantoms fleeing as he approached, but he thought that they were mirages of his mind caused by fatigue and excitement.

It had been several days since Joël had seen any sign of human life, and he felt that he was about to die of it. Darkness covered the earth, his feet were bleeding, his brain was empty and bleak—and then he perceived a light.

He marched rapidly in that direction and reached a little house. Around it there were trees and a garden with flowers. The door stood ajar; he opened it and went in. He found a bed, a table, a stool, a loaf of bread and a pitcher of water. In the ashes of the fire a black dog was whining. Joël sat down and shared the bread and water with the dog; then the latter licked his hands and died.

Joël was ready to go to bed, but he went outside to see whether the master of the house was in the garden. He took a few steps along a path; roses were shedding their petals there and he took great pleasure in respiring them. He continued walking and saw a ditch as narrow and deep as a grave. A little further on, he stumbled over a recumbent man, and a terrible fear gripped him. He felt him with his trembling hands; he was dead. He must have been extraordinarily old.

Then, although he was exhausted by fatigue and chilled by terror, he dragged the dead man to the grave and covered him with pious earth. Then he went back into the house and went to sleep.

After he had slept for a few hours, a strange light filled the room and woke him up, Joël saw the old man that he had buried standing beside him. He was handsome and seemed just; his rags were radiant. He spoke.

"This evening, you have laid beneath the clement earth the body of the most indefatigable pilgrim that the sun has ever illuminated. My name is Isaac Laquedem. I am the man who said to Jesus Christ: 'Go on your way, my dwelling is not yours.' He avenged himself on me cruelly although he professed to forgive sins. Since then I have traveled the vast world, I have listened to people cursing me in various tongues and I became more powerful than God, my master, because I have seen men suffering.

"Then I set down my staff and I cried: 'My task is concluded, Lord! I want to see three last sunsets, in a flowery garden, near a house at the limits of the world, only having the amity of a dog, and to die thereafter.' My wish has been granted. You arrived, child, as I died. You gave bread to my dog and earth to my remains. I want to recompense you and terminate your journey. You have been searching for seven years for the flower of youth without knowing that the flower in question was against your breast. It was given to you on a shore by a siren who loved you, and fatality has laughed at you."

Joël put his hand into his doublet; there was indeed a little flower there; it as gray and devoid of beauty. He remembered, then, that he had taken it unthinkingly from the hands of the siren Genofa, one evening when he had gone to sleep on the shore.

There it was, then, the flower that the mariner Sinbad had dropped into the sea, and which the waves must have tossed until Genofa had made an ornament for her hair with it.

For seven years he had been traveling the world in search of a prize that he had on his person. For seven years, instead of wandering miserably, he could have tasted the happiness of which he dreamed.

Dolor took possession of him at that thought, but the old man went on:

"I will take you back to the town where you were born, but on condition that you always remain good. Know that if you ever cause the death of a child, a maiden or a beggar—which is to say, a pure soul—on that day I will take back the life that I have given you, and on that day you will be no more than a pinch of dust carried away by the evening breeze..."

Joël remained motionless, prey to astonishment. The old man took him in his arms and carried him away through the air.

XII

Joël found himself sitting on the side of a road. He must have been traveling for a night and a day, for the sun was setting. He was holding the flower of youth in his hand; he was alone. He looked around; the woods and the fields were familiar to him; a friendly perfume rose from the fields; his native earth embalmed his soul. Close by, there was a clump of trees, where he had often dreamed in his youth. The steeple rose up in the azure in the distance, like a benevolent and ironic smile.

Bewildered by joy, Joël started running along the road. He would have liked to kiss those objects, the sight of which was so sweet to him, to hug the rude soil to his breast. An infinite emotion invaded him, a happiness of which he had not believed his human nature capable.

The sea was paling on the horizon; the sun gilded the wheat; he saw doves in a field. They started to laugh and greeted him: "*Bonjour! Bonjour!*" they said "We recognize you, student Joël; you've been on a long journey! One of our companions died last year, weeping for you copiously..."

A little further on he saw a dog passing by and heard it murmuring in its own language: "Isn't that the student Joël who left seven years ago? Ombre, my brother, won't lick his hands and face, for I saw him die last winter..."

Then there was an old woman carrying a faggot of dead wood, who crossed herself on seeing him, and said: "Phantom of student Joël, it's doubtless your punishment to wander the earth. How remorse must be making you suffer! Old Silence, who loved you so much, shed tears as numerous as the leaves of spring, and dolor caused her death..."

Joël stopped, his heart lacerated. All the beings that were dear to him had departed from his house, then, taken away by a pitiless destiny. Had his amour not been inconsiderate? Had he not been bound to sacrifice the dove, the dog and the old woman to it? He thought that one cannot struggle against one's passions, that at that very moment, his amour was triumphing over his misfortunes.

He held the flower of youth in his right hand and he marched, his eyes fixed, toward Princess Raphaële's château.

He saw a young woman coming toward him; she had eyes the color of the sea. It was the little siren Genofa.

For seven years she had been waiting for the student Joël. She lived in a sheepfold near the road and was desolate, every evening, when the footsteps of a traveler resounded.

This evening, her eyes were full of tears, but those tears became a smile, and the smile an ecstasy, and she ran forward, her arms extended, toward the man who was approaching.

O joy! It really was the student Joël, the student Joël who had been thinking about her, who loved her, since he was holding like a talisman, as he returned to his village, the flower that she had once given him. So they were finally going to love one another! She was mute with joy.

But why was he not saying anything? Why was he not crying out: "It's me!" and taking her in his arms?

He looked at her with astonishment, searching his memories in vain. Then, with a gesture to evoke the entire past, she said: "Would you like to return that flower to me, Monsieur Student?"

But he started to laugh, and replied: "It's the flower of youth, for which I've been searching for seven years, and which I'm taking to Princess Raphaële, Mademoiselle Shepherdess..."

And, saluting her with his hand, he passed on.

The sea breeze inflated his cloak and he marked his footprints in the sand of the shore joyfully. He was very close to the princess's château. He saw the first stars born over the sea; he heard a delightful music of harps and, raising his eyes, he perceived instrument-players on the high terrace. And in front of them, beneath her loose black hair and her sky blue dress, in the mirage of the nascent moon, as beautiful as the waves and dreams, Princess Raphaële was gazing at the horizon.

Joël arrived at the stone stairway. One more minute and he would be at the feet of his beloved and a little joy would redeem his long woes. He had reached the end of his journey, and an infinite happiness filled his soul. He fell to his knees and thanked God.

At that same instant, in the distance, on the edge of the white road, the little siren Genofa, her hands crossed over her chaste and patient heart, expired.

And the prediction of the Wandering Jew was accomplished.

Joël had caused a virgin to die of love, and in the place where he had been kneeling, praising the Lord, there was no longer anything but a pinch of dust, which the evening breeze blew into the sea.

Thus destiny and amour play cruelly with men...

THE STORY OF AN UNLUCKY GRENADIER

To Monsieur Vaz de Carvalhaès.[10]

There was once a child for whom nothing succeeded. If he went to guard the flocks he infallibly allowed the most beautiful ewes to go astray; if he carried a fragile vase he invariably dropped it; he stained his new clothes on the day of his first communion. So he was perpetually scolded and beaten by his parents. The other children, knowing that he was unlucky, laughed at him. He was not unhappy, however, because he thought that some day, he would receive compensation for his woes. Why did he believe that? He did not know, but he believed it. His name was Martin.

In the meantime, the French Revolution broke out.

His father and mother, who lived in a small house and owned a small field, wrongly accused of having shouted "Long live the King!" were guillotined in consequence of that error.

Before going to his death, his father, who was old and had a long white beard, said to him: "My son you're unlucky, but don't be discouraged. Work hard and be good. You'll find me and your poor mother again in Heaven."

Marin lived alone from that day on, with an old servant who labored the soil.

Some time after that his house caught fire. Everything was destroyed. The old servant built a hut in which they lived, exposed to the wind and the rain.

---

[10] The Vaz de Carvalhaes family was an important Brazilian political dynasty; the present dedication is not to one of its more prominent members.

When Martin was twenty years old he fell in love with a young woman and was loved by her, but because of his bad luck her parents would not consent to him marrying her. Then they became secretly engaged.

One day, Martin said to his fiancée: "There are great wars with foreign nations. I'm going to take part in them and try to render myself illustrious by my bravery. Who knows? Perhaps I'll become the friend of the Emperor Napoléon and he will write a letter to your parents personally to advise them to grant me your hand. Whatever happens, I shall bring you back a flower picked on foreign soil."

He kissed his fiancée, said adieu to the old servant, and was engaged in the grenadiers.

He made war; he fired rifle shots, marched barefoot, went several days without eating, and entered joyfully into conquered towns.

Once, the Emperor Napoléon, after seeing him at a distance through his telescope mounting an assault on a tower, said: "I want to decorate that brave grenadier." And he summoned his captain. But the captain made a mistake and Napoleon decorated another grenadier, who was not at all brave.

And Martin did not protest, for, fundamentally, he was timid.

Another time, on a morning of victory, he was a sentinel at the corner of a wood, and the Emperor passed by, followed by a single aide-de-camp. How proud and handsome he was! He had won the battle the day before, and was the most joyful emperor that had ever been seen.

"Grenadier," he said to Martin, "strike your briquette and give me a light. You're a good soldier!"

And Martin struck his briquette, trembling. Oh, certainly, if he had mentioned the letter to his fiancée's parents, the Emperor would have written it there and then with a pencil, standing up in his stirrups, and he would have said: *He's a good soldier!*

But by the time Martin thought about it, the Emperor had disappeared in the distance, in the dust, and the opportunity had fled with him.

One evening, Martin was asleep next to a cannon. They were in Austria and the night was full of stars. The cannon next to which Martin was asleep was terrible, sad and black, but on looking at it closely, one could see that it had an air of benevolence.

Martin woke up on hearing a slight rustle beside him. It was the cannon sighing. It was sighing because it was sad and weary. It saw Martin and spoke to him.

"In truth, I'm tired of making war. How wicked men are! They load me with powder and iron in order to kill one another and they drag me after them like a slave. Once, I lived in a marvelous subterranean palace; there were all sorts of metals there of splendid colors, rivers unknown to humans and tenebrous shores, Now I have the form of a cannon and I cause harm, although I'm benevolent by nature."

"We resemble one another," said Martin. "I too don't kill with a glad heart. I'm only here because of a fiancée who is waiting for me in France."

And in the silence, only interrupted at intervals by the cry of a wounded man, he told the cannon about his fiancée.

They became friends. In battle, Martin recognized the voice of the cannon, he followed it during marches, found it again in the evening, and opened his heart to it.

Napoléon had just declared war in Russia, and it was the most terrible campaign that had ever been seen.

They traversed several counties, each more astonishing than the last. The sky changed over the army's head. They marched in the midst of forests of firs, rocks, precipices and high mountains. One day, when they had fought with men carrying pikes, with fur bonnets and clothes that rendered them similar to the local trees, the cannon's wheels were broken by an enemy cannonball.

The army was in a mountainous region, on a road that overlooked a somber lake.

A general who was passing by ordered the artillerymen and the grenadiers who were present to push the canon into the lake, so that the enemy did not take possession of it in order to put their own wheels on it.

Martin was full of dolor on seeing his friend lying on the ground, but he too was obliged to push the cannon toward the lake. Seeing that, the cannon was very sad, for it was not unaware of the severe discipline that obliged Martin to do that, and it said:

"Is this conduct worthy of a friend? Because I'm wounded, you're abandoning me in these unknown mountains and only giving me this solitary lake for a tomb. What can a cannon do lying beneath these dormant waters? You're ingrate, like all men, but I forgive you because I'm your friend and I don't want the memory of this action to cause you any distress."

Having said that, the cannon rolled down the steep slope; it broke a tree, dragged a thousand stones with it, and fell with a dull noise into the water of the lake. And a long time thereafter, leaning on his rifle and bending over the place where his friend had disappeared, Martin could still hear a great sigh.

Napoléon's army traversed snowy plains where wolves and Cossacks were roaming, and Martin and all the other soldiers suffered a great deal from hunger and cold. But Martin was unhappier than the others because the snow had killed all the flowers in Russia and he could not find one to take back to his fiancée. He always fought with great bravery, in the hope of being noticed by the Emperor and finally obtaining the letter for his fiancée's parents. In any case, the supported all his woes with tranquility, because he said to himself: *One day, I'll have my recompense.*

He saved the life of an old soldier, who was naturally jovial, but whose face had been so disfigured by a cannonball that he always seemed to be weeping. They drank from the same water-bottle and were companions. The jovial old soldier told Martin a thousand pleasant stories to cheer him up, and Martin talked to him about his fiancée.

Seeing that Moscow, their capital, was about to be captured by the French, the Russians set fire to it. The flames escaping from the houses, doubtless made of wood, were so high that they rose all the way to the snowy sky and the clouds took flight, fearing that their robes of mist might catch fire.

The French were very sad, seeing that, for they had counted on finding warm houses, nourishment and beautiful Russian women in the city.

And the Emperor Napoléon said to his soldiers: "Since that's the way it is, let's return to France." And, tightly wrapped in his gray garment because of the cold, like the images engraved on gold coins, he drew away with his guard.

Martin said to the jovial old soldier: "Let's go as far as Moscow. I'll get a flower for my fiancée from some house, we'll warm ourselves a little with the heat of the blaze and we'll catch up with the army afterwards."

So they set off at a run and went into the city. The temperature there was stifling because of the burning houses. The streets were deserted. The two grenadiers ran around a random, looking for a public garden where they might have found the flower for which they were searching. But at that time, there were none in Moscow.

They were becoming discouraged when Martin finally perceived a tiny flower in a pot on a window sill. It was as white as a snowflake that had become a flower; it was sad, and it was thinking: *My God! What sudden heat! What has become of the young woman who cared for me? What a fate for a little flower to be abandoned like this and not to know anything!*

Martin picked it and put it in his buttonhole; followed by the jovial old soldier he left the city in haste, where the heat had become unbearable.

They both ran through the snow for several hours, and they were about to rejoin the army when Martin perceived that he had lost the little flower.

"Always unlucky!" he said. "Let's go back; we'll find it."

But how could such a tiny flower be perceived, lost in such a vast snowy plain?

In vain the little flower, terrified by the cold and the solitude, said: "Here I am! Here I am!" Martin and the jovial old soldier went past it twenty times without seeing it.

Then night fell. The two grenadiers looked at one another and understood their folly, thinking that they would never be able to find the French army again, because of the distance, the fog and the great rivers...

They shouted, uselessly, and ran in all directions. In the end, exhausted by fatigue, they sat down in the snow in the middle of a forest of fir-trees. And Martin aid to his companion: "Leave me, jovial old soldier. On your own, you'll catch up with the French army. Bad luck is attached to me like a spider to a fly."

The old soldier made a horrible grimace, as if he were about to burst into sobs, and he replied, laughing: "We're the playthings of destiny. These Russian landscapes please me a great deal; I find the cries of the wolves and the sound of the wind full of harmonies, and this forest, most of all, is infinitely agreeable to behold."

They went to sleep wrapped in their cloaks. Then Martin had a dream.

Someone touched his shoulder with a fingertip; he opened his eyes, sat up and saw a man motionless in the snow, who was looking at him. The moonlight filtered through the firs and Martin recognized the Emperor Napoléon with his gray coat and his marble features. He made a sign, snow crackled, branches broke, and Martin saw, to his amazement, his friend the cannon, whom he had precipitated into the lake. The Emperor leapt on to it as if on to a horse. Martin did the same and the cannon flew away with two great black wings that the grenadier had never noticed before.

A second later, Martin heard a great rumor behind him. It was the entire French my, with its Maréchals, its artillery and its cavaliers, who were galloping behind the cannon, sometimes leaping and sometimes flying. It was an extraordinary charge! How proud he was to be leading it! Suddenly, a bell rang. It was the first church in France. The canon stopped, along with the whole army, which lined up in a vast square. All the windows of the houses were decked with flags.

On the threshold of the church Martin saw his fiancée and her parents in their best clothes, and also recognized neighbors and friends. The Maréchals' horses pranced, the drums rolled and all the soldiers presented arms. How blue the sky was! How sweet his fiancée's smile was! Then Napoléon took his fiancée by the hands, and the parents and the neighbors whispered and drew themselves up proudly. At that moment, Martin heard an immense sigh. The cannon had just rolled into a precipice that had suddenly opened up.

Martin looked at Napoléon; the latter was as motionless as a statue; he had turned to marble. The houses, the crowd and the army were as transparent as glass. The Maréchals, the hussars and the artillerymen seemed to be made of a light mist, which the wind stretched and shredded. The fiancée's face was covered by a thick beard and had taken on the appearance of a frightful Cossack; the parents and the neighbors were nudging one another and laughing ironically, except for one, who resembled in a marvelous fashion the jovial old soldier, on whose face Martin remarked with amazement an unusual expression of grief.

Then he woke up and cried out in terror. His hands were bound; he were surrounded by Cossacks, who were striking him rudely with their pikes and forcing him to march in their midst.

Those men had come across the two grenadiers during the night; they had cut off the head of the jovial old soldier because they had thought him ugly, and they had taken Martin prisoner.

He asked: "What have you done with my dear companion?"

The captain of the Cossacks, in order to play with him and render his captivity crueler, replied: "It's your companion who betrayed you and delivered you to us, and now he's a Cossack too."

And the thought of that treason was a thousand times more bitter to Martin than the cold or the thrusts of the Cossacks' pikes. The shade of the jovial old soldier, who could see all that, would have liked to cry out: "They've cut off my head, Martin, otherwise I'd be with you." but he was invisible and mute, like all the shades of the dead.

Martin was locked in a high tower, from which he could only see the sky through a very narrow skylight fitted with thick iron bars. The Cossacks strove to make him suffer a great deal. They left him to endure cold and hunger, they made him believe that the French army had been destroyed, the Emperor Napoléon crucified and that France had become a Russian province. Martin, who loved his country, was greatly saddened by that.

His belief in justice did not weaken, however. He did not despair of seeing his fiancée once again some day, and being recompensed for all his woes by a little happiness.

One day, when he was gazing in a melancholy fashion at the skylight of his prison, a stork went by, and seeing him so sad, was seized by sympathy for him. She came to alight behind the iron bars and they talked.

"Can you tell me, beautiful white bird who has traveled far, whether it is true that the Emperor Napoléon has been crucified and that France is now a province of Russia?"

The stork began to laugh and replied: "You've been deceived, poor prisoner. I don't understand anything of the wars of men, but I know Napoléon well. He's still alive, and he lives, solitary, on a little island in the middle of the sea, where, no doubt, he's finally resting after long labors. France is still France, have no doubt of that. I, who inhabit the summit of towers, prefer the harmony of French bells to any music and I heard them recently singing marvelously over a joyful people in the church of Notre Dame."

The stork adopted the custom of coming every day to chat with the prisoner and they were soon linked together by a close friendship. She told him about her travels in lands where there were there are fountains, sand and palm trees, and where an eternal heat reigns. And he caressed her with his hand and the bird's heart was infinitely touched by that mark of affection.

Now, the guard, a cruel man, discovered the stork's visits. One day, without being heard, he slipped into Marin's prison at the moment when the bird, having passed her long neck through the bars, was talking to the prisoner in a low voice, saying: "My companions will be migrating to other lands soon, but if you wish, poor prisoner, I will build my nest in these gray stones in order to live with you, and I shall watch without regret their white column diminishing on the horizon."

The guard leapt forward, saber in hand, and struck so rudely that she fell dead at Martin's feet.

The latter looked for a moment, dazedly, at the flowing blood, and heard the ferocious laughter of the guard, in whose grimace he saw the ill luck of his entire life.

Then he seized a heavy key that was hanging from the man's waist and struck him such a blow, with all his might, that his skull was cleaved in two.

Martin undressed the dead guard, put on his garments, took the body of the stork under his cloak, as darkness fell he left the tower without being recognized, making an amicable salute to the Cossacks guarding the door.

He walked for a long time and arrived in a solitary place near a little wood. There he hollowed out the hard ground near an old fir-tree with his hands and he buried the white body of his faithful friend, begging her pardon from the bottom of his heart for having caused her death.

He traveled, staff in hand, in order to return to the land of France. He traversed terrible forests, and swam across rivers that were carrying ice-floes. Rain soaked his hair and beard, thorn-bushes caught his garments, pebbles lacerated his feet, and the wind tipped him into ditches. He climbed mountains, struggled against tempests, darkness and sunlight. His bad luck followed him everywhere. When he hesitated between two roads, one good and one bad, he always followed the bad one. He only knocked on the doors of inhospitable people, or if, by chance, he slept under a roof, the house collapsed or caught fire during the night.

He was never discouraged.

When I reach French soil, he thought, *I'll go to see the Emperor Napoléon. I'll tell him about all my misfortunes, and he won't fail to write he letter for my fiancée's parents.*

Once, in a forest in Germany, he was attacked by wolves, which devoured his left hand. Another time, in an outlying district of a city, he fought with beggars, who broke his teeth.

Finally, one day, while traversing a region of woods and hills, he encountered an old woodcutter who spoke to him in French.

He uttered loud cries of joy and asked him if France was far away.

The old man smiled maliciously and replied: "The frontier is at the summit of that hill. Go up to the top and you can contemplate the French countryside."

Martin ran forward; he no longer had any fatigue; he was drunk with joy.

Dusk having come, night advanced from the horizon and covered the earth with a thick veil. When Martin reached the top of the hill, his eyes could not distinguish a tree, a village or a steeple, so great was the obscurity.

It was a mild spring night. Martin thought: *Let's sleep here, and at dawn, I'll finally see my homeland.*

That dawn was never to come for him. When he woke up the next day his eyes contemplated a darkness even more intense than that of the previous night. The damp night air had rendered him blind.

He went along the roads, living on alms, finally beginning to sense the weight of his destiny.

He enquired as to the direction of Paris and headed for that city. As he was about to arrive there he heard two men sitting outside their doors, who were talking about Napoléon. He approached them and questioned them

"How can a blind grenadier reach the Emperor and ask him for a simple letter in exchange for his services?"

The two men started to laugh at his ignorance and told him that the Emperor had been a prisoner of the English on a distant island for a long time, and they were talking about him at that moment because he was near death.

Then Martin's heart broke; our hero sat down on the side of the road and wept.

He traveled; he wandered through France, but he did not seek out his own village because he knew that without Napoléon's letter, his fiancée's parents would be inflexible.

He conserved, however, a vague hope in providence.

So many woes will be compensated, he often thought.

Weary of walking, old and stopped, he stopped one day in a little town, bought a wooden bowl, and installed himself at a street corner not far from the church, asking passers-by for charity.

"Have pity on a poor blind man," he said.

He never mentioned his former status as a grenadier because he thought his decline too great.

He stayed there for thirty years. Every day, from the house against which he sat, a woman clad in black emerged in order to go to church, and every day, she deposited a sou in Martin's bowl.

The grenadier ended up recognizing her footsteps and he addressed a smile to her, for in spite of so much misery, he had remained benevolent and he did not hate those who gave him alms.

With time, the woman clad in black had been obliged to lean on a cane, and then a crutch, and the click of that crutch on the pavement of the street was a joyful song for Martin.

One day, in winter—he was then very old and his soul had become obscure with time—the lady dressed in black did not go along the street. Martin waited for her for three days in great sadness, for without him being aware of it, that tremulous tread and that sou in his bowl had become indispensable to his poor life.

After three days, an old woman came to find Martin and say to him: "The lady who put a sou in your bowl every day has asked me to bring you all these silver coins. She's just died and her soul has gone to Paradise."

"My God! My God!" said Martin. "Tell me who that lady was, who was so good. Did she have a happy life? Has she sons in the French army?"

The old woman told Martin the lady's name and added: "All her life she waited for her fiancée, who left as a grenadier with Napoléon. As she died in my arms she said: 'If he is still alive somewhere on earth, might I only see him again, even old and broken by age?"

So Martin had remained for thirty years, without knowing it, alongside his fiancée, the unique goal of his life. His bad luck had pursued him to the end. It was too much! Destiny weighed too heavily on such a poor man! He raised his fist toward the heavens and blasphemed God.

The church bells rang at full tilt, the wind caused the snow to swirl, an icy night descended upon the earth and just then, Death passed by. She saw Martin sitting on the ground at the corner of the street, stopped for a moment and touched his pale forehead with her stony finger.

Then a great light appeared to Martin. The houses, the church, the snow and everything else disappeared. He saw himself in a grenadier's uniform his rifle on his shoulder, as in the time of his youth, on a road that rose up toward Paradise. A great joy filled his heart. He heard other dead people whispering:

"In truth, that's a handsome grenadier!"

And almost all the dead were hesitating over the road to take. Martin deliberately headed for Paradise and knocked on the door without trepidation.

It opened, and Saint Peter appeared. Martin said to him: "Here I am!" thinking that he was expected.

And through the open door, Martin perceived Paradise. His mother and father were there, and his fiancée, as pretty as in her sixteenth year, the cannon, which had emerged from the lake, the faithful white stork, the jovial old soldier grimacing and winking, and all the others he had loved. And they all recognized him, being very content to see him, and beckoned to him to come.

And he also saw unfurling before him in a vast tableau, in which all the characters were animated as if they were alive, the fine actions possible and the beautiful dreams unrealized on earth. There was Napoléon's letter to his fiancée's parents; he could read it distinctly, and it contained the words: *He's a good soldier!* He perceived a long procession of people whose faces were familiar to him, and then a feast, and dancing, and he was there, holding his fiancée's hand; they were young and in love. Then he was in his house, the fire was bright; his wife was changing and rocking a child; a traveler knocked on the door, alone and covered in snow; he came in and sat down; it was Napoléon, who had come to ask his grenadier for hospitality. And that tableau, which had the movement and color of life, represented a host of other fortunate and admirable things which might have happened to the grenadier if he had not been unlucky.

Martin extended his arms. But Saint Peter said to him, lifting his key, with great severity: "Grenadier, you have blasphemed God as you died, and you have not expiated that sin. It's necessary, in consequence, that you have to go and spend a century in Purgatory."

"Have pity on me, Saint Peter," Martin replied. "I've endured great suffering, I have done no harm to anyone, and I have known nothing on earth but misfortune. I blasphemed God, but I was a poor old man whose soul was blind, like his visage. I can see all my friends gathered there in this abode and I lack the heart to think of quitting them. Forgive me, you who are a saint, and remember he tears that you shed when the cock crew."

But Saint Peter replied: "Such is the divine law."

And with that, he closed the heavy door.

"There's no justice, either on earth or in Heaven," cried a hardened sinner, whose soul was wandering in space.

And the poor grenadier, his head bowed, with his rifle on his shoulder, descended toward Purgatory, where he was to burn and suffer for another hundred years.

THE DOLL

I

There was once an actress who played comedy and drama in a great theater in Paris. She had a great deal of success and everyone applauded her enthusiastically. Listening to her on Sunday, good women dropped the chocolate and oranges they had brought and their tears flowed in abundance.

"How well she plays!" they said.

"What sincerity in the emotion!" said competent men.

My fortune is assured! thought the theater manager.

Who would have believed that little Rosette would be capable of that? thought her mother.

For she had a mother, which we can observe without causing the reader any surprise. When Rosette appeared on the stage, her face was animated marvelously, her voice had heart-rending tones, and she seemed possessed by the most ardent human passions. But as soon as the curtain came down, life seemed to abandon her; the carmine and the powder made an insensible mask on her face, she experienced nothing further, and she was indifferent to everything.

For that reason, her friends had nicknamed her "the doll." She had a rosy and regular beauty, which made one think of a perfected plaything.

And many men loved her, some out of vanity, because a portrait of her in color, in which she was represented smiling and semi-naked, was displayed near the Opéra; others because her eyes did not reflect any thought, and they assumed that that would dispense them of any intellectual effort to conquer her; others because they supposed her to be very intelligent; others without any apparent reason, because of the unknown force that obliges men to love actresses.

She gave herself very often, without sadness or pleasure, for money, for a gift, for a role or for a bouquet. She did not attach any importance to the act and was greatly astonished to see men suffering because of it.

She was ignorant of love, and only wept over petty things, having no emotions. Her mother sometimes said, in jest: "Rosette has a stone instead of a heart." And she thought that it might be true, in fact.

A poor fireman, who came to the theater every night because of the requirements of his service, saw Rosette and fell in love with her. He loved her with an infinite amour, tender and profound, as it is not customary for firemen to love. It was her voice that he heard in the raucous screech of the vehicles setting off for blazes; it as her eyes that he saw in the red windows of burning houses; flames made him think of her lips, ashes of her hair.

The fireman was twenty years old. His name was Eloi and he had a simple heart.

Oh, he thought, *I'm the most unfortunate man on earth! That celebrated actress would never consent to love a humble fireman like me!*

He suffered a great deal and had no hope.

Every evening, motionless at the foot of a stage-set that might be either a palace, a park or a street, he savored the only joy of his life, which was seeing and hearing the woman he loved declaiming and acting.

It seemed to him then that his soul was magnified, that he emerged from himself, participating in a superior life. And he remembered that he had once had an analogous sensation, one feast day, when the captain of his regiment had made a speech about the flag and the fatherland.

His love was such that he saw without sadness Rosette's face, on leaving the stage, resume the cold expression that rendered her similar to a doll. There were other thoughts that penetrated him then: the vision of a mute fay whose eyes devoid of gaze, under the lamps of the theater, poured out an exceedingly sweet enchantment.

One day, Eloi the fireman knew the greatest joy of his life. Rosette's eyes had posed on his and had caused a divine flame to penetrate into his heart. The next day and all the evenings that followed, Rosette looked at him again. And every time, her eyes spread a mysterious warmth, which troubled our hero to the point that he ran through the streets afterwards, bewildered, mad with desire and hope.

Then, one evening, he bought a little two-sou bouquet and hid it over his heart.

It's necessary to have audacity, he thought. *I'll give her this bouquet and confess my love to her. I'm not handsome, it's true, but after all, perhaps she's sensible to the prestige of the uniform.*

The performance ended. Rosette went past our hero, as usual, looked at him, and disappeared into the corridor that led to her dressing room.

This is the opportunity, Eloi said to himself, *and he slipped behind her, bouquet in hand.*

He stopped before the door, very emotional. The door was ajar, and this is the spectacle that he beheld: Rosette was sitting on the knees of an old man. He was a celebrated poet, the author of sublime tragedies, in which Rosette hoped to act.

"There's a fireman looking at us," said the celebrated poet.

"No," said Rosette, looking out into the corridor. "There's only a two-sou bouquet that someone has dropped."

II

Eloi gave up the job of fireman. He bought books and began to study with great ardor.

If I became a famous poet, he said to himself, *Rosette would love me and she would also swear an eternal love to me.*

He therefore labored to be a poet and learned how ingrate that career is. He rented a mansard in an old house where Alfred de Musset had lived in his youth, he had a lamp and a large notebook in which he wrote his verses. He frequented other poets, who had long hair and black garments like ushers; they were very learned, spending their time chatting and smoking; they were poets by the grace of God and were honored as such, but no one ever saw their writings. They laughed a great deal when Eloi asked them humbly for their opinion of his verses, and said to one another: "He's a *pompier*!"

And Eloi was ashamed, thinking that they were making allusion to his former profession.[11]

However, he worked obstinately, and as patience is the foremost of virtues, the form of his verses was gradually purified, and thoughts appeared there confusedly, possessed of a vague harmony.

And one winter evening, when Eloi was alone in his icy room, a muse saw him through the keyhole and came to sit down beside him. It was a muse of the Latin Quarter who had the custom of wandering the deserted quais around Notre Dame, in old houses. She had assisted de Musset by night in that same room; she had watched over Hégésippe Moreau agonizing in a hospital bed; she had given genius to misunderstood poets whose names are now unknown to humankind. She knew all sorts of beautiful songs and poetic stories.

She became Eloi's friend and companion. The soul of books, mute until then, emerged from the pages and whirled around his head, alive and delectable. Our hero's mind filled with extraordinary fictions and charming tales.

He was about to take his tales to the *Mercure de France*, which was then the greatest periodical of the era. Other poets wrote for it, natives of America, Holland, Rumania and Turkey. In those lands there are to muses, as in France; they persisted nevertheless, without any reason in writing poems devoid of harmony, and even of sense. So Eloi's verses, dictated

---

[11] The French *pompier*, which usually means "fireman" when used as a noun, is also used as an adjective meaning "pompous" or "pretentious," and can be used as a noun to refer to a person of that inclination.

by a genuine muse of the Latin Quarter, seemed admirable to everyone. Many of them were published and their author became illustrious.

The director of the Comédie-Française, having heard mention of Eloi, wrote to him in haste to bring him a play for the theater. He was just finishing a tragedy, the principal role in which had been written for Rosette. He went to the Comédie-Française joyfully, his manuscript under his arm, and when the concierge tried to prevent him from going in he replied with pride: "The director has written to me and I'm going to read him my tragedy, the principal role in which will be played by the celebrated actress Rosette."

"It's a fine work, worthy of our great literary tradition," said the director of the Comédie-Française, when he had heard Eloi's play. "We'll put it on right away. You're certainly a great poet."

And he rang in order to send for the costume-designer and the set-designer.

Then Eloi expressed his desire to see Rosette act in his play.

"That's an unfortunate coincidence," the director replied. "I received a letter from her this morning in which she informs me that she's giving up the theater. She's been living with an explorer for some time and is about to depart with him on a long voyage. In truth, women are strange!"

Someone knocked on the door. It was the prompter, the stage-manager, the costume-designer and the painter, who wanted to put themselves at the disposal of the author of the new play.

But Eloi had risen to his feet, prey to an extraordinary agitation. He cried: "You can go home, Messieurs; I apologize for having disturbed you. I'm not a great poet, my verses are bad, since it won't be Rosette who will speak them. Refrain from putting on the play without her. The audience would die of boredom and you'd blush to have had anything to do with such great stupidity."

With that, he left precipitately.

"Poets are singular," said the prompter.

"But I've never seen one like that," said the director of the Comédie-Française.

III

Eloi discovered a few days later the name of the explorer who was taking Rosette away. He had just left with her for Marseille. Eloi bid farewell to the muse who had been his companion and had enabled him to know the joys of thought. The latter was very sad, and said to him:

"Modern days are cruel to muses, Where are the May nights of old, the lovers in crinolines and the poets with blue frock-coats in Balzac's mansards? Disinterest, love of poetry, youth of the heart, what has become of you? Ingrate friend, my last hope, you're leaving me too. But I don't want to lavish my treasures any longer on wretched souls. I know an old well near the Odéon, in an ancient courtyard. Its blue water will be my tomb; and if, later, a face that I recognize leans over the rim, perhaps my light form will float between the stones like a testimony of the beauty that does not die."

But Eloi was thinking about Rosette and was not touched by that speech.

He took the train and went to Marseille. He was already too late. Rosette and the explorer had just left on a ship bound or Africa. He embarked in his turn on another ship that had the same destination. His surprise was great, for he was contemplating the sea for the first time; the sea breeze stirred his hair and filled his lungs, and he sensed his soul enlarge all the way to the horizons that he perceived in the distance, bathed in blue vapor.

In the evening, sitting on the deck, he made little paper boats, which he threw into the sea in order to watch hem draw away in the waves. The paper that he used was that of the manuscript of his tragedy. Every little boat carried away a few verses, which the fish came to read, mocking them, for fish are ignorant of the beautiful things conceived by humans. Then the little boats descended to the sea-bed, in a strange light, and every verse became a little submarine flower, a flower that would never see the light of day again.

In Algiers, Eloi learned that the explorer and Rosette had already departed in search of the great lakes that are found in Africa. Then he cut a traveler's staff and set forth. He traveled, he got to know the immense land.

His footprints were impressed in the desert sands, he drank from springs that resembled those of the Bible, slept under palm trees, and ate unknown fruits. He was bitten by snakes, battled with wild beasts, and crossed rivers full of crocodiles swimming, feeling their damp skin on his body.

On his way he found traces of the explorer and Rosette, who were traveling with a numerous armed troop. Camp fires and paths traced through the forest guided his steps.

One evening when he was asleep, savage negroes captured him and tied him solidly to the foot of a tree. Then they lit a great fire, resolved to cook their prisoner and eat him, for they were cannibals. Eloi understood their intention and judged his fate very bitter.

Before dying, he cried Rosette's name one last time, and suddenly, at that name, all the negroes uttered cries of joy, prostrated themselves before him, started dancing and hastened to break his bonds. Eloi thought that perhaps all those men had conceived a simple and marvelous amour for Rosette, and that he owed his deliverance to the magic of her name.

He always carried with him a portrait of the object of his love. He showed it to them. Then the negroes threw themselves on the ground; some struck themselves with their weapons. They carried Eloi in triumph to their village and appointed him king.

Eloi's reign only lasted three days because, after that time, he fled the palace in order to resume his errant course. And he had more adventures without number among extraordinary peoples. He was mistaken for a god by people of superhuman stature who were good and child-like. He was reduced to harsh slavery by other people who were dwarfish and had enormous heads on their debilitated bodies.

Finally, he saw the towers of a civilized city on the edge of the sea. Rosette and the explorer had already passed through it, but no one knew for which country they had headed.

Eloi embarked again and wandered at hazard over the world.

He saw Egypt and its pyramids; the Red Sea, in which enormous sharks swam and where an unbearable heat reigns; Persia, where the sabers and warriors are curved in a circular arc; India where there are ferocious tigers and where domesticated elephants dance to the sound of a flute like children; and the island of Ceylon, where men have oily skin and long hair like that of women, in which they plant tortoiseshell combs. He ate rice with the Chinese, made drawings with the Japanese, great lovers of that art, and dressed in furs in Siberia.

One evening he was traversing a glacial region of that country and had begun to despair of ever finding those for whom he was searching when he perceived a man lying in the snow. He was not moving, and his face seemed crystalline, like the flowers of pools imprisoned in the ice. Eloi drew closer, and saw that he was dead.

One might think that he was an explorer, our hero thought.

Then he saw that Rosette's name had been traced in the snow, and he understood. He understood that the latter had doubtless passed this way and that she had abandoned the body of her dead friend without a sepulcher.

Eloi considered the explorer. An obscure fraternity connected him to that man. He dug a hole in the snow with his staff and laid him in it.

Then he set out for France.

IV

Having returned to Paris, Eloi bought a newspaper in order to see what the principal events were that had agitated his country in his absence. There was much mention there of Rosette. Her voyages had rendered her illustrious. She had returned with all kinds of weapons, collections and riches, with which she filled her house. The newspapers published her portrait, with lavish praises, and scarcely devoted a line to the death of the explorer.

What can I do, Eloi said to himself, *to get to know her and to make her love me? She's followed an explorer, but if I were to make an extraordinary invention, she would certainly distinguish me among men.*

He studied science. He familiarized himself with the mysteries of calculation, how gases combined, under what laws the stars moved. His mind, which travel had cultivated, became more skillful in understanding every day. Soon, by means of his experiments and his labor, he acquired a great notoriety among specialists in mechanics, but people strove to harm him because he had not emerged from any official school.

He invented a dirigible balloon and the newspapers talked about him, described his projects and published his plans. One day, having completed the construction of his balloon, he summoned the academies and official personages to witness its first aerial voyage. The Champ-de-Mars was filled by an immense crowd, and everyone said: "This man does honor to science and France."

Eloi was moved by so much glory, and in his heart, he paid homage to Rosette. He had prepared a large flag that he was going to unfurl when the balloon rose into the air, and on which he had written Rosette's name in letters of fire.

He climbed into the nacelle and gave the signal. But at that moment, Eloi perceived Rosette, who was leaning over of a balcony and seemed to be looking in his direction. He made a movement of surprise and joy. His hand caused the rudder of the balloon to deviate and it shattered into a thousand pieces on the chimney of a tall house.

Eloi was pulled out of the wreckage safe and sound; the academicians and the inventors of other balloons were filled with delight.

What can I do now, Eloi thought, *to succeed in reaching Rosette?*

He started wandering miserably around his dwelling. In a neighboring tavern, he made the acquaintance of a fat and red-faced individual who was Rosette's coachman. He questioned the man, who said:

"How singular women are, Monsieur. I, who am speaking, have been called by a profession to many good fortunes in the elegant world, and I take no vanity from it. It's not the man that the women I've served have loved in me but the inferior class to which I belong. Rosette, for example, whose carriage I drive and whose horses I care for, is only capable of weakness for the rich banker who pays for her luxury, or for her coachman. I shan't say any more; a natural delicacy forbids me to do so."

I'll become a rich banker then, Eloi said to himself. He left the tavern and went to the Bourse.

He still had five francs on him. He bought a share that was greatly depreciated at that moment. He came back every day, mingled with the crowd of men who live there, shouted and counted like them. The share he had bought for five francs was worth ten thousand some time thereafter. He hastened to sell it in order to buy others which he sold again. He soon became very rich, and his rapid fortune won the admiration of everyone.

He had a fine town house, servants, carriages and a yacht.

The banker who lived with Rosette, who had had to make considerable expenses in order to purchase dresses, jewels and furniture, saw his affairs decline sharply. Having heard mention of Eloi as a very skillful speculator, he came to propose a partnership to him. That was what the later ardently desired. He therefore accepted, glad to be able to participate in Rosette's life.

He was reaching his life's goal; he was about to be able to speak to the woman he loved, to tell her about his efforts, his long toil.

"Come and dine with me at Rosette's," the banker said to Eloi one evening.

And Eloi went with his associate, trembling. When he went into the drawing room and was introduced to the woman he loved, he saw nothing and heard nothing. The furniture danced around him and he had in his memory the marvelous vision of the theater where he had once been a fireman and where Rosette had acted. It was so precise that he heard the three bells, and the voice of the stage-manager speaking to the cast members.

Rosette pronounced a few politely banal words, and no attention appeared on her waxen face.

The meal concluded and a letter arrived for the banker; he was summoned elsewhere for a very important business meeting. He excused himself and left, leaving Eloi with Rosette.

They chatted about indifferent things; they were alone; Eloi's dream was therefore realized. Words dictated by his heart pressed upon his lips.

Thanks to you I've emerged from my obscure condition; my intelligence has awakened, I've suffered, I've thought, I've striven toward superior things. I've known poetry and its marvels, voyages and the unfurling of the horizons of the world, science and fortune. You are the ambition and the motive force of my life, my sadness, my pride and my hope. Let me put a kiss on your lips, in order that it should be the seal of the virtues that you have inspired.

But Eloi did not pronounce those useful and veritable words, because a rich man cannot say the things that a poor man can, and our hero's heart was different since fortune had smiled on him.

"I'm from a noble and ancient family and my opulence is extreme," he said. "I have a house finer than this one, servants, carriages and a yacht. If you would like to augment your luxury, I will give you jewels of an inestimable price, and your magnificence will surpass that which you have seen until now. 'There goes the richest woman in Paris,' people will say when they see you. That will be realized if you will only give me a little love in exchange."

"Of love," said Rosette, "there is none in my heart and I cannot give you any. You talk to me about your wealth. That wearies me now as I once wearied of the theater and voyages. Life appears to me to be monotonous and empty; all the men I have known have only inspired indifference in me. I regret very bitterly the love of a fireman that I once saw in the theater and who dropped a two-sour bouquet outside my dressing room one evening. In truth, he is the only man that I could have loved."

Eloi stood up, took his leave of Rosette and left precipitately. He wandered through the night like a madman. In the morning he sat down on a bench in an avenue, and the vanity of everything appeared to him clearly. It was in his nature, however, never to despair.

He saw his valet de chambre, who had come in search of him, anxiously.

Eloi ran toward him. "I make you a gift," he cried, "of my house, my yacht and my entire fortune. Give me a piece of paper quickly, so that I can sign a definitive donation. But believe me, if you love a woman, know that luxury and riches and everything one can procure, are poor weapons with which to conquer her."

With that he drew away, leaving the valet de chambre full of surprise.

He headed toward a firemen's barracks. There was one in the neighborhood and they had a vacancy for a fireman. Eloi was hired on the spot. He found one of his old comrades there, who said to him: "You haven't succeeded in life, since you're returning to your former estate?"

"That's true, I haven't succeeded," Eloi said.

And that evening, in his shiny helmet and his leather belt, he headed for Rosette's house.

As he approached it, however, he saw people running and a great glow in the sky,. He heard people shouting: "Fire!" and ran in the direction from which they were coming. It was Rosette's house that was burning.

The flames were rising toward the sky in a whirlwind. The crowd was watching, full of admiration and terror. His fireman's uniform permitted Eloi to fray a path to the foot of the house, where there were other firemen. Then he took a ladder, leaned it against the wall, climbed it, reached a window and launched himself inside the house. The floor was creaking and the smoke obscured his vision. He traversed several rooms in vain. Finally, he saw Rosette. The fire had doubtless surprised her in her sleep; she was moaning, extending her arms toward Eloi and seemed to be imploring him.

The light of the blaze illuminated Rosette's face marvelously. Finally, he was about to embrace the woman who was the cause of his elevation, his intelligence and his will; he was about to save the woman he loved from death.

The heat was increasingly great. Eloi took Rosette in his arms, and then perceived that she was, in truth, no more than a doll, a poor waxen doll who was melted softly by the ardor of the blaze, and whose glass eyes, like two blue tears, fell at his feet with a dry click.

THE GOATHERD KING

"Little Eloi, who are descending the mountain followed by your goats, singing a love song, you must go to consult the witch who lives up there in the trunk of a fir-tree hollowed out by the storm. In truth, she knows everything, the past and the future. Tell her that I, Gudule, who was present on the day of your birth, saw a bloody comet in the sky that day; I saw it with my own eyes for the space of a second. Add that the toads in the pond began to cry out in a strange fashion. Those are marvelous things of which she will give you a veritable explanation, from which you will derive great profit."

Thus spoke old Gudule to little Eloi. And the next day, by way of a lost path on the mountain, he went, followed by his goats, to the solitary place where the witch lived, in the trunk of a hollow fir-tree.

The witch had a very bad reputation throughout the land. She had, it was said, turned many young folk away from the straight path. She had been amorous in her time. Eloi knew that and he was full of apprehension, fearing that she might demand too much of him in exchange for her predictions.

He found her in the process of mixing the blood of a scorpion with the juice of crushed herbs. She was old and frightful to behold. On perceiving Eloi she darted a glance at the bed of ferns where he was accustomed to sleep and her face expressed a great melancholy.

And when Eloi had interrogated her, she traced figures on the ground while pronouncing magic words. Meanwhile, she smiled at the little goatherd and twice she took his hand.

"Little goatherd," she said, finally, "Little goatherd, you shall be a king."

And, auguring for herself the favorable meaning of her words, she tried to draw Eloi toward her.

But the latter had no more to learn. He pulled away and fled, joyfully, over the mountain.

He would be a king! One does not learn such news without conceiving pride. His condition as a goatherd suddenly seemed despicable to him, and he thought that he could no longer guard the goats on the mountain. He therefore went to find the master in whose pay he was and he said to him:

"Here's my herdsman's crook, I'm returning it to you. But keep it preciously. You'll be able to sell it dear when I've become the greatest king in the world and I shall traverse the land with a thousand cavaliers and a beautiful princess in a white robe."

Little Eloi has gone mad, thought the man.

A goat that loved little Eloi dearly followed him on the path as he drew away, but he chased it away by throwing stones at it, thinking that it was inappropriate that a future king should be followed by a humble goat.

Eloi encountered his fiancée and said to her:

"I'm leaving this region and going to the capital of the realm in order to favor and hasten destiny, for I'm going to be a king. Naturally, I'll be obliged to marry the Princess of Bavaria or the Spanish Infanta, in accordance with the politics of the moment, but I'll appoint you as a maid of honor in the court and your apartments will be next to mine in the royal palace."

And the fiancée burst into tears.

On the way, Eloi admired the prosperity of the land that he was traversing and rejoiced in thinking that all of it would soon be part of his domains. He even took note of a château that seemed to him to be very favorably situated, in order to make it a residence later where he would come with his court.

He soon arrived in Paris and headed for the king's palace. The sovereign had a daughter of great beauty. Eloi saw her passing in her carriage and thought:

Doubtless that's the instrument of my fortune. She'll fall in love with me and I'll marry her, and thus the witch's prediction will be fulfilled.

In order to make her fall in love with him he went every evening, at the same time, to post himself close to the palace, and watch the king's daughter go past. After a few days he thought he recognized by certain signs that the heart of the princess had been touched by amour. Once, she had designated him, smiling, to her jester, and the next day, he clearly saw her sending him a kiss with her fingertips.

The princess loved him, and he would be king, but it was necessary to hasten events. During the night he scaled the wall that enclosed the park of the king's gardens and headed for a place where a light was shining. It was the princess's window, slightly open to the night air.

She's thinking about me and waiting for me, Eloi said to himself. *The time has come to act.*

And he entered the princess's bedroom resolutely.

A great scream rang out. Eloi recoiled, full of horror. The princess did not love him, or, if she did love him, it was in a strange fashion. She was in the arms of her jester; she was holding him tightly embraced, and terror mingled with amour rendered the latter's face simultaneously grotesque and pitiful.

A chamberlain came running and went to inform the king that two men were in the princess's bedroom. There was a great scandal; Eloi was put in prison, judged and condemned to be hanged.

That did not frighten him at all. He had too much sentiment of the grandeur of his destiny.

"Monsieur Jailer," he said to his guard, on the eve of the execution, "it is written that one day I shall be king. A witch predicted it. She had no interest in lying to me; it is marked in the stars. Let me escape, and when the scepter has finally fallen to me, I won't forget you and I'll appoint you minister of police, which is the highest rank you can attain."

The jailer had no chance of ameliorating his lot. He thought that a man who had been found in the princess's bedroom was a connection worth having, and he let him escape.

I've taken a false path, Eloi said to himself. *It's not by amour that I'll arrive at conquering my kingdom but by war.*

Let's accomplish great military exploits, and once I'm a general in chief, it will be easy for me to stage a coup d'état. *Then the king's daughter will repent bitterly of having neglected me, and perhaps I'll marry her out of generosity.*

He joined the army and made war. He battled with great courage. He was the first to assault fortresses; he underwent great proofs; he was wounded several times. But he was pursued by bad luck. He great deeds were not noticed by anyone. He remained obscure in the host of combatants and when the war was over he had not won the slightest promotion or the slightest distinction.

The coup d'état *is impossible, he said to himself. The witch didn't lie, though. Perhaps it isn't the land of France of which I'm to become king. Let's travel, and perhaps, on the way I'll encounter an empty throne on to which I'll only have to climb.*

The he traveled over the immense world. He climbed mountains, passed over seas, and respired over arid sands the intoxication of his ambition. He saw innumerable peoples, but they all had kings who governed them harshly. He was flagellated in Constantinople, circumcised in Jerusalem, and attached elsewhere to a furious horse that was launched into the desert. Remembering Mazeppa, he had some hope then, but it was in vain; the people who rescued him reduced him to slavery. Later, he had another disappointment when a negro tribe shut him in a palace with all kinds of precious dishes and slaves to serve him. Alas, it was not to appoint him king; he was able to escape on the very day when they were going to eat him.

The years passed, his hair went white; his condition was still that of a beggar.

What! he thought. *The witch lied, then? Old Gudule cannot have seen a bloody comet in the sky, on the day of my birth, or heard the toads crying strangely?*

He was still walking, seeking his kingdom. He became very old. He arrived, one evening, in a mountain village, and he was so weary of the errant life that he knocked on the door of a house and hired himself out as a herdsman. He was given a gray cloak, a long staff and a herd of goats to guard.

He climbed the mountain, and was full of astonishment to hear the trees murmuring, which he recognized in spite of his old age. Then he looked from a distance at the paths descending the mountain and recognized his homeland.

His shadow was projected a long way, immense and admirable designed. And that shadow was strange. The staff that Eloi was carrying in his hand looked like a scepter, the bushy hair around his had made a crown, his gray cloak resembled a royal mantle; in sum, that shadow seemed to be the shadow of a king. The goatherd considered it, stupefied, and an old crow on rock started to sing in its own language: "The fish is master of the stream, the crow reigns over the forest, and the goatherd is the king of his flock."

Then Eloi understood his error, and wept.

THE LAST SIREN

"Beautiful flowers for your little friend...," said an old woman to Jean Noël, holding out a bouquet of roses.

And Jean Noël took the bouquet and gave it to his friend. As he put his hand into his pocket to pay the flower-seller he felt that the coin he took out was the last one. That coin was a golden louis. Jean Noël looked at it for a second; the setting sun made the metal shine with a gleam that seemed to our hero to be of inestimable beauty. He gave the coin to the old woman and thought:

I've lived mindfully and without counting. Life has been a happy dream for me. And this is the supreme reality. For the last time, I shall shake the hand of Rosette, my mistress. I've consumed all my fortune; I've spent all the money that my friends and my father's friends were capable of lending me. Let's accomplish without sadness and without regret the sole gratuitous action that I can accomplish henceforth.

"Let's go to dinner," said Rosette. "I'm very hungry."

Jean Noël smiled. Nearby there was an expensive restaurant where gypsies played violins and which was full of beautiful and elegant people.

"Go in there and wait for me," he said. "I need, this very instant, a volume of the history of philosophy that is at home, in order to elucidate a certain point, doubtful in my mind, regarding the life of Plato."

"Plato is insupportable," said Rosette. "Hurry up."

They separated. Rosette went into the restaurant. Night fell.

Jean Noël went down the Avenue de l'Opéra lightly, saluted the Théâtre Français and reached the Seine. A great rumor resounded. Trams with huge red and green eyes were circulating, screeching and huffing. The Institut extended its solemn shadow. Jean Noël had a moment of sadness on thinking that he would never be seated in that monument, as an old man. But he was consoled by the thought that Rosette would wait in vain all evening in the restaurant, and he would thus be avenged for her lies and deceits.

He had accustomed himself a long time ago to the idea of death. However, he hesitated between the Pont des Arts and the Pont Neuf. He finally chose the Pont des Arts, remembering that one summer day, a young woman passing over it with her mother had smiled at him. He reviewed that charming and disinterested memory and thought that, in sum, his life had been unexpected and happy.

The bridge was deserted. The black water was splashing down below and, meekly, he let himself fall.

There was a second of frightful anguish; confusedly, he heard a voice say: "How mad that man is!"

It was a fish that was passing by. Jean Noël struggled, thought inexplicably about the watch that he had in his waistcoat pocket, suddenly gripped by the urge to know the exact time, and then lost consciousness.

When he woke up, an exquisite music was resounding. It was a song, the song of a human voice, but a voice softer than any of those he had ever heard.

Is it possible, he thought, *that the fictions of religion are true? Am I in the paradise of Christians; am I going to see God the Father; is it the voice of the angels that I can hear? How can I be here, a man who doesn't believe in God and accomplished on earth a thousand sins in which I rejoiced?*

He opened his eyes, and his surprise was enormous. He was lying in a subterranean cave, on a bed of heaped-up fabrics, in the midst of objects of every sort, which rendered the place similar to both a museum and a brigand's lair. There were weapons, men's garments, sparkling jewels and chipped statues. And beside him, a woman of marvelous beauty was lying and singing.

She had put her arms around Jean Noël's neck, and he could feel the quivering of her skin. He could see that the skin in question was incomparably white and pleasant to the touch.

Long blonde hair streamed like a delightful wave over our hero's face and hands.

He made a movement to get up, but then the woman stopped singing, the grip of her arms tightened, and Jean Noël felt upon his own lips the caress of two moist, profound lips that enabled him to know a kiss softer than all the kisses he had known on earth.

Shortly thereafter, when their embrace relaxed, Jean Noël, full of astonishment, pleasure and bliss, spoke as follows:

"I certainly cannot believe that I have entered into the supernatural domain of death. I cannot imagine it so sweet. A purely terrestrial grace ornaments your face. But tell me, by means of what combination of circumstances, having thrown myself from the height of the Pont des Arts into the profound Seine, am I savoring your presence and your kisses in this unknown place?"

"That's men all over," she replied. "Always wanting to know! Thus, they kill a little of their happiness every day, Do I care about your name and your life? But no matter; you shall know everything. I'm the one who saved you as you were about to perish under the water, and who brought you here to my subterranean dwelling. I'm not a woman. Know that here, in the very heart of Paris, not far from the place you call the Louvre, a short distance from the temple of stone and iron full of strange monsters known as the Gare d'Orsay, the last of the sirens lives!"

As she spoke these words she drew side the veil that covered her, and Jean Noël, stupefied, was able to see that half of her body was covered in scales and similar in form and color to that of a fish.

"All my companions have been dead for a long time. And I, the last of my race, have fled the sad modern seas and swum up this river, for the sight and the company of men has always been necessary to our life. Sirens are amorous; they need caresses and kisses. But since you have been traversing the waves in high iron ships, the tempests have been very rare that permitted me to hold a living mariner in my arms. When my last sister died, the solitude was too burdensome for me and I came here I watch the drowned pass by with their glaucous eyes and their open arms.

"I see some who have been thrown involuntarily into the water with knives in their breasts. I see some who are lamentable and ugly, and excite my pity. There are the bodies of little children who have hardly seen the sun, and whose mothers have thrown them into the water immediately. Often, I've seen madmen throw themselves from the height of bridges, and I've been able, as I did for you, to collect them and save them. I've known their amour. They've told me their stories. There were gamblers, ambitious men, and beggars. There were lovers who were committing suicide because they had been abandoned by their mistress. The kisses of those were the best; the bitterness of tears was mingled with them, as well as I know not what terrible ardor engendered by the desire to forget. I can say without pride that I've often consoled them for their chagrins..."

"I can easily believe that," replied Jean Noël.

"Once, there was a poet who read me his works. They caused me great tedium, for I heard no art in his words. His verses spoke of nothing but amour, and I saw with surprise, at the first kiss, that he was unfamiliar with it. But I educated him, and it was drunk on caresses that he left my dwelling..."

Jean Noël made a movement of surprise.

"I divine your thought," said the siren. "You're astonished that the poet of whom I'm speaking left my arms. You share the prejudices of your fellows regarding me and my race. You believe that we cause those we attract toward us to die. That is an unjust calumny; it is reported in the voyages of Ulysses by the old poet Homer. That storyteller, famous among you, was a liar. He slandered us because he was blind, because he could not contemplate us, and one detests the good things that one cannot enjoy. We are, on the contrary, good and compassionate, and I shall give you proof of it. Take from among my riches those that you desire; I'll take you out of this cave and out of the water, and you'll be free."

Full of joy, Jean Noël, to whom the proximity of death had rendered an appetite for life, thanked the siren effusively. He took a purse of gold and a precious ring, and exchanged a last kiss with the person who had saved him.

"Adieu," she said, "my lover of an hour. Be happy, but sometimes think, as you go along the bank of the river, that between the black waters and the screech of the locomotives, her senses burning with desire for beings of a different race, the last of the amorous sirens is wandering in the darkness."

A nocturnal wind was blowing. Jean Noël found himself back on the bank of the Seine. His garments were wet. He had a purse of gold in his pocket and a precious ring on his finger, made of a pearl similar to a teardrop.

Was it a dream or a reality? he wondered.

At a slow pace he went back to the restaurant, where Rosette was waiting for him. She was still there, a little anxious and very irritated, but he did not listen to her reproaches.

"I was delayed reading the life of Plato," he said.

It was midnight.

"That's too implausible. I've had a dream."

They went home. Rosette did not remain rancorous for long. She said to him: "I forgive you!" Then she kissed him and pressed herself against him.

But Jean Noël, having pushed her away for the first time, understood then that he had not had a dream, and that he had known the amour of the last siren.

JEANNET'S THREE PROFESSIONS

That evening, Clodoche the cobbler called his three sons and spoke to them thus:

"Although I nail clogs all day long, I can't succeed in earning my living and yours. People don't want to recognize the importance of having their feet shod, since they give me so little money in exchange for the beautiful clogs I make for them. In any case, it isn't just that you live without working. Leave, then, to seek your fortune in the world. I shall try to forget, to the sound of my hammer, the chagrin of your departure."

And the three sons, having embraced their father, set forth along the road.

Now Jeannet, the youngest, who was much the most intelligent, was detested because of that by his two elders.

So, when they were alone, far from Clodoche's house, they started to throw stones at their brother, and chased him away, obliging him to take another road.

He's only fifteen, they thought. *He'll never get out of difficulty, and we'll be rid of him.*

Very sad, Jeannet went on his way. He walked for several days, and at the end of that time, the air round him resonated with the noise of clarions and drums. It was an army going to war.

"Where are you going, little man?" said the drum-major, who was marching at the head.

"I'm seeking my fortune," Jeannet replied.

"Come with us, then. You'll see great battles and you'll enter behind me into captured cities."

So Jeannet learned the profession of the soldier. He did not have much difficulty, for he was naturally brave. He soon knew how to handle an harquebus and a sword.

Now, the army was stopped by a fortress of extreme height. The enemies, hidden behind the battlements, were exterminating the attackers. They were about to fight one final battle.

"It's necessary to place this ladder against the fortress," said the general, "But who will dare to get close enough?"

Jeannet seized he ladder and launched himself forward first in the attack. He succeeded in placing it in a good spot and was the first to climb it. His companions followed him and, thanks to him, the fortress was taken.

The war ended; Jeannet left the army. When he took his leave of the general, the latter said to him: "You've certainly been a good soldier, and to thank you, I'll make you a gift. Take this rope ladder in memory of the one that you used to mount the assault on the fortress, and put it on your back. An enchanter gave it to me to give to the most valiant. Every time you throw it against a wall, no matter how high it is, it will enable you to reach the top."

Jeannet took the ladder, said adieu to the general, and went away.

He soon reached a big city, and there he engaged himself as an apprentice to a tailor. He worked hard and learned to make garments.

Now, the governor of the city, who was about to get married, had it announced that he would give a rich reward to the master tailor who brought him the most beautiful suit for his wedding day.

The tailor in whose house Jeannet worked was very sad; old age had weakened his eyesight and he could not attempt to win the prize. But Jeannet worked so hard and so well that the suit he sowed with his hands was judged the most beautiful of all, and his master was the winner. A year had gone by; Jeannet, weary of the sedentary life, decided to leave.

To thank him, he old tailor gave him some scissors as a reward.

"Look after them carefully," he added, "for they're enchanted, and in young fingers they can cut stone and iron as easily as silk or cloth."

Jeannet put the scissors in his pocket and continued his journey.

He went past an old solitary castle where an astrologer lived who was standing outside the door at the time, dreaming.

"Stop," he said to Jeannet, on seeing him go by. "Would you like to study the movement of the stars with me? I need a pupil at present. I'm making a map of the sky, which will contain all the planets; you can help me. Come in. You'll see that science is a beautiful thing."

Jeannet lived there for a year and worked with the astrologer. He was the one who drew up the star map, because the astrologer was distracted, and confused the stars with one another. Jeannet even discovered a comet for which his master had been searching in vain for a long time.

In spite of the latter's supplications however, he decided to go back to his father's house.

When he left, to thank him, the astrologer gave him a marvelous telescope that permitted him to see at an extraordinary distance and through opaque objects.

All these gifts don't enable their man to live, thought Jeannet. *My father will scarcely be content when he sees me return with scissors, a ladder and a telescope.*

When he arrived close to the cobbler's house, he learned that the daughter of the king had been abducted by a powerful genie, who had taken her to a tower of prodigious height, built in the middle of the sea, where he kept her night and day. The hand of the princess was promised to whoever could set her free.

Jeannet decided to attempt the adventure. He learned that a host of men of all conditions had departed with the same aim and had never come back, but that did not frighten him. He took a small boat and started rowing in the direction that had been indicated to him.

He rowed all day, and at nightfall he perceived an enormous shadow in the distance outlined in the sky. It was the genie's tower.

I'll never succeed in freeing the unfortunate princess, he said to himself. *That tower is too high.*

However, he had the idea of examining it with the astrologer's telescope. And he saw the king's daughter through the stones of which it was built, who was very beautiful and very sad.

He also saw the genie, who was frightful to behold and who slept in the large room in which the princess was in chains.

Jeannet rowed on and arrived at the foot of the tower. He threw his ladder against the stone that was beaten by the waves.

The ladder grew of its own accord and reached the summit of the tower, where the young man was in a trice. He went down a dark stairway and went into the room where he princess and the genie were.

The genie was woken up by the noise he made and was about to strike Jeannet with his wand when our hero remembered the scissors of his former master the tailor. He took them out, and with a single snip, he cut off the genie's head, which he threw into the sea. Then he cut through the princess's chain easily, and took her down to the boat.

The princess put a ring on Jeannet's finger to thank him. But the sea was rough, the darkness thick, and it was necessary to get back to the shore. They both employed all their strength. Finally, the boat reached land at daybreak.

The first fisherman they met recognized the young man and cried: "Great God! The king's daughter has been freed!"

The news spread so rapidly through that he adventure was known before they arrived at the palace, where the monarch immediately had a great feast prepared to welcome them. All the ladies and gentlemen put on their best clothes.

After such a long journey, though, Jeannet was very badly dressed, and he was refused entry to the castle. He was not embarrassed for so little and pushing the high chamberlain aside, he went in by force, shouting: "Make way! Make way! I'm the son of the cobbler Clodoche, and I'm bringing back the king's daughter!"

A short time afterwards, the old cobbler Clodoche, dressed in a beautiful suit, went out full of joy. He was going to attend the wedding of his son Jeannet and the princess. He would no longer have to make clogs except to distract himself. As for the other two sons, no one ever heard mention of them, and as they were nasty and idle, no one in the land cared about them, except for Clodoche, who mourned them for a long time, because he had an excellent heart.

Jeannet's adventures became famous. The people rejoiced in having a prince skilled in all professions, who could equally well be a soldier, a scholar or a tailor.

And fathers, telling this story to their children added by way of conclusion: "You see, my son, that it matters little what estate one chooses; one always succeeds when one is active and hard-working; as a soldier, one wins battles; as a scholar, one discovers marvelous things; as a modest artisan, one is useful to one's fellow citizens, providing footwear if one is a cobbler and clothes if one is a tailor. And one always marries the king's daughter, which tells you, more simply, that one finds happiness by doing one's duty well."

SF & FANTASY

Adolphe Alhaiza. *Cybele*

Alphonse Allais. *The Adventures of Captain Cap*

Henri Allorge. *The Great Cataclysm*

Guy d'Armen. *Doc Ardan: The City of Gold and Lepers; The Troglodytes of Mount Everest/The Giants of Black Lake; The Abominable Snowman*

G.-J. Arnaud. *The Ice Company*

André Arnyvelde. *The Ark; The Mutilated Bacchus*

Charles Asselineau. *The Double Life*

Henri Austruy. *The Eupantophone; The Olotelepan; The Petitpaon Era*

Barillet-Lagargousse. *The Final War*

Barbot de Villeneuve.*The Naiads/Beauty & The Beast*

Cyprien Bérard. *The Vampire Lord Ruthwen*

S. Henry Berthoud. *Martyrs of Science; The Angel Asrael*

Aloysius Bertrand. *Gaspard de la Nuit*

Richard Bessière. *The Gardens of the Apocalypse; The Masters of Silence*

Chevalier de Béthune. *The World of Mercury*

Albert Bleunard. *Ever Smaller*

Félix Bodin. *The Novel of the Future*

Pierre Boitard. *Journey to the Sun*

Louis Boussenard. *Monsieur Synthesis*

Alphonse Brown. *City of Glass; The Conquest of the Air*

Émile Calvet. *In a Thousand Years*

André Caroff. *The Terror of Madame Atomos; Miss Atomos; The Return of Madame Atomos; The Mistake of Madame Atomos; The Monsters of Madame Atomos; The Revenge of Madame Atomos; The Resurrection of Madame Atomos; The Mark of Madame Atomos; The Spheres of Madame Atomos; The Wrath of Madame Atomos* (w/M. & Sylvie Stéphan)

Jean Carrère. *The End of Atlantis*

Félicien Champsaur. *Homo-Deus; The Human Arrow; Nora, The Ape-Woman; Ouha, King of the Apes; Pharaoh's Wife*

Didier de Chousy. *Ignis*

Jules Clarétie. *Obsession*

Jacques Collin de Plancy. *Voyage to the Center of the Earth*

Michel Corday. *The Eternal Flame; The Lynx* (w/André Couvreur)

André Couvreur. *Caresco, Superman; The Exploits of Professor Tornada* (3 vols.); *The Necessary Evil*
Gaston Danville. *The Perfume of Lust*
Camille Debans. *The Misfortunes of John Bull*
Captain Danrit. *Undersea Odyssey*
C. I. Defontenay. *Star (Psi Cassiopeia)*
Charles Derennes. *The People of the Pole*
Georges Dodds (anthologist). *The Missing Link*
Charles Dodeman. *The Silent Bomb*
Harry Dickson. *The Heir of Dracula; Harry Dickson vs. The Spider*
Jules Dornay. *Lord Ruthven Begins*
Alfred Driou. *The Adventures of a Parisian Aeronaut*
Odette Dulac. *The War of the Sexes*
Alexandre Dumas. *The Return of Lord Ruthven; The Man who Married a Mermaid* (w/P. Lacroix)
Renée Dunan. *Baal; The Ultimate Pleasure*
J.-C. Dunyach. *The Night Orchid; The Thieves of Silence*
Henri Duvernois. *The Man Who Found Himself*
Achille Eyraud. *Voyage to Venus*
Henri Falk. *The Age of Lead*
Paul Féval. *Anne of the Isles; Knightshade; Revenants; Vampire City; The Vampire Countess; The Wandering Jew's Daughter*
Paul Féval, *fils. Felifax, the Tiger-Man*
Charles de Fieux. *Lamékis*
Fernand Fleuret. *Jim Click*
Charles-Marie Flor O'Squarr. *Phantoms*
Louis Forest. *Someone is Stealing Children in Paris*
Arnould Galopin. *Doctor Omega*; *Doctor Omega and the Shadowmen* (anthology)
Judith Gautier. *Isoline and the Serpent-Flower*
H. Gayar. *The Marvelous Adventures of Serge Myrandhal on Mars*
Louis Geoffroy. *The Apocryphal Napoleon*
G.L. Gick. *Harry Dickson and the Werewolf of Rutherford Grange*
Raoul Gineste. *The Second Life of Doctor Albin*
Delphine de Girardin. *Balzac's Cane*
Léon Gozlan. *The Vampire of the Val-de-Grâce*
Jules Gros. *The Fossil Man*
Jimmy Guieu. *The Polarian-Denebian War* (2 vols.)
Edmond Haraucourt. *Daah, the First Human; Illusions of Immortality*
Nathalie Henneberg. *The Green Gods*
Eugène Hennebert. *The Enchanted City*

Jules Hoche. *The Maker of Men and His Formula*

V. Hugo, P. Foucher & P. Meurice. *The Hunchback of Notre-Dame*

Romain d'Huissier. *Hexagon: Dark Matter*

Jules Janin. *The Magnetized Corpse*

Gustave Kahn. *The Tale of Gold and Silence*

Gérard Klein. *The Mote in Time's Eye*

Fernand Kolney. *Love in 5000 Years*

Paul Lacroix. *Danse Macabre; The Man who Married a Mermaid* (w/Alexandre Dumas)

Louis-Guillaume de La Follie. *The Unpretentious Philosopher*

Jean de La Hire. *The Fiery Wheel; Enter the Nyctalope; The Nyctalope on Mars; The Nyctalope vs. Lucifer; The Nyctalope Steps In; Night of the Nyctalope; Return of the Nyctalope*

Etienne-Léon de Lamothe-Langon. *The Virgin Vampire*

André Laurie. *Spiridon*

Gabriel de Lautrec. *The Vengeance of the Oval Portrait*

Alain le Drimeur. *The Future City*

Georges Le Faure & Henri de Graffigny. *The Extraordinary Adventures of a Russian Scientist Across the Solar System* (2 vols.)

Gustave Le Rouge. *The Dominion of the World* (w/Gustave Guitton) (4 vols.); *The Mysterious Doctor Cornelius* (3 vols.); *The Vampires of Mars*

Jules Lermina. *The Battle of Strasbourg; Mysteryville; Panic in Paris; The Secret of Zippelius; To-Ho and the Gold Destroyers*

Maurice Level. *The Gates of Hell*

André Lichtenberger. *The Centaurs; The Children of the Crab*

Maurice Limat. *Mephista*

Listonai. *The Philosophical Voyager*

Jean-Marc & Randy Lofficier. *Edgar Allan Poe on Mars; The Katrina Protocol; Pacifica 1, 2; Robonocchio; Return of the Nyctalope;* (anthologists) *Tales of the Shadowmen 1-13; The Vampire Almanac* (2 vols.)

Ch. Lomon & P.-B. Gheuzi. *The Last Days of Atlantis*

Camille Mauclair. *The Virgin Orient*

Xavier Mauméjean. *The League of Heroes*

Joseph Méry. *The Tower of Destiny*

Hippolyte Mettais. *Paris Before the Deluge; The Year 5865*

Louise Michel. *The Human Microbes; The New World*

Tony Moilin. *Paris in the Year 2000*

Michael Moorcock's *Legends of the Multiverse*

José Moselli. *Illa's End*

Norbert Sevestre. *Sâr Dubnotal: Vs. Jack the Ripper; The Astral Trail*

Angelo de Sorr. *The Vampires of London*

Brian Stableford. *The Empire of the Necromancers (1. The Shadow of Frankenstein; 2. Frankenstein and the Vampire Countess; 3. Frankenstein in London); The Wayward Muse; Eurydice's Lament; The Mirror of Dionysius; The New Faust at the Tragicomique; Sherlock Holmes and The Vampires of Eternity; The Stones of Camelot* (anthologist) *News from the Moon; The Germans on Venus; The Supreme Progress; The World Above the World; Nemoville; Investigations of the Future; The Conqueror of Death; The Revolt of the Machines; The Man With the Blue Face; The Aerial Valley; The New Moon; The Nickel Man; On the Brink of the World's End; The Mirror of Present Events; The Humanisphere*

Jacques Spitz. *The Eye of Purgatory*

Kurt Steiner. *Ortog*

Eugène Thébault. *Radio-Terror*

C.-F. Tiphaigne de La Roche. *Amilec*

Simon Tyssot de Patot. *The Strange Voyages of Jacques Massé and Pierre de Mésange*

Louis Ulbach. *Prince Bonifacio*

Théo Varlet. *The Castaways of Eros; The Golden Rock.; The Martian Epic* (w/Octave Joncquel); *Timeslip Troopers* (w/André Blandin); *The Xenobiotic Invasion*

Pierre Véron. *The Merchants of Health*

Paul Vibert. *The Mysterious Fluid*

Villiers de l'Isle-Adam. *The Scaffold; The Vampire Soul*

Gaston de Wailly. *The Murderer of the World*

Philippe Ward. *Artahe; Manhattan Ghost* (w/Mickael Laguerre); *The Song of Montségur* (w/Sylvie Miller)

Victor Margueritte. *The Bacheloress; The Companion; The Couple*